Prodigy of Flame

By Beth Connor

Prodigy of Flame

Published by:
Wolf Grove Media, LLC

Typesetting: Beth Connor

Cover Design: Eve Hard

Editor: Anne Ramallo editsbyanne.com

ISBN-10: 1-958329-07-8

ISBN-13: 978-1-958329-07-8

Thank you for reading *Prodigy of Flame*. If you enjoyed it, please leave a review, it makes a big difference.

The
Isdralan Chronicles

Micah and The Candles of Time

Prodigy of Flame

Chapter 1

Under the Shade of Arba Vitae

"Magic is a force that flows through every-
thing, connecting all things in the universe. We must
learn how to harness its power for good or for evil."
- Bataku Raama, *The Birth of Magic*

Molten steel dripped from the cliffs into the basin below, filling every crack and crevice. A whisper echoed off the burning walls: From fire we are forged, and from fire we are destroyed. An Earthborn man plunged into the flames, where the liquid magma consumed him. Above, an Elven girl watched—herself, hair as red as the fire that engulfed him. Her mouth ripped open in a silent scream as she reached for him. Or had she pushed him?

"Kaci?" Was that Elena or the vision? Kaci wasn't sure.

Darkness enclosed the world until a flash of lightning revealed a decrepit, old tomb. Disarray, decay. A voice echoed through her mind: This was no way to respect the dead.

"Child, snap out of it!"

Just a moment longer, Kaci silently pleaded. She was close. Close to something meaningful.

A long journey. Concealed faces accompanied her deeper into the caverns. They searched for something she wasn't sure they should find. An entire village hidden—shrouded in shadows. Did they do this?

Kaci tried to ignore the poking at her ribs. This was important. Deep down, she knew it. It was unheard of to see yourself in your own visions.

Notes of a flute lilted in the air as she sat with an Orcish woman, tall and regal in velvet skirts, and a boy in front of a quaint home surrounded by forest, many years from now.

Feeling a sudden, sharp pain on her cheek, Kaci flinched and rubbed her face, attempting to ease the sting while also trying to suppress her wounded pride. Why did Elena still treat her like a mere child? If Kaci were human, she might have already settled down, started a family, and had her own children by now. However, as an elf and an apprentice to a great elder, Elena constantly reminded Kaci that she was still a child, having only experienced twenty-five summers. Kaci wondered if the other apprentices faced the same mistreatment as they endured the training and education that would molded them into individuals wiser than their peers.

Tendrils of moonlight peeked through the clouds as she gazed into the flickering light of the campfire. The moonbeams joined tiny embers, like the ones in her vision, drifting and mixing with images of people and places she did not know or understand.

"What do you see in the fire, child?" Elena's words were harsh but not unkind. Still, Kaci felt the weight of them crushing her frail body. She squeezed her eyes closed, pushing away frustration as she tried to make sense of her vision. She didn't want to tell Elena about the man in the lava. What if she *had* pushed him? After what happened at the last gathering, she was not sure Elena would trust her to go to another one. The scene in front of the little cottage had felt safe and peaceful, and that version of herself was much older and wiser. That seemed safe to share.

"A woman. I think," she whispered, careful not to sound like she was withholding information. That would only make the session worse. The elder was a harsh mistress, but not unfair, provided Kaci tried her best.

Elena used to make many journeys of exploration and knowledge. It was during one of them that she met Kaci's birth parents. They had recognized Kaci's destined path and entrusted their baby to Elena's care. According to the stories, during her mother's delivery, Kaci's gifts with fire manifested in force. When Elena returned home with the infant as her protégé, she ceased her travels entirely. Kaci couldn't help but feel that Elena held a lingering bitterness in her heart because she could no longer explore the world.

"What do you mean, *you think*?" The wise woman's fingers tightened on the child's shoulder as though her grip could squeeze the knowledge out. Kaci tensed, and the flames from the campfire flared, singeing her auburn hair as she collapsed, embarrassed. Not again!

Kaci had heard whispers all her life that the community had been hesitant to accept a stranger as Elena's apprentice. However, the matriarch had always reassured them that this was a matter of fate and that Kaci would ultimately fulfill her intended role. Unfortunately, the girl was doing an excellent job of proving Elena wrong.

"I don't know," came her tiny voice buried under the sea of hair. "There was music. A sad song floating through the air like a butterfly."

"Forget the music. You said there was a woman. Tell me about her."

"But it was hard to see. The music was too loud!" Kaci puffed her cheeks. "She was pale gray. I think. With tusks like a boar."

"An Orcish woman." Elena frowned, tapping a finger on her lips. "What else? Sometimes the smallest of details can help interpret visions."

Pushing herself to a sitting position, Kaci sniffled once before speaking. She was tired of trying to pick apart every part of her vision, and she did not want Elena to suspect there was more. Years of practice had taught her to give only enough detail to make herself look capable, but not exceptional. "There was the gray woman and a young human boy, eleven or twelve years old, under a tree. We were supposed to do something, but the loud music drowned everything else out."

"Wait, you said *we*," Elena interrupted. "What do you mean *we*? Were you there?"

"No! Yes?" Kaci's jaw trembled. "I don't know."

She certainly didn't want Elena to know she could see herself in visions.

"Focus, child. It is easy." The older woman's lips thinned, and her eyes narrowed. "At this rate, you will never be ready for the conclave. I swear the Great Mother tested me when she chose you as my successor."

The silence was thick, and Kaci's body tightened at the mention of the conclave. She shook her head. "It's gone, Mistress." She gave the woman a crooked smile. "At least I saw something this time."

Firelight danced over a smattering of freckles as Kaci's smile faltered. Sticks and dirt littered her mop of wild hair and, despite the warmth, her thin frame shivered under the loose tunic.

The older woman sighed. She rose and departed without a word, leaving Kaci to extinguish the fire herself. Elena's shoulders hunched forward, and her feet seemed to drag toward the small thatched hut she shared with Kaci.

Letting the air escape her lips, Kaci relaxed and pulled forth a tiny flame from the embers she had just doused. Without Elena here judging her, she would take a moment and enjoy the warmth as it washed over her.

Elena wasn't cruel, but she was a hard mistress. Lessons often began before dawn and went until well after the sun had set. She would preach that as leaders, they would always be apart from the others, but Kaci didn't want to be apart. All she had ever wanted was to fit in. Maybe that is why she was such a failure. After last year's incident at the conclave, Elena was pushing her to prove herself at this summer's gathering of elders—*no more embarrassment.*

Kaci didn't want to let her down. She tried to be an excellent student, but everything she did seemed to need correction. When she was supposed to listen to the wind, visions of the future clouded her brain. When she was supposed to scry for revelation and guidance, the answers left her worse off than when she began. All she got was a jumble of confusion, like tonight.

Elena told her that the signs and omens had always been right about a future successor, but Kaci saw how the elder looked at her. Worry was plain to see in the older woman's furrowed brow.

People confused Kaci. So often, their faces betrayed what was actually in their hearts. Elena was the same. Her teacher told her repeatedly that everything would be okay—that one day it would just click—but her eyes told a different story. Kaci was a failure and a disappointment.

She had never seemed to belong in her homeland of Aeloria. This hidden realm, cradled deep within the forests of Elyndris, had a stringent social structure. Every elf had a role, from elders to healers, sentinels, and artisans. They all fit perfectly, like pieces of a complex puzzle—every piece except Kaci.

Having been handed to Elena, Kaci was fortunate to know her place in this world and the path she must walk. This should have been enough to soothe her worries. But where her kin found solace, Kaci found restraint. She was a wildfire in a serene forest, a gale in a calm sea. Her fiery spirit refused to be quenched, and her impatient nature disrupted the tranquil equilibrium of the village.

As a small child, she often felt a fiery anger boiling inside her. Once, when she was barely old enough to leave her mistress's side, some village kids asked her to play with them. They had finally invited her along! Then she lost a game. Being a small thing who had not yet mastered her emotions, she had slammed her hand down on the board, and, to her horror, it burst into flames.

The other children had been terrified. This was the

first time of many that Kaci felt a deep sense of shame over her ability with flame. She knew she had crossed a line and could have hurt someone. From that day on, she became an outcast. None of the other kids wanted to play with the girl who could conjure fire with just a touch. Magic was supposed to be something you commune with, like speaking with nature and seeing what may come in visions, not burning things to ashes.

Kaci turned to the forest for refuge. The forest took her in, loving her unconditionally. It became her playground, and she spent her days climbing trees and picking violets. She loved the scent of the flowers and the way they felt soft against her skin.

Once, after one particularly horrible day, she stumbled upon a massive tree that seemed to glow with vibrant green light. Elena had found her there. "Arba Vitae," she informed her. "She is the physical manifestation of the Great Mother, the center of our people. Our job as keeper is to protect her."

Kaci asked, "But if the tree is so important, why isn't it guarded?"

Elena replied, "An ancient magic protects The Arba Vitae. Only the pure of heart can find her. The tree has its own way of selecting to whom she will reveal herself.

She chooses those who are worthy and will care for her. The guardians of the tree are the spirits of nature themselves."

Kaci knew she wasn't worthy and wondered why Arba Vitae had revealed herself to a child, but she returned as often as possible. She often sought solace beneath the branches of the ancient tree. It was a place where she felt safe, loved, and cared for in a way she had never experienced before. The tree was her mother, who provided comfort and protection that Elena never could. In the dappled light beneath the leaves, Kaci sometimes imagined that she could hear the tree whispering secrets and words of wisdom meant only for her. She would lean against the rough bark and close her eyes, feeling the gentle sway of the branches and the rustling of the leaves, letting the tree's loving presence wash over her.

An ember popped, and Kaci snapped out of her memory. She quickly put out the fire, then tucked a strand of wild hair behind her ear.

Elena deserved a more suitable protégé, not some dangerous fire child. Despite her efforts to blend in, Kaci always felt like an outsider in her clan. She knew the elders did not consider her fit to lead, and the villagers feared her. Kaci was a burden. No one would miss her at the gathering if she left tonight.

The girl sighed. The plan had been forming in her mind since the last gathering. Leaving now was the right thing to do. The only thing to do. If she stayed, Elena would keep trying to teach her, and Kaci would keep failing. It was an unending cycle. If she left, Elena could find a different wise woman—one that would be much more likable than Kaci with her fiery temper. Meanwhile, Kaci might find her true self and her purpose in the world. Once she knew, maybe she could return and take on some unobtrusive role in the village.

With a leap, Kaci was off at a sprint, legs pumping as she wound her way through the ancient forest. Tonight, after such harrowing visions, it was the Great Mother's advice Kaci sought. Now and then, she would stop to rest a tiny hand on one of the massive trees, whisper a few words, then continue. Her forest was a living entity that sheltered her through many tears and troubles. There was nowhere in the world she felt safer.

The sheltered clearing was alive with nocturnal music, and fireflies blinked and danced between the giant's branches. Kaci felt the warm embrace of her sanctuary as her bare toes sunk into the deep moss. A cleansing breath filled her lungs with the earthy musk, calming her soul.

Kaci slowed as she approached Arba Vitae. She touched a patch of scorched bark and a small wave of guilt washed over her before she felt its warmth beneath her fingers. "I'm leaving," she whispered, leaning in close. "I can't stay here anymore. When I am gone, Elena will find someone worthy of you."

Kaci vowed to leave her village tomorrow. She wanted to find her true self.

The tree was silent, but Kaci sensed comfort and sorrow, as if it understood her need to leave. Kaci closed her eyes, took a deep breath, and let Arba Vitae's energy wash over her. Something darker had been mixed with its energy since the last enclave, and Kaci knew it was her fault.

As she turned to leave, Kaci felt a pang of sadness in her chest. She didn't want to leave her forest behind. It had always been there for her, a constant presence in her life. But she couldn't stay.

Back in the hut, sleep was like a distant dream for Kaci. She lay awake in bed, staring at the ceiling, her thoughts racing. Why did it feel so difficult to leave behind the village? She had no friends, no one to miss her. Still, the familiarity of her surroundings and the routine of her daily life had become a source of comfort. But

Kaci knew that staying would mean she would become what Elena expected her to become: forever alone, the fiery heart that no one would go near. This was not her path. As much as Elena tried to convince her otherwise, deep down, she knew leaving was the right choice.

Kaci got out of bed, her heart pounding. She packed her bag with essentials and supplies, careful not to make a sound.

Her lungs burned as she held in a breath and tip-toed into the cabin's main room, careful not to step on the third floorboard from the left. The wood was old. It groaned and creaked, but Kaci maneuvered the living area expertly. She pulled open the drawer containing all the coins and gifts earned from the villagers they had helped, hating that she was stealing from Elena. Kaci would only take what was necessary, although she felt like her own hard work had earned most of the coin.

Her journey had to be now, as the clan meeting was coming with the full moon. She wouldn't give Cird-en and the others the chance to shun her again. Kaci shuddered at the memory of last year's gathering. It had begun with so much hope. She'd thought she might even gain a friend or two. But it had ended with her almost being banished. She couldn't face the other clans again after the fire incident.

The elders always held the clan gathering in her village, nestled in the vivid greens with Arba Vitae watching over them. The wind had carried the damp, mossy fragrance as it mingled with the bonfire smoke around which the apprentices huddled, their faces half-hidden in shadows.

She had attempted to befriend some of the others, but they laughed at her stammering words. Their mockery hung in the air like a dissonant note against the comforting crackle of the fire. Humiliation blazed within her, brighter than the flames that danced nearby. Then something strange and uncontrollable welled inside her—a surge of raw energy that made her heart hammer in her chest.

Without warning, the bonfire had flared violently, searing heat radiating outwards in a cataclysmic wave. She remembered the others crying out in surprise and pain. Their smug expressions transformed into masks of horror and disbelief. Cirden's apprentice took the worst of it. The young woman had been close to the fire, her wide eyes reflecting the violent, incandescent flare before she fell back, skin marred by the cruel kiss of the flames. She had almost succumbed to her wounds, and would be forever marred. Kaci's shame was made deeper by her suffering.

Cirden's face had been a mask of disappointment. His condemnation carried a harsh bitterness that tasted of ash and shame as he advocated for Kaci's banishment. His words still echoed in her ears, a jarring melody that she could not let go of. She cringed each time she remembered it. He had wanted Kaci to pay for her recklessness and it had taken Elena's intervention to prevent Kaci from being cast out of the village. Kaci would not let this happen again.

She closed the door to the life she knew, feet treading lightly on the well-worn path leading away from the small cabin. Fading stars melted into the gray predawn sky as she scanned the road ahead—the road to the future.

To her surprise, Kaci was not alone. Ahead, a woman stood still and silhouetted in shadows at the gate leading out of town. *Elena.* Wasn't she in bed? She waved in greeting, and Kaci's shoulders slumped as she approached her teacher.

"Leaving without a goodbye?" Elena's voice was as cold as the morning air. This was not how her exit was supposed to go!

"I thought it would be easier," Kaci replied, her voice no louder than a whisper. "You can find someone better."

"Oh, Kaci, if it were that easy, I would have re-placed you years ago." Elena sighed.

Kaci's heart broke into a million pieces. She knew Elena didn't want her, but to hear it was too much. "Why didn't you then?"

"I've known of this day before it was even the spark of an idea in your mind." Elena studied her. "I saw it in the flames when you were very young."

"Then why didn't you stop me?" Kaci felt the frustration rise in her throat. She couldn't even run away right.

"Don't you understand? This is the way the Great Mother wants it to be. You have a duty to fulfill. A destiny. And you won't be returning to us until it's complete." Even now, Elena remained cool and distant, but Kaci noticed something else in her eyes—something she had never seen before.

The lines on her mentor's face seemed more profound than ever, but Kaci couldn't bring herself to ask what Elena was feeling. What if she was wrong and learned the woman never loved her?

"I don't care about my duty or destiny," Kaci lied.

All she wanted was for Elena and the others to love her. If her mentor always knew Kaci would leave, why had she pushed her so hard to learn the ways of the elders? Elena would never do anything without good reason. Kaci knew that much to be true. She could feel the fire rising in her voice, and she struggled to control her frustration. "I will never come back!" Perhaps it was easier to play the roles they had always assumed.

Elena's face fell, and she gave a stiff nod. "May the road rise to meet you, child."

Giving no reply, Kaci turned her back on her former mistress and walked past the gate, down the dusty dirt road. After attempting to quell the anger, Kaci opened her mind to the surrounding land, her sanctuary. She felt the forest's gentle thrum. Just off the path, a small tributary wound its way south to meet a greater river. The water's song created a beautiful harmony with the forest, but there was a strangeness to the undercurrent, like a single note out of tune. Probably just her fear.

Following the water would be the perfect path to start a new life. It seemed to still the fire within and wash away the pain. And so Kaci began her journey—onward to find herself and her destiny, whatever it may be.

Chapter 2

Shelter from the Storm

"Sometimes the most treacherous storms can lead us to the greatest treasures." - Bataku Raama, *The Birth of Magic*

Kaci's auburn hair whipped about in the squall as heavy raindrops lashed across her face. She cursed under her breath at the unexpected storm. Usually, she was adept at picking up on weather patterns, but something about this tempest was uncanny. It felt as if the wind were forcefully propelling her, like a majestic ship swept into a storm, its billowing sails steering it dangerously close to the rocks. As lightning split a nearby tree, the air crackled with electricity. Kaci knew she needed to find somewhere safe, and she needed to find it soon.

After months on the road, Kaci had come no closer to finding herself. (Who created that term, anyway?)

Perhaps it was everyone else that needed to find her. As if there were little bits scattered around the land to collect! Goodness. Even if she scooped them all together, this rain would only wash everything away.

As she slogged forward, her boots squished in the thick mud, each step a battle against the sucking earth. Blinking away the rain that fell in her face, she reached the top of the hill. As she scanned the next valley through the deluge, her sharp eyes landed on a small cave nestled in a dirt mound. It looked like there may have been a door at one point, but now only the crumbled remains of a stone entryway remained, worn down by centuries of erosion. The cave reminded her of the holy barrows where clan elders would perform ancient sacred rites. She felt a pang of nostalgia for home, but for now, this would be a gift—a haven to weather out the storm.

Half running, half sliding, Kaci made her way down the hill and inside the shelter. She was pleased to find it spacious and dry, with a hidden crevice far from the rain that would accommodate a good night's sleep. It had a view of the entrance, should anyone try to enter.

The last few months had been trying, but she attempted to keep a brave and cheerful face. Thieves had tried to take her meager food stocks and coins on three separate occasions. But Elena's warnings had served her well. A simple trick with fire magic and their bellies had sent them running for the privy.

The people who had deceived her were even more detestable. Driven by their stories of misery and anguish, she had given away many valuable coins, only to witness the destitute, famished person squandering them at a pub. She could hear Elena's voice scolding her for her inability to discern human intentions.

The large human cities and towns scattered throughout the lands had been the hardest to cope with. There were so many people, so close together. While elves were common in these parts, most people gave her a wide berth, reminding her that she was different when all she wanted to do was blend in. Everyone had such potent feelings that they seemed to wear like heavy cloaks draped over their souls. Anger and sorrow hung in the air like a dark cloud. Now and then, she would encounter light and happiness, but they were as fleeting as a glimpse of a unicorn between trees.

The large stretches between towns, such as this, had been her favorite. Great forests with trees vibrating the song of life. While the animals were wary of her, their essence was familiar and comforting. At one point, she attempted a conversation with a young owl, but it just stared at her with its wide yellow eyes before flying away.

The rain outside her shelter was muffled, and every so often thunder rumbled across the forest. Kaci hummed a cheerful tune as she set out her bedroll and made a small fire. The room lit up as a bolt struck right outside the cave, and a tremendous crash split her eardrums.

She looked up as the lightning flashed again, illuminating a gigantic humanoid silhouette in the doorway. Kaci gasped and scrambled backward, attempting to melt herself into the corner.

A gruff cough rattled in the entrance. Who else would be about on such a night with eyes good enough to find this place?

"Hello!" she called out, hoping her voice sounded unthreatening yet fearless.

"Ahem, are you setting up camp for the night?" a husky voice called. "Do you have room for one more?"

"Of course." Kaci exhaled slowly as the gigantic form ducked under the doorway and entered the shelter. "There is plenty of room here." Kaci tried to convince herself that it would be nice to share a meal and conversation with another being. She had not seen another soul in ages, but this creature was terrifying. She cringed and wished she could kick herself.

The stooped figure tried to straighten and stand tall, then gave up, resigned to an awkward, hunched position. As the owner of the voice stepped into the firelight, Kaci let out a small gasp. It was a girl, perhaps a woman. She was large, at least three feet taller than Kaci. Her skin was a deep shade of gray, and two curled horns sat atop her head. From the smoothness of her skin, Kaci deduced that she couldn't have been far into adulthood. Most orcs began fighting campaigns in their early years, and the scars of battle would show well before adulthood. This one had skin as smooth as glass.

Kaci was startled to recognize the woman she had seen, many months ago, in her vision with Elena. A younger version, certainly, but she was unmistakable. Though she had the tusks that normally accompanied the orc kind, her clothing was regal, almost like something a human noble would wear—a confusing mix of nobility and monster.

"Are you going to say something or just stare all night?" the woman bellowed.

"Uh, um…Hello, I'm Kaci!" she sputtered. "Girl of

the—" She cut herself off, remembering how the others had laughed at that title.

"Charmed," the woman said with icy air. "You may call me Lady Durya, or Baroness."

Kaci nodded, feeling awkward. She had never been good at conversing, and now she faced this intimidating creature, and not exactly for the first time. The Great Mother must be testing her.

"Did your horns hurt when they grew in?" Kaci blurted out. She knew the moment the words left her mouth that she shouldn't have spoken them. What had she been thinking? She looked down and hunched her shoulders, trying to look as small as possible. Being short in stature, this was easy.

The lady looked at her and sniffed.

Kaci's face heated, and the blush crept into her cheeks, brighter than the hair on her head. She had obviously screwed up again. Somehow, she had alienated every friendly person she had met on this journey within the first few minutes of the introduction, like the farmer offering her a warm night's sleep and a hot meal in exchange for some work. Kaci had tried to teach him the technique of crop rotation to help his harvest. He just got angry and shouted about how he had been a farmer longer than she had been alive.

"I'm sorry," Kaci whispered. "I didn't mean to offend."

Before Lady Durya could reply, another voice echoed from the entryway. "Hello? Is anybody in there?"

Grateful for the distraction, Kaci responded immediately, "Yes!"

A flash of lightning illuminated the sheets of rain coming down as the thunder crashed outside. From the dark doorway, a young man entered. His eyes were the palest blue, like ocean foam, with little black specks. He pushed back a dark flop of hair, giving an impish grin.

"Mind if I take shelter? The weather outside is rather unbearable."

His voice was rich, and something about him seemed oddly familiar. Kaci straightened, feigning confidence, and told herself she would not screw up this time. No stupid questions. Although he was strange and very dry. Too dry for being caught up in such a storm. She opened her mouth to comment, but Lady Durya cut her off.

"How is it you are so dry?" the woman asked, her eyes shooting daggers at the newcomer.

"You must be The Baroness of Marshfield," the man stated, sidestepping the question with a slight bow.

Durya blinked twice before answering, "Why yes. Of course, you would know of me." She straightened, almost bumping her head on the low ceiling. "With whom do I have the pleasure of meeting?"

Kaci poked at their small fire a few times, trying to understand the strange dynamic. The man glanced at Kaci, and a broad smile grew on his face. Then he looked Durya up and down and gave a snort.

"Names are meaningless." He gave another charming smile and bowed with a flourish. "But you may call me Micah."

"Micah of?" Lady Durya frowned. "To what house do you belong? Surely a powerful one if you feel you may address me so casually."

"Oh, no house as great as yours, lovely lady."

"I see," Durya replied curtly. She frowned, and her eyebrows knitted together in deep thought. "Well then, I'll set up my bedroll way, way over there and will leave at first light."

"Of course, milady." Micah inclined his head and cleared a corner of his own.

Kaci's head darted back and forth as she observed her new companions setting up for the night, pointedly ignoring each other. She was lost in this bustle of activity when a tentative voice croaked from the darkness.

"Storm peace?" Shadows gathered at the crumbling entrance, and three figures emerged, looking at each other and the group inside.

"Vermin!" Lady Durya spat. "You will not pack me into this tiny space with the likes of goblins. They are disgusting creatures."

Kaci's small cave had become a refuge for the downtrodden and was now quite crowded. It surprised her to see goblins. Though most of the land feared and shunned them, Kaci had learned that they played a vital role in society. They were expert scavengers and knew how to find food and supplies that others could not. Humans often hired them as workers in their mines because of their natural affinity for metals and minerals. However, their love of shiny objects, especially gold, made them difficult to trust. Kaci had heard stories of goblins stealing from their employers, hoarding treasures in secret stashes deep within the mountains. But these goblins seemed harmless enough.

One of them uttered a few words in the strange

language and reached a hand toward Lady Durya. A dead rat hung from his fingers, skillfully skinned and ready to be cooked. Kaci giggled, grateful for Elena's instructions in many languages. The goblin had inquired if Durya was hungry and, in a strikingly un-goblin-like action, had offered to share its dinner.

Lady Durya was not impressed. She let out a horrendous squeal and nearly crushed Kaci as she retreated into the corner.

"It was a peace offering, Lady Durya," Kaci informed her after skillfully stepping out of the large woman's way.

"Kaci, do you understand them?" Durya demanded. She turned to the goblins and spoke loudly and slowly: "Back away, fiends."

"Um, yes," Kaci replied, trying to sound meek but feeling rather proud of her skills. Goblin was a complex language, but she could pick up enough.

Lady Durya scoffed and turned toward the goblins. Her voice grew louder and climbed an octave. "Well, what do you want?"

Kaci did her best to translate the question to the trio. The goblins chattered among themselves before the largest of the three sneered in an attempt to smile at Kaci. He turned to Durya and repeated in the common language, "Storm Peace?"

Letting out a low growl, Lady Durya gritted her teeth in frustration. "What is he even talking about?"

Kaci shrugged and watched the standoff uncomfortably until Micah interjected. "I'd think an orc should understand the meaning of storm peace. Do you not understand your culture, Lady Durya? They are asking you for peace in the storm. They promise not to kill you if you promise not to kill them."

"Argh," Lady Durya finally cried, "for the love of the gods, yes, storm peace if you set up on the opposite side of the cave." She glared at Micah and her voice turned icy. "You can go stay on their side."

Micah chuckled, which further infuriated Durya, and Kaci wished she could melt into the wall. This situation had escalated quickly. A few minutes ago, she was worried about social niceties. Now she wasn't sure if she would survive the night. On their own, each of these people seemed nice enough, but all together, the storm brewing inside seemed about to be as bad as the one outside.

Turning to the goblins, Kaci gave a reassuring

smile and whispered in their language, "The scary lady says you can sleep over there."

The large one answered for everyone. "Arrg, we understand all words." His voice was gruff and guttural, but clear and easy to decipher.

"Do you have names?" Kaci asked, facing the largest of the three, who seemed to be the only one that would speak to them.

"Smeadon," he replied, baring his teeth in what could only be a smile. "My companions be Jeth and Meshach."

"Pleased to meet you. I am Kaci." Kaci smiled, searching her memories on what to do when meeting a goblin, but all she could remember was that they loved shiny things. Finally, she offered a slight inclination of her head.

Laying a hand on her arm, Lady Durya whispered in a cool voice, "Dear Kaci, goblins are not intelligent creatures. It's best to let them go over there and ignore them."

Smeadon's face shifted, and his teeth baring seemed to take on a menacing tone.

"You may be mistaken." Kaci swallowed hard and

glanced at Micah to see if he would offer help, but he pretended to be distracted, digging through his pack. Lady Durya, busy setting out her extravagant bedroll, turned back to Smeadon. "You three sleep comfortably. You will be safe."

A strange noise came from the large goblin that could only be a laugh. "We keep watch," he replied. "I watch over you too, small elf." He patted her head and then turned to his companions, spouting clipped instructions in their own language that Kaci couldn't fully make out.

The storm ebbed, and before long, the slow breathing of sleep filled the chamber as Smeadon sat watching the entryway. Kaci drifted between the twilight of sleep and wakefulness. Intense visions barraged her senses. Lady Durya seemed surrounded by visions of a ship in a storm, and treasure surrounded the goblin trio.

The strangest was Micah. Something emanated from him that she could not quite grasp. It was as though a shroud of black covered him. Normally, she would associate this with something evil, but that was not the feeling she got from Micah. It was nothing bad, but it was immense.

A low rumble interrupted Kaci's thoughts. More

thunder, she thought drowsily, but the vibrations surrounded them, and the whole cavern shook for almost a minute before the quiet returned.

"Smeadon, are you still awake?" Kaci whispered, trying not to wake anyone else up. "Did you feel the earth shaking?"

The rumbles started again, and Smeadon was silent a moment, his head tilted in concentration. Finally, in a gruff voice, he said, "I feel it. We wake others."

But before Kaci could move, the shaking intensified, and the cave emitted loud and terrifying cracks. She heard the echo of rocks falling, then the ground below her dropped out. She was falling.

Chapter 3

Beneath the Surface

*"The earth trembled, and from its fiery heart
rose beings unlike any the world had ever seen. They
were the Earthborn, children of flame and stone,
and with them came the power of the land itself." –*
Bataku Raama, *Birth of Magic*

Agony coursed through Kaci's body and a crushing weight pressed down on her chest. Voices echoed around her as if she were submerged in a surreal dream. She tried to call out, but only a faint groan escaped her lips. Her lungs burned for air, yet all she could manage were shallow gasps. As the darkness grew more intense, a dazzling display of stars pirouetted behind her closed eyelids.

"Here," a muffled voice called. "Give me a hand with this boulder."

Her body flooded with air and Kaci gasped sharply, her lungs exploding into a fit of coughs. Strong arms pulled her into an upright position, and she found herself face-to-face with Lady Durya. The concern on the Lady's face was clear, even in the dimness, and Kaci felt grateful for her rescuer.

"Easy," Micah said from behind her. His voice was soothing as he inspected her face, pulling open her droopy eyelids. "Not sure if elves get concussions, but your pupils seem normal. How do you feel?"

"Urrgh…" Kaci muttered, "I hurt everywhere."

"It seems as if you got the worst of it. The lady and I have a few cuts and bruises, but aside from that, we came out unscathed." He pushed a strand of hair out of his face, still studying her.

"Smeadon and the others. Are they okay?" Kaci asked, trying to sit up straight when a sharp pain split through her head.

"Aye," came the guttural voice from further back in the room. "We be fine, small one."

Someone handed her a water skin. After a few moments, the burning pain subsided and Kaci felt more like herself. She tried to scan the room, but darkness wrapped her surroundings in secrecy. The fire had been extinguished in the collapse.

"If you can find my pack, I have some candles," Kaci offered.

"I have a taper here." Lady Durya's rich voice, echoing against the stone walls, took on an ominous sound. "But I have not found a tinder yet."

"Hand it here," Kaci groaned, reaching into the dark. "I can light it."

Her voice was confident, but her head protested. As Durya placed the smooth candle into her hand, Kaci reached for the wick in her mind, sending tiny wisps of emotion and willing the fibers to accept the heat until they burst into flame. The lady sniffed, and her face looked unimpressed in the flickering light. "Well, that is a useful skill to have."

Kaci nodded. The pain in her head was throbbing, and she was positive her voice would betray her if she tried to speak.

Long shadows danced on the walls of the crumbled room as the group surveyed the extent of the damage. They had fallen at least twenty-five feet into an immense chamber. It must have been directly below the cave, Kaci thought as she gazed up into the hole in the ceiling.

"There is no way we are getting out that way," Micah sighed. "Unless any of you can fly and toss down a rope?" He looked around, hopefully.

Kaci shook her head and studied their space. Tall stone pillars lined the long chamber, alternating with giant statues of rugged Earthborn with axes and battle gear.

"I think this was some sort of Earthborn meeting hall," she whispered. "It doesn't look like it's been used for ages, though."

"What are Earthborn?" Micah asked, his brow furrowed in confusion.

"They're a race of people who live deep within the earth and are known for their skills with metalworking."

Micah nodded slowly, still seeming unsure. "We have people like that where I am from, but they are called dwarves. Why do you call them Earthborn?"

Kaci shrugged. "Legend says that they are birthed from the fire deep beneath, emerging into existence through the very stones and soil they mine, and so they're known as the Earthborn."

"Eww, it's not a meeting hall. It is a mausoleum," Lady Durya interrupted. "Come." She beckoned to the

group without stopping to see if they followed, and
pointed to the plaque at the base of one statue.

*King Dundry Ironfist. His axe was sharp, but his
mind was sharper.*

Eyes widening, Kaci ran her fingertips along
the words. "I've never met an Earthborn, but El—I
mean—I studied their culture and history. There should
be a door nearby that houses King Dundry's family."
She scanned the area around the statue and pointed.
"There, on the wall." She felt terrible for excluding
Elena's name but wasn't ready to reveal her past to her
new friends. This was an opportunity for a fresh start, an
unblemished record.

There was so much dirt and lichen that one could
hardly see the door's outline. The bronze handle pro-
truded slightly. Kaci grabbed at it and gave a pull.
Durya was at her side in a flash, swiping the hand away.

"What do you think you are doing? There are bodies in there." Durya frowned and gagged. "*Dead bodies.*"

"I know!" Kaci replied, forgetting to feel self-con-
scious. "I have never seen one of those either!"

"Are you insane?" Durya stomped, her raised heel barely missing Kaci's foot. "This is no way to respect the dead. We need to focus on getting out of here!"

Kaci felt her face heat. It was never her intention to be disrespectful. She was only curious.

The goblins, who had alternated between conversing together and watching the women, fell quiet. Smeadon approached the rest of the group. "Look there. Way out, maybe?" His long finger pointed toward a massive stone archway with gold veins snaking through it. The area beyond was mostly dark. Only a small pinprick of light cut through the distance. "We go?"

Micah's face was pale, and his eyes darted from the room's shadows to the dark archway. "I don't like it. We should probably just try to climb out." He eyed the giant hole above their heads. "Maybe we could pile the rubble up and jump."

"That is preposterous! There is no way we can jump that high, even *if* we had rope and stacked all the stones." Lady Durya's hands were on her hips. "There is obviously another exit. A king with any self-worth would have a grand entrance for others to pay him reverence."

"Still," Micah continued, "before we go wandering

through some house of the dead, uninvited, we should weigh our options."

As Durya and Micah continued to argue, Kaci lit another taper and headed toward the next statue.

Queen Balora. Ruled with an iron fist and a heart of gold.

The statue depicted a stout woman with long, flowing hair tied into a ponytail and an intricately braided beard. Fascinating. She wondered if she could ever grow a beard like that.

"Kaci!" Durya's voice echoed against the cavern walls. "Don't go wandering off! What if you wake the dead?"

Kaci felt a twinge of annoyance as Lady Durya spoke to her with a tone that made her feel like a child listening to Elena's lessons. With a pout, she returned to the group, feeling a little foolish for her internal outburst. As she approached, she failed to notice the small, shadowed hole in the ground. Before she knew it, she had stumbled right into a rat's nest, disturbing the tiny creatures and sending them scrambling in all directions. Kaci let out a yelp and tried to regain her footing, but her arms flailed wildly, causing even more chaos among the rodents.

A few small squeaks were quickly joined by what could have been hundreds. Rats ran from every crack and crevice in a massive exodus to the giant archway.

The Baroness's bloodcurdling scream caused the massive hole above to litter more debris onto their heads. Goblins scurried this way and that, dodging the tidal wave of rats, and Micah held his backpack up to protect himself from the falling rocks.

"Eeeeeee! You woke the dead!" Lady Durya screamed, trying to stomp on the tiny creatures scurrying past her.

"Oh, stop! Don't hurt them," Kaci cried. "It wasn't their fault!"

One goblin pulled a spear from his back and skewed a rat, a gleeful grin spreading on his face. Smeadon passed a few gold coins to Jeth and gave Meshach a hearty pat on the back.

Kaci was bawling now, big tears falling down her face. Smeadon glanced at her and grabbed the spear from Mesach's hand. Turning to Kaci, he gave her back an awkward pat. "You eat prize?"

Kaci snuffled, shaking her head weakly, and fell backward onto her rump. She buried her face in her hands. What had she done? Kaci felt a pang of sadness in her chest as she watched the goblins remove the rat from the skewer. She understood everything played its part in the circle of life, but if she hadn't stumbled into their nest and disturbed their peaceful existence, the little creature wouldn't have met such a gruesome end. She couldn't shake the guilt that gnawed at her insides and she vowed to be more careful in the future.

Smeadon stared at her in bewilderment as Kaci sighed and shook her head. "I'm not hungry," she whispered as she said a small prayer in her mind willing the Great Mother to honor the creature's contribution to the group. By now, everyone was staring at her. With an impish grin, Micah offered a hand, and she rose to her feet.

"You need help, child," Lady Durya started, then snapped her lips shut and paced. "Have you ever lived outside Aeloria?" she finally asked, raising an eyebrow.

Kaci blushed, bracing herself for the barrage of disdain for never leaving the lands of her people, but when her eyes met The Baroness's face, she saw a slow smile spreading across it.

"My darling child," Lady Durya cooed, "have you ever considered becoming a lady-in-waiting? I need to fill out my staff."

"A waiting lady?" Kaci asked, forgetting her tears for a moment. "That sounds utterly boring!"

"No…" The Baroness started, then just rolled her eyes. A low rumble sounded in the distance, and she placed a hand on Micah's shoulder to steady herself before quickly pulling it away. "Never mind all that. We should focus on getting out of here."

"Agreed." Micah gave her a wry smile. "Unfortu-nately, my guess is the main entrance is through there." He pointed a slender finger at the darkened marble archway. "But we could still try to climb." He looked at the group, full of hope.

One of the smaller goblins passed some coins to Smeadon, and he licked his lips as a slow smile spread across his face. The coin purse seemed ready to burst as he shoved the prize into it.

"Why is that unfortunate? I don't understand why you don't want to go that way!" Lady Durya stomped her foot. "There is a perfectly good door up ahead, and you want us to get all disheveled and dirty again?"

Kaci placed a hand over her mouth to stifle a gig-gle. The tall lady was already covered in dirt and debris.

She could not possibly get any worse.

Micah sighed. "Fine. Let's get this over with."

The rag-tag group picked its way across the rubble toward the grand arch. The shadows grew larger as they approached the door, and a terrible vision filled Kaci with fear—the large maw of some sea creature or giant beast looked like it was about to swallow them whole. Her steps faltered, and Micah laid a reassuring hand on her shoulder as they stepped through.

The archway led to a long stone hallway flecked with the same gold vein. No one spoke as they continued. Only Lady Durya's tall heels echoed through the empty space. Several doors and alcoves lined the corridor, and the goblins began whispering privately. As always, it was Smeadon who spoke to the group.

"We explore," he said, stroking his coin purse as one would caress a favorite pet. "We safe. We go now."

Before anyone could protest, the trio disappeared into one alcove, their guttural voices speaking fast.

"Good riddance," Durya scoffed. "Smelly gross things."

Kaci opened her mouth to defend her newfound friends, but closed it just as quickly. It wasn't worth it, and Smeadon didn't seem to care what anyone thought of him. Maybe she could learn something from that.

The speck of light was now growing bigger. Its glow seemed to flicker and dance on the walls, and the smell of smoke drifted their way. It must be a small campfire, Kaci mused. This meant more people ahead, and if there were others, there must be a way out.

Micah and Durya seemed to reach the same conclusion as their pace quickened, and Kaci found it hard to keep up. She felt a bit like a small child chasing after a parent or an older sibling.

"Thank goodness," Lady Durya breathed. "I thought this hallway would never end."

As they approached the light, Kaci made out four human figures surrounding the fire. Three of them faced the last, who gestured and moved as if telling a tale or giving instructions. He had a golden crown on his brow, covered in rich jewels. Was he some sort of king? Strangely, none of the men spoke. The cavern was deathly quiet. Kaci placed a hand on Durya's forearm. "Something is off here."

Lady Durya shook her off and cleared her throat as she approached the silent huddle. "Excuse me. I am Lady Durya, and we have been involved in an unfortunate accident. Can you direct us to the way out?"

The four men rose in unison. The one wearing the crown spoke in a raspy voice. "They are here to steal my crown. Seize them!" The other three men pulled rusty weapons from their belts and waved them wildly as they advanced.

Durya took a step back, bracing herself. "I have no need of your crown." Her voice was regal, yet Kaci couldn't help but notice how Durya's gaze lingered on the large jewels.

The first man approached, thrusting his dagger at her. Durya easily sidestepped, kicking his legs out from under him and grabbing his weapon as he crumpled to the ground.

"We should help her," Kaci whispered, dancing from foot to foot. The two other men were still advancing on the lady. The one with the crown stood apart, eyes wild like a feral animal trapped in a corner.

Micah laughed. "She seems fine on her own," he said as the second man dropped.

Before Kaci could react, a cold rush of air blasted her, and something odd tickled her brain. It was a subtle murmur, like a soft whisper drifting through the corridors of her thoughts. As she followed it, she felt black and empty, like her soul was being sucked away. Part of her recognized it as a curse or spell, but she could not control it.

A powerful urge to help the man with the crown came upon her, as if the Great Mother were reminding her of this man's inherent connection to everything. Without thinking, Kaci stepped in front of him. Suddenly, she felt a familiar heat building in her chest—that same explosive tumult she'd felt before things went awry at the bonfire. The whispers in her mind quickened their pace, responding to this raw power with fascination and fear, like a moth drawn to the mesmerizing flame, yet aware of the dual-edged sword it held—its destruction and its extraordinary power. This was all wrong. She wanted to cry out for The Baroness to step back, but her voice wouldn't come.

In an instant, the heat released, along with the spell. The small campfire flared into a massive flame, engulfing everything around it. Kaci threw her body in front of The Baroness just in time to protect her new friend from the fiery burst, but the four men were not as lucky. The smell of charred skin permeated the hall and Kaci dropped to her knees.

"No, not again!" Kaci swallowed her sobs as she

assessed the blackened bodies on the cave floor. She had been learning to control her temper and the fire. Why did this happen? Perhaps it would be better if she just found some cave in the wilderness and became a hermit, living the rest of her days in solitude.

Lady Durya moved closer. In a surprisingly quick motion, she wrapped Kaci in a tight hug. Once she released her, she spoke earnestly, "You really *should* consider my offer to become a lady-in-waiting."

"Micah!" Kaci called, ignoring Durya. "Where are you? Are you okay?" She could never forgive herself if she had hurt Micah. The thought of it put her feelings in perspective. She could deal with harming the four men. It may not have been her choice, but they were trying to harm her. But Micah?

"I'm here," came a soft voice. He stepped from the shadows, pulling a piece of cloth from his pack and gingerly lifting the crown. Its pristine state was starkly odd against the backdrop of the man's charred form.

"Wait!," Durya hissed. "The crown should be mine. I fought off more men."

"Oh?" Micah raised an eyebrow. "If we are counting bodies, the crown clearly belongs to Kaci."

Kaci shuddered. Even from a distance, she could feel waves of cold emanating from the crown. "Keep that thing away from me. It's cursed."

"Clearly," Micah replied, wrapping it in the cloth.

Just then, more voices echoed in the hall. *Down here! They went this way.*

Before anyone had time to react, a troop of Earthborn guards approached. "Halt in the name of King Thorlyn of the Mountain Kingdom. You are under arrest for theft and trespassing!"

Kaci turned to see if they could make a break for it, but several more Earthborn had closed in behind them. The group was trapped, with nowhere to run!

"Excuse me. We are *not* thieves, and this is *clearly* a misunderstanding." Lady Durya shoved her way forward, nearly knocking Micah over. The crown tumbled from his hands onto the stone ground, its clatter echoing off the walls.

"I can explain that," Durya added, her voice sounding less confident than before.

Two guards moved quickly to restrain Micah, and the remaining three pointed their weapons at Lady Durya.

"You don't say?" the leader remarked, his voice dripping with sarcasm.

No one seemed to pay attention to Kaci, and she wondered if she could use this to her advantage. She wanted to do what was right, but it was doubtful that these guards would believe anything they had to say. Before she had time to devise a plan, another Earthborn stepped out from the shadows. He scooped up the fallen crown with gloved hands, careful not to touch the metal with any exposed skin. Instead of the guards' leather armor, this man wore a dark-lined cloak with a hood that shadowed his face.

"You know it's cursed," Kaci whispered. The man stopped in his tracks and turned to her, his eyes widening.

Durya was arguing loudly with the guards, proclaiming her innocence—"I didn't know any of these people before today!"—when the hooded man raised a hand. Everyone fell silent. He pushed back the cowl revealing his features—an Earthborn with a robust beard that spilled over his chest in a meticulous braid. His face, weathered by age and wisdom, held an air of confidence that seemed to permeate the room.

His gaze wandered over the crowd, taking a meticulous survey of each face, as though reading the unspoken narratives etched in their expressions. Eventually, his eyes rested on Kaci. His head tilted ever so slightly, the fingers of one hand threading through his braided beard as he assessed her.

When he finally spoke, his voice was low and soft. "Perhaps there is more to this story than meets the eye. We will take them to King Thorlyn."

"*NO!*" the head guard and Lady Durya said in unison.

Micah smirked, and something about the way his lips turned up ever so slightly tugged at one of Kaci's memories. But when she tried to grasp at it, she found nothing. The thought just poofed into a cloud of dust.

The armorless Earthborn turned back to Kaci and gave her a gentle smile. "What do you know of this crown?"

Kaci blinked twice before stammering, "N—nothing. I mean, I can tell it has some sort of curse on it, but I have never seen the thing before now."

The man inclined his head in acknowledgment, but Kaci couldn't tell if he believed her. He took a step back as he evaluated the three of them. "My name is Belan, high priest to King Thorlyn of the Mountain Kingdom. You will all accompany us to hold an audience with the king."

"You are not taking me anywhere," Lady Durya sniffed. "I would rather die."

"We can arrange that," the lead guard sneered.

"You will join us as guests of honor," Belan told the lady.

"No—" The guard interjected.

"Hush, Tomas. It's decided." The guard scowled but stood down, frowning as he kicked at a loose stone on the floor.

Belan turned to Lady Durya. "You do not have a choice in this matter."

Heat flared up in Kaci. "There is always a choice!" The words flew out of her mouth before she had the chance to stop them. Why did she always have to be so impulsive? She was going to get them killed.

Belan let out a deep, rumbling chuckle and gave the girl a wink. "You may join us as guests of honor or as prisoners. That's your choice."

A rumble sounded from deeper in the mausoleum.

The earth groaned and shifted like a great beast stirring from its slumber deep within the earth. Kaci could detect an unearthly growl of something much older. Everyone turned to the sound, and Kaci felt her heart drop to her feet. It was as if everyone was frozen in time. She tried to move, but found her body stuck. Out of the corner of her eye, she detected movement. Was that Micah? Did he have the crown?

And in a flash, it was done. It was like nothing odd at all had happened. What was going on? What was wrong with her?

Micah turned with a flourish, and the image of the young boy from her vision flashed into Kaci's mind. But the boy in her vision was so much younger than this man. Perhaps he had a son?

"Honored guests, then! Let us leave." Micah grinned back at Kaci and she had the sinking feeling that he knew something she didn't.

"Did you just say *lettuce leaf?*" Kaci asked.

Micah threw his head back and howled before turning to follow the guards.

Chapter 4

Cursed Crown

"Cling not to power, for it is fleeting and corruptible. Instead, seek knowledge, for it is eternal and liberating." - Bataku Raama, *Birth of Magic*

Kaci's heart pounded in her chest as she studied the figure on the throne—the Mountain King. Elena had taught her about the leader of the Earthborn in their studies of the world outside Aeloria. This once-formidable king seemed to have withered to a skeletal shadow of his former self. Despite his frailty, there was a predatory danger to him. He was like a cornered animal, unpredictable and deadly.

A low murmur ran through the room, jolting Kaci from her thoughts. She watched the priest, who had escorted them to this place, approaching the throne.

"Brother!" The king had been a warrior, but now his

skin lay loose over his once-muscled body. "My Crown! Have you returned it to me?"

"I have it with me, Brother." Belan sighed and gave a curt nod, waving the guard, Tomas, over. "Hand me my pack."

"In this matter, I am NOT your brother. I am your sovereign!" The old man spat as he struggled to rise to his feet. "I. Want. My. CROWN!" he sputtered.

Tomas paled as he passed the large rucksack to the king with a stoic expression. Belan's face, too, grew whiter by the moment as he rummaged through the pack, but failed to produce the coveted crown.

Kaci watched the others, wondering if they could see what she saw. Micah fidgeted, his hands wringing and his eyes everywhere except Belan's backpack. Lady Durya stood tall, her nose in the air, towering above the rest in attitude and stature. Something about her stance was a little too rigid. A little too stiff.

Perhaps Kaci was the only one who could see what was happening. Her studies with Elena had taught her enough about corrupted magic to know its dangers. The cursed crown had done something to the king's mind, and the corruption seemed to have spread to his body, as well.

The king's face grew hot, like a volcano getting ready to blow, and his hand reached for the great axe that hung from his belt. "What is this trickery? Has my brother betrayed me?"

"No, Thorlyn." Belan's voice was calm, but his eyes were not. "I had it right here!"

Lady Durya stepped forward like she was going to say something, but Micah grabbed her wrist before the king swung his great axe recklessly through the air.

A breath escaped Kaci's lips as she turned to the others. They were in grave danger here. Someone had to do something, and fast.

Her voice trembled and cracked as she spoke. "It was there. I never took my eyes off the crown, from the moment it came off the thief's head until *he* had it." She pointed at Belan.

The king looked from Kaci to Durya to Micah, then back to Belan. When he finally spoke, his voice was deadly quiet. "These must be the ones you hired to plot against me."

"Thorlyn, you are wrong," Belan's calm voice cut through the tension in the throne room. His eyes never wavered from his brother as he continued, "I have no desire for the crown. Use your head—I was born to the crown and gave it up, Brother. Why would I want to be king now?"

"Lies!" the king hissed. "All lies to confuse and mislead me. Kill them all!" he commanded the waiting guards.

"You're sick, Brother, can't you see?" Belan's voice was a blend of frustration and concern. He turned, casting a sidelong glance at the head of the guards, who stood nearby. Their eyes met, and a silent understanding seemed to pass between them. Tomas gave a slight nod. "You need help," Belan added.

An icy dread built in Kaci's chest as the guards closed in on them. What was happening?

"Do you know who I am?" Lady Durya scolded. "If you lay a finger on me, the wrath of Marshfield will rain down on you!"

The king laughed a hollow laugh. "The humans have coveted my realm since I was in swaddling clothes. Do they think sending an orc in a dress will frighten me?" He turned to Tomas. "Kill them all!"

"Sir," Tomas stammered. "This is your brother. Perhaps we—perhaps a tribunal would be called for?"

Kaci held her breath as the king paused.

"Silence!" King Thorlyn roared. "You would just as soon steal the crown for yourself!"

Belan opened his mouth, then closed it quickly.

"I tire." King Thorlyn gave a dismissal, waving everyone out. "Take them to the dungeon to rot." His face was hollow and gaunt, and his skin was like a dried husk. But for a brief moment, the king's eyes flared bright and blue, and Kaci glimpsed his former vigor. "DO not return without my crown." He sank back into the massive throne like a tiny boy pretending at war. Kaci could swear she saw a small black shadow hovering over the king. Then it was gone.

"Question each of them until you find my crown, and if you don't find my crown, you all die."

"Yes, sir." Tomas made a show of waving his sword at the group.

Tomas escorted them unceremoniously out of the great hall and led them down a spiral staircase that plunged into the heart of the mountain. Finally, they stopped before a set of double doors. Kaci watched as Micah snapped his fingers repeatedly, looking at them curiously. She returned her attention to the guard.

"Is this the dungeon?" Kaci asked, looking from Tomas to Belan.

The old guard let out a hearty laugh, and Belan answered. "No, child. These are my apartments. We were never in any danger."

"You were about to give your shell of a king a cursed crown," Lady Durya scoffed. "It seems like you were setting us up for a lot of trouble!"

Belan shook his head. "No, my lady. He would not receive that crown. Many months ago I had a replica made. I planned to swap the replica with the cursed crown until I could make him better. Tomas?"

With a practiced hand, the guard chose a key from his belt, unlocking the heavy door. It groaned as it opened to a comfortable sitting room with plush chairs and a small shrine to the Allfather.

"Thank you, old friend. Please be safe. I do not want you caught up in this mess, ya?"

Tomas sniffed, disregarding Belan's advice. "I had word that a scouting group has returned. I'll send any intel your way." His voice held a tone of camaraderie and shared burden. It was clear to Kaci that, while the king was the face of the kingdom, Belan was its spine.

"But don't take too long, Belan," Tomas continued, his words underscored with urgency. "The guards tell me he has grown worse, not better, since the crown was stolen."

Belan sighed and gave his friend a pat on the back. "Be safe, Tomas. We will set this right." The guard turned and closed the great doors behind him.

In the privacy of the chamber, Lady Durya began to pace, eyes full of fire. "Do you want to tell us what is happening, Earthborn? Here we are minding our own business when you kidnap us, accused us of stealing, drag us deep into dangerous territory, and place us in front of an insane king."

Belan opened his mouth to reply, but she cut him off. "I have the mind to arrest you right here and place you before a war tribunal."

Belan crossed his arms "Lady—"

"Do you even know who I am? What power I hold?" Lady Durya's voice echoed through the chamber, her large frame towering over those around her. "That king insulted me. He called me an orc in a dress! What do you have to say for yourself?" She paced the floor, her footfalls heavy, a storm in the room.

"The king—" Belan began.

"I am the *Lady* of Marshfield Estates. My foster father is the Duke of Westerfield, second only to the King."

She punctuated her words with a powerful thump of her fist against her chest. "Believe me, a human king is more important than your piddly little mountain king. We could crush you in the blink of an eye."

Belan sank into one of the plush chairs scattered about the room, resigned. His lips remained a thin line under the bushy beard that hid his face.

To Kaci's horror, Micah pealed into a fit of laughter. Lady Durya placed her hands on her hips and glared at him in rage.

"Are you done?" Belan asked Lady Durya.

The lady blinked twice before nodding abruptly. "Yes."

"Please, have a seat then." He waved at the chairs around the sitting room.

"About six months ago, my brother received that crown as a gift from Aeloria."

Kaci's eyes widened. Why would her people give

the Earthborn a crown? Aelorians didn't even use crowns.

"Thorlyn ruled with truth and honor," Belan continued. "He had always been a wise ruler, right up to the time the crown entered our lives. No one saw it, but things changed when Thorlyn placed it on his head. No longer did we stay up all night drinking ale and talking about times past and future. The king was suspicious of everyone. Every dark corner hid some threat of danger. One by one, our allies and friends dropped away until the only ones left in the grand hall were a few grizzled old warriors with nowhere else to turn. And me. I worry the Aelorians have cursed us."

"I understand your concern, Belan, but I know my people," Kaci's voice was heated. She may have left Aeloria, but she would always defend her people. "They have cursed no one and certainly not a crown. Perhaps it was lost or stolen, but it is unfair to blame the Aelorians without proof." She felt a twinge of guilt for her outburst. Belan was clearly worried for his brother, but she couldn't shake off the hurt that someone would falsely accuse the Aelorians.

"I don't blame your people, child." Belan gestured to the door. "I rode north with Tomas and the others to speak with the Aelorian council of elders and prayed they had not fallen to the same corruption as my brother. I planned to solve the mystery, but no one knew anything about the crown. They thanked me for my time and sent me on my way."

Kaci closed her eyes and imagined how Belan's meeting with the elders would have gone. She pictured her people gathered in a circle, speaking softly in their musical language, while the Earthborn barged in with their loud voices and harsh accents. Elena would be dismissive, Kaci knew, and her people would be passive and secretive as usual, only sharing what was necessary. Kaci wondered if her people had anything to do with the crown, but it seemed unlikely. The elves were not known for their greed or thirst for power. They preferred to keep to themselves and live in harmony with the natural world. She opened her eyes, listening intently to Belan's continued explanation.

"I returned home to find that the crown was making Thorlyn sicker and sicker. I was afraid he would not survive much longer. I had the replica made and hired men to swap it for the cursed crown while he slept. Unfortunately, things did not go as planned; instead of bringing me the cursed crown, they stole it and escaped into the night. Tomas and I tracked them to the old mausoleum."

Kaci studied the Earthborn priest. Belan stood contrary to the stereotype of the gruff and warrior-like Earthborn. His rough brown robes hung loosely over his frame, and a simple wooden staff rested in his hand. He exuded a quiet strength and wisdom that was hard to ignore. Though his voice was gentle and measured, he commanded respect from those around him. It was easy to see why he was a revered leader. He took Micah's and Lady Durya's many questions in stride, drawing a deep breath between each answer.

He had adorned the room with lavish but tasteful furnishings. Soft, plush cushions were strewn across the floor, providing comfortable places to sit. A beautiful, handcrafted mahogany table rested in the corner. Its intricate carvings and rich color drew Kaci's eye. On top of the table sat an imposing black bowl, much larger than any washbasin she had ever seen. Its smooth surface reflected the light in a strange, otherworldly way. Kaci felt a sense of unease as she looked from the bowl to the man sitting in front of her.

"Earthborn, don't scry!" she blurted out, regretting her impulsivity immediately.

Belan broke into a peal of warm laughter that seemed to fill the room and envelop her in its warmth. It was the first time she had felt safe since leaving her village, and probably the first time she had felt accepted by an elder. The comfort felt strange on her skin, but she liked it.

"You are right, child. It is rare to see one such as I." He spoke in a soft voice. "But, the Allfather willed it, and who am I to question his gifts?"

Kaci smiled. Belan had called her child again. Elena often called her child, as if all her years of learning meant nothing and she was just a little thing with no knowledge. But when Belan said it, it felt warm, like he was some wise and knowing grandfather.

"I question the Great Mother too much." Kaci smiled and met the Earthborn's eyes. "Elena said that would be my downfall."

"Questions are important. Curiosity exists for a reason. Life is full of mystery, and we do our gods a disservice if we do not explore it."

"Didn't Einstein say something like that?" Micah mused.

"Who is that?" Lady Durya asked.

"No one you would know." Micah's face reddened. "I'm not sure your education would be that vast."

"Are you calling me uneducated?" Durya rose to her feet and took a step toward Micah.

"No, of course not. I am just from far away." Micah gave a bow, and Lady Durya returned to her seat.

Belan rose and waved Kaci over to the scrying bowl. "This is how I found the crown after the thieves stole it from the king. I had a mind to let them keep it, but my brother continued to worsen. I'm positive that whatever curse the crown holds must be destroyed at its source before he can be restored."

He reached for a large water pitcher and poured it into the bowl. "Would you like to try? I was going to look after you all retired for the night, but maybe your skills surpass mine."

Kaci peered over the edge of the obsidian bowl, and her insides turned to jelly. "I—I can't. I scry with fire, anyway. The water never seems to work for me," she whispered. Kaci remember the last time she had tried scrying. *An Earthborn man plunged into the flames, where the liquid magma consumed him.* She looked at Belan, sure now that this Earthborn was the man from her vision.

The charred faces from the enclave came rushing back to her. Even though the other apprentices had been cruel, no one deserved to be burned that way. It was no wonder everyone back home hated her. She was a monster. Her breath caught in her throat as she looked around the room. "I shouldn't even be here. I need to leave."

Her throat was closing, and she couldn't breathe. There was no way out. Where were the trees? Blood pounded in her ears. She was going to be the death of them all. A fire crackled in a small stone fireplace on the west side of the room. Was it getting bigger? Should she warn them?

Then she felt a gentle hand on her shoulder. "Breathe," Belan's soothing voice instructed. "Inhale, count to five, then let it out slowly."

Air flooded her lungs, and she counted slowly. The fire was fine, just the right size—not too big or small. Kaci let the air slip between her lips as it escaped her body, then took another large breath.

"There now," Belan said. "It's going to be all right. How does everyone feel about getting a good night's rest and developing a plan in the morning?"

"You expect me to spend another night as your prisoner?" Lady Durya frowned, and Micah smacked her, pointing at Kaci. "Oh well, that will be fine," she continued.

Kaci sniffled and felt the corner of her lips turn up. No one had ever cared about her. This was nice. She watched Belan rise from his chair and show the others to the spare sleeping chambers. Micah hugged his leather satchel close as he headed into his room, and Lady Durya had to duck under the low doorway. Kaci covered her mouth to hold in a laugh.

With the other two settled into their rooms, Belan turned to Kaci and waved her toward the largest door.

"How big is this place?" Kaci asked. Her voice still wavered slightly, but she felt much more steady than before.

"It's adequately sized," Belan managed a smile. "The sitting room, my sleeping quarters, and sleeping rooms for two apprentices. I gave the smaller rooms to Micah and Lady Durya. You can rest in my quarters. I sleep out here more often than in my bed, anyway. I have work yet to do."

Kaci followed his stare to the obsidian bowl and took a deep breath.

"Do you…" Kaci paused, looking at the scrying bowl again. "Do you think you could teach me to use the water? Elena never had the patience to train me. She mostly directed me to what came naturally."

"Come." His voice warmed her like the sunrise over her forest.

Belan tapped the water's black surface a few times, and Kaci watched as the ripples spread from his fingertip. Little waves pulsed like a heartbeat.

"What do you see when you look into the fire?" Belan asked, turning to meet her gaze.

"It's hard to explain," Kaci mused. "It's less like seeing and more like…" she turned back to the bowl. "Becoming?"

"Are you asking me?" Belan laughed. "There is no right or wrong. You do not need to impress me."

Kaci laughed uncomfortably. "It starts deep in my belly, like a warmth. When I am sad, it is easier. It's like that emotion lives inside me, and staring at the fire brings it out. The flames consume me until I am somewhere else. Like I am watching a scene, but I cannot hear what anyone says. Usually, the music is too loud, and the colors too bright. Elena said to push that down, but the more I push, the louder and brighter it gets, and then I fall out of the vision."

A hearty laugh escaped Belan's chest, brightening the room. "Why would you push that down? You are filled with light and music, my child. If you let it out, you just might change the world!"

"Oh, no, you are wrong. I am a failure and not full of joy—only sorrow," Kaci told the man. "I mean no disrespect, but you cannot see inside of me."

Belan was still laughing, but he got in a few words between breaths. "You are as bright as the sun," he gasped. "You are a super-nova, child. I would have to be blind to miss that."

"But won't I hurt someone?" Kaci frowned. The man was obviously crazy. Maybe she shouldn't have asked for help.

"Look into the water, Kaci. See the sun rising over a pristine lake?"

She gazed at the surface and felt it within herself. The pressure building. Her fists clenched, and she turned to Belan in a panic. She was going to blow them all up. She knew it.

"Breathe," he whispered. "Bring your focus back to the water. This time, don't push away what's down there. Become it."

So she did. The music started faintly but grew into a beautiful crescendo of notes and colors, and the sun burst forth over the water's edge. She let go, and a warmth spread through her body.

Kaci was no longer in a dark room but surrounded by trees and the sky.

Bathed in the open embrace of the sunrise. The heart of an unknown village pulsed, its human inhabitants bustling, an odd rhythm to their daily tasks. Strangeness hung in the air, an unseen veil that turned the merry tunes into dark symphonies, that twisted smiles into wary glances.

Invisible to the world, Kaci drifted, compelled toward the bustling town square like a leaf in the wind.

The throng surged, and a shadowy figure emerged at the helm of the town hall, a visage veiled by obscurity. No matter how Kaci pushed through the crowd or how she strained her eyes, the figure remained frustratingly elusive. Amid the chaos, the hum of the crowd, the ominous music, one word pierced through—Westerfield.

Silence hung in the air, thick and suffocating. The crowd vanished. The music ceased. All that remained was Kaci and the woman shrouded in shadows. The figure lifted a delicate crown, crafted with fine precision, a symbol at its heart. Three intertwining lines were etched into the met-

al, their colors distinctly radiant, each line gleaming gold, silver, and onyx.

Shadows swelled around them, threatening to consume everything. The woman crowned herself. Her voice, dark as the oncoming night, echoed through the eerie silence, "By the dark of the new moon, I will touch the gods!" The darkness detonated, an explosion of shadows engulfing the town, consuming everything in its path.

"NO!" Kaci screamed.

She was back in the room, with Belan's powerful arms pulling her up. "Find your light, child. Find your light."

When she looked, it was there, pushing deep within. Hope, love, and the answer.

"I know where to find the crown," she whispered.

Chapter 5

The Road to Marshfield

"True magic lies not in the spells we cast, but in the connections we make with others. To truly know someone, we must look beyond the surface and delve into the depths of their soul. Only then can we unlock the true power of friendship." - Bataku Raama, *The Birth of Magic*

The weight of the vision pressed on Kaci's mind, pointing her toward Westerfield and the terrifying shadow woman. Something awful was unfolding in that place, and Kaci couldn't bear the thought of abandoning Belan to face the shadows unassisted. She was torn between her fears and the knowledge that she shouldn't turn away from this impending darkness.

A piercing scream interrupted her thoughts, and a loud thud followed by the scuffling of feet.

"What's going on?" Kaci asked with concern.

Belan's brow furrowed with worry.

As they approached the source of the commotion, Lady Durya's shrill voice demanded attention. "I knew you were up to no good," she yelled from inside the room.

Micah responded, his voice muffled, "You have it all wrong. Let me go!"

Lady Durya retorted, "Not until you give it back!"

"It's not yours!" he protested.

"It's not yours either!"

Belan swung the door open to reveal Lady Durya holding Micah's pack, with Thorlyn's crown in plain sight. Kaci gasped in surprise. She would have sworn her vision told her it was hidden somewhere else. But when she looked closer, she could see this crown differed from the one in her vision.

The crown in Micah's possession was sturdy and well crafted, with intricate designs etched along its surface. It had a regal presence, fit for a ruler of great power and authority. The centerpiece of the crown was a symbol made of three interconnected spirals, like the one from her vision. Each element flowed seamlessly into the next. It was a symbol of great significance, and Kaci felt drawn to it, even without knowing its meaning.

Belan looked from Lady Durya to Micah and shook his head. "You are playing with forces you don't understand."

"But I understand!" Micah protested. "More than you know!"

The Lady rolled her eyes. "Of course you understand. You understand how valuable it is."

"No…" Micah signed, then flopped down on a narrow bed.

"Why were you going through his things?" Kaci interrupted, eyeing Lady Durya.

"To rescue the crown, of course," she sniffed. "So we could get out of here."

"If you knew he had the crown, why didn't you tell Belan?" Kaci pressed. "He probably has better control of this situation. This is his home!"

"I didn't *know* he had the crown. I simply knew this fellow was shifty," Lady Durya retorted.

"It seems you were the one being shifty by going through his stuff," Kaci pointed out.

"Who are you to judge my actions?" Durya frowned. "I demand that you stand down!"

It was Belan's soothing voice that finally diffused the situation. "What's done is done. The crown is dangerous and must be taken care of. And that is what we will do. But it is not something that can simply be destroyed. We must return it to where it came from."

"That is what I was trying to do." Micah sighed. "With no one else getting hurt."

"Wait, if you knew about the crown already, why didn't you tell us?" Lady Durya's voice was low and menacing. "When we were in the Earthborn mausoleum."

His gaze shifted between Kaci and Lady Durya. Then opened his mouth as if about to speak, but sighed before finally muttering, "I couldn't, I can't explain. I just need to do this."

His eyes turned up, pleading as Lady Durya stomped a foot.

"Let it be, lady. His heart is true," Belan said.

"How do you know?" the lady asked.

"Call it a gift," Belan replied with a smile.

Kaci had remained quiet as she examined the crown from a distance. Suddenly, she spoke up. "I don't think this is the same crown from my vision. The one I saw was more delicate. This one is sturdier." She paused. "I don't know for sure, but I have a feeling that there might be two crowns."

"Visions?" Lady Durya blinked. "Two crowns?"

"New information has come to the surface," Belan said. "I believe we can find a piece of this puzzle and perhaps another crown in Westerfield, near the village of Marshfield."

The lady's lips thinned. "Marshfield?"

"Yes." Belan smiled. "Hand me the crown, son. We must have them all before they can be cleansed."

"All?" Kaci asked, curiosity getting the better of her. "How many do you think there are?"

The silence was heavy, and Kaci wasn't sure that Belan would answer her, but after a moment, he did. "I don't know for sure, but I suspect there are three crowns, child. One for each of the powers in our land."

Kaci gaped in surprise. "Three crowns?" she repeated. "So, if there's one for the Earthborn and one for the humans, that would mean there's one in Aeloria?" Her mind raced with possibilities. Where could it be? Was Elena safe?

"What about the orcs?" Lady Durya added, crossing her arms.

Belan chuckled at Lady Durya's question. "You and I both know the orcs are not organized enough to hold significant power, my lady," he said, with a hint of amusement in his voice. "Their strength lies in their numbers and fierce fighting skills, but they do not possess the political prowess to hold a throne."

Lady Durya turned to Belan with a steely gaze. "Since you are going in the direction of Marshfield, you will escort me home," she demanded.

Belan's amusement was clear in his smile. "As you wish, my lady," he replied.

Kaci's mind was elsewhere. "Would that mean the third crown is near Arba Vitae?" She swallowed hard.

"That is the conclusion I came to as well," Belan answered. "I'm sorry, child."

"I need to go back! I must warn Elena!" Kaci could feel the panic rising. Was it too late? It had been six months since she left, right before the conclave. Any of the elders could have it.

"Child, the water showed you Marshfield," Belan said. "Would you like to join us on our journey to

Marshfield? Your vision guided me to the answer, and your skills may be useful to us."

Kaci's heart sank as thoughts of home pulled at her. They might all be in danger, and even if they didn't love her, she loved them. However, she had to go where she was needed most. With a deep sigh, she resolved to focus on the crowns she'd already located and put her worries about her home aside for now.

"I will arrange for our departure," Belan told everyone, then looked at Micah. "Once we clear the mountain, you are free to go."

Micah rose from the bed. "I will come with you," he stated simply.

"Sure." Lady Durya's voice dripped with sarcasm. "Three crowns are more valuable than one."

"It's not like that," Micah insisted. "Their value is not in the coin they will bring."

"Then what is it?" Durya asked.

"I can't tell you," Micah replied. All Lady Durya could do was roll her eyes.

Belan studied them both and interrupted the exchange. "Marshfield is not an Orcish territory. What ties do you have with them?"

Lady Durya let out a bitter laugh. "By right, I am the baroness of Marshfield Estates. But I know what you are thinking, and they certainly do not follow me for my beauty."

Kaci's head snapped up at the mention of the estate. "Baroness? How are you a baroness to a human territory?" she asked, tilting her head. "No offense."

Lady Durya smiled wryly. "Oddly enough, I am not offended," she said, patting Kaci's head gently. "I am the youngest child of Lord Maxwell Conwyn. He granted me the title and the estate as a reward for my services to our people."

A slow smile spread across Micah's face. "Marshfield Estates, mmm?"

"What is that to you?" Lady Durya frowned. "It's the truth!" She ripped open her satchel, retrieved a letter, and waved it in Micah's face. "They called me home!"

"So how did you end up in a cave, alone? Don't you get escorts for that sort of thing?" The young man laughed.

Lady Durya's fists tightened, crumpling the letter.

She squeezed her eyes shut as if to push back tears or anger. Kaci was not sure which.

"Please stop, Micah," Kaci interjected. "Lady Durya, may I see your letter?"

The large woman let out a breath and handed the crumpled paper to Kaci, who smoothed it and read.

To My Dearest Foster Daughter, Lady Durya Barclay of Seaside,

With the greatest sadness, I write to inform you of the death of your father, Lord Maxwell Conwyn. My grief knows no bounds, and I beg you and your husband, Lord Barclay, to return to your childhood home and help us in our time of need.

I am afraid I can tell you no more in writing. I only ask that you hurry.

Yours Truly and With Much Love,

Lady Evelyn Conwyn, Duchess of Marshfield

"Oh," was all that escaped Micah's lips.

"I'm so sorry, Lady Durya!" Kaci cried, wrapping

her arms around the large woman. Lady Durya stiffened but did not pull away. "You have a husband? Where is he?"

The Baroness froze and pulled away from Kaci's hug. "There was a storm, and the ship sank to the bottom of the sea."

"Oh, my goodness!" Kaci blinked. "What happened to the people? Where is your husband?"

"Well, I imagine at the bottom of the sea," the woman retorted. "He was not much of a swimmer."

Cocking her head, Kaci opened her mouth to say more but shut it quickly.

"I was making my way to Marshfield on my own when the storm arose. That is when I came upon you people. It would seem in my best interests to travel as a group." She sniffed.

"So be it," Belan answered, looking the tall woman up and down. "I suspect time is of the essence and suggest we leave immediately."

Belan made his way to a large cupboard, opening it to reveal enough supplies and rations for months. "Fill your packs and we will be on our way!"

"How are we going to get past the king?" Kaci asked, raising an eyebrow. "I doubt he will just let us leave."

"Earthborn are a pragmatic race and always well prepared." Belan chuckled, pushing a rich carpet aside to reveal a trapdoor. "This will get us well away from the mountain and on our way."

The wooden door creaked and groaned as Belan pulled it open. He dusted some old cobwebs from the entrance, and Lady Durya squealed as a few spiders skittered away into the cracks.

"Eww, spiders! I hate spiders."

Micah's eyes landed on a large feather that had fallen from a nearby quill. Without thinking, he picked it up and twirled it between his fingers, contemplating its softness. Then he waved it at the back of Lady Durya's neck. She shrieked and whipped around, her arm lashing out and striking Micah square in the face. The force of the blow sent him tumbling across the room, where he landed in a heap on the floor.

"OUCH!" he screamed. "What was that for?"

"Oh," she sniffed, "I thought you were a spider."

"Enough play. Let us be on our way," Belan said as

he descended the ladder into the tunnel below.

When they all reached the bottom, he passed out torches.

"Keep mine as a spare," Kaci said, grinning. She felt the pressure building as she summoned a small ball of light that hung in the air in front of her. It was fun to show off for once.

"My dear," The Baroness chimed in, "do remember, when this is over, you still have an open invitation to be one of my ladies-in-waiting."

Kaci sighed. When would the lady understand she hated waiting?

As they continued down the dry and well-maintained tunnel under the mountain, Kaci's thoughts drifted back to her home, Arba Vitae, and the forest. She longed for its comforting embrace and whispered a prayer to the Great Mother for Elena's safety.

As the group walked on in silence, Kaci's gaze drifted to her new companions. Each seemed to glow with an inner light. Belan radiated a calming blue aura, his wisdom surpassing even that of Elena. Already, Kaci admitted to herself with a pang of guilt that she held Belan in higher regard than her own mentor. She had known Belan for less than a day, yet his teachings had made a deep impact on her. With Elena, she had always felt unsure, afraid of failure, doubtful of her own capabilities; but with Belan, her sense of confidence had surged.

Lady Durya was a study of contradictions. She strived to present herself as a proper noblewoman, with a bold demeanor matching her high station. However, this facade was often shattered by her quick and explosive temper, which seemed to always bubble beneath the surface. Despite her attempts at decorum, Lady Durya's emotions often got the best of her. Kaci stifled a giggle as she recalled some of the woman's impulsive outbursts. It seemed Lady Durya couldn't quite decide what kind of person she wanted to be and was constantly struggling to reconcile these conflicting aspects of herself. Kaci found herself inexplicably drawn to this complex woman.

"What are you looking at?" The Baroness spat.

"Nothing, just thinking," Kaci replied.

"Well, think more quietly!" The woman crossed her arms and sniffed.

Micah, for some reason Kaci couldn't put her finger on, projected a sense of familiarity that put her at ease.

Maybe it was the way he carried himself—with an air of nonchalance that suggested he didn't take life too seriously. Or maybe it was the twinkle in his eyes when he looked at her, as if he already knew her secrets and loved her for them. But this gaze also held a hint of sadness, a lurking darkness. Kaci wondered what demons he was hiding, what past he was running from. She couldn't help but feel connected to him, wanting to know more about this man who seemed to have a world of his own. She vowed to keep his secrets and to be his friend in the strange and uncertain days to come.

Ahead, a pinprick of gray light showed they would soon exit the tunnels. Kaci let out a breath she hadn't known she was holding. Soon she would see the trees and the great sky again. And even if they were not her own trees, they would be better than that dungeon of a mountain. She wondered if the Allfather liked it dark, like the bowels of the earth.

"Hey, Belan," Kaci called out, jogging to catch up with him. "Why do the Earthborn live so deep in the mountains? Does the Allfather will it?"

Belan laughed a rich and hearty chuckle. "Oh, no child," he said. "The Allfather is the god of the sky and air. He lives on the highest peaks and loves to take the form of a stag."

"Huh. Then why do the Earthborn worship him? Wouldn't they choose a god more rooted in the earth."

"Then what would we reach for?" Belan asked, a smile stretching across his face.

Kaci beamed, feeling a warmth spread through her. "Will you tell me about him? The Allfather. While we travel."

"Of course, child," Belan replied. "I would be honored."

As they continued toward the light, Belan told Kaci about the god of hunters and warriors, known for his love of freedom. The Allfather had shaped the world—created the winds that swept across the mountains and given the Earthborn their love for the depths of the earth. Kaci listened intently, fascinated by tales of the powerful deity. She gazed down the path as they walked through the dark tunnel, wondering if the Allfather was watching them.

Belan's eyes sparkled with a glint of nostalgia as he gazed ahead. "To touch the sky," he smiled, "is the goal for us Earthborn. It represents the pinnacle of our existence and the essence of our being."

Kaci listened intently, her curiosity piqued by Belan's words. "But how can you touch the sky?" she asked.

Belan's smile widened. "Some Earthborn strive to climb the highest mountains, to reach the peaks where the Allfather dwells. Others aim to create something that will last beyond their time, reaching toward the heavens in their own way."

Kaci nodded. She could see in Belan's determination the unyielding spirit that drove the Earthborn toward their lofty goal. She, too, felt the pull of something greater, something beyond her reach but still within her grasp. A pang of sorrow clutched her heart as she realized how much she missed the sky above her beloved Arba Vitae.

The light brightened until the group no longer needed their torches, and the tunnel widened into a large stone archway. They entered a dappled forest, where the morning sun peeked through the tree branches. Kaci bounded into the fresh air, dancing under the great sky while the others watched.

"Oh, thank you, Great Mother, for the sun and the sky!" Kaci sang, stopping to pick a wildflower, then skipping back to tuck it behind Lady Durya's ear. The Baroness rolled her eyes but left the flower where it was. "Oh! Look at this!" On the ground in front of them was

the largest, brightest feather Kaci had ever seen. "I wonder what bird lost this!" She tucked the plume into her
pack. "It must be a sign of good fortune." She grinned.

"The road lies ahead," Belan's voice was soft, "It is
at least a day's walk until we reach Marshfield. We must
make haste if we are to get there before the dark of the
moon." He was fast for someone with such short legs.

All forests had a voice. A symphony of sounds
breathing in and out in harmony. Within this forest,
Kaci began to tune in to a single distinct noise. It didn't
feel frightening, just a bit off—as though one voice in
the chorus was unrehearsed, yet trying to mimic the
beautiful melody.

Kaci skipped up to Belan. "Someone is following
us," she whispered so no one else could hear. "Act normal." Then she skipped nonchalantly to the back of the
group.

The forest had been Kaci's playground since she
was a small child, so she was an expert at disappearing
into the woods. This group was too lost in their own
thoughts to miss her, anyway, Kaci reasoned. Without
a second thought, she scurried up a tree and sat back
in its branches to observe. The group continued onward, but she had no worries about losing them. As fast

as they were, she was faster, and this road seemed to meander back and forth. She would take a more direct approach to catch up.

It wasn't long before she caught sight of the interlopers. Three figures emerged from the woods, backpacks laden and heavy. The tallest of the three scanned the road and waved the other two on. It wasn't until they were right upon her that Kaci jumped from her tree.

"Smeadon!" She squealed and gave the goblin a hug. He looked at the other two, mumbled something, and shrugged. "What are you doing following us?"

The old goblin smiled (or at least she thought it was a smile) and patted his rucksack. It clattered and clanged. When he opened it, the pack was full of treasure.

Smeadon's sharp teeth gleamed in the sunlight as he grinned at Kaci. "Your crazy group lead us to many prizes," he said, his voice laced with appreciation. "And leave the treasures ripe for pickin's."

Kaci raised an eyebrow in concern. "I don't think the Earthborn would want you taking their offerings," she said, peering into the backpack.

"The dead don't need it," Smeadon replied matter-of-factly. "And you people don't either, or you would have taken it."

Kaci sighed, acknowledging his point. "Well, I suppose they don't," she said with a shrug. "But I wouldn't show that to Belan if I were you."

Smeadon's grin faltered slightly, and he glanced over his shoulder at his fellow goblins. "You no tell the others we here?" he asked, his voice low. "Thems type don't understand our type. We trying to collect enough treasure that our clan be takin' us back."

Kaci's eyes widened in surprise and sympathy. "You lost your clan?" she asked softly.

"We the shunned ones, li'l lady elf," Smeadon replied, his tone bitter. "But you bring lots of luck and treasure."

Kaci felt a pang of sadness for the goblins. "Well, I suppose if you promise not to hurt us, I won't say that you are following," she said, offering a small smile.

"We no hurt, right Jeth? Right, Meshach?" Smeadon turned to his companions, who both nodded in agreement.

"Okay then, be careful. We are approaching a human city, and they are not very kind to the likes of you," Kaci warned.

"We know, li'l lady elf. We be safe," Smeadon assured her, attempting to smile again.

Kaci suddenly remembered something and rummaged through her pack. "Oh, wait! I have a gift for you," she exclaimed, pulling out a bright red plume. "This will bring you luck. May it find you lots of treasure!" She handed the feather to Smeadon before bounding into the forest toward the others.

Chapter 6

Secrets in the Shadows

"Those who seek power above all else will often find themselves consumed by it, for the cost of greatness is often greater than one can bear." - Bataku Raama, *The Birth of Magic*

At first glance, Marshfield looked like any other bustling human settlement. But something was off. Kaci recognized so much from her vision—the air thick with tension, the residents who seemed to go about their business as usual, yet with suspicion in their eyes. As the group walked further into the village, Kaci felt a growing sense of unease, and she couldn't shake the feeling that her group was being watched.

Kaci recognized even more landmarks as they approached the town hall. The dirt path leading up to it was just as she remembered, and she noted the towering manor with its protective stone wall. They were on the right track, and it filled her with dread. What secrets lay hidden within its walls?

This was where Lady Durya had grown up. Kaci looked at her friend, surprised to see the usually confident Lady Durya looking uncomfortable and on edge.

As they neared the town hall, the locals' suspicious glances morphed into outright hostility. Kaci could feel their eyes boring into her back, and it made her skin crawl. It was as if they knew who she was and why she was there.

"Lady Durya," Kaci asked her friend, "Shouldn't these people recognize you? I mean, you are their baroness, right?"

The lady blinked as she searched the faces and then looked at her feet. "I did not leave the manor all that often," she finally answered. "My brother, Marcus, would make public appearances. He had thicker skin and could take their stares and unkind words. We were nothing," she sighed. "Mere war casualties."

"What do you mean?" Kaci asked.

Lady Durya gestured toward the marshlands in the distance. "Long ago, the humans and orcs in this area were at war. People lived in fear of the sieges. It was brutal and unending. The constant battles had taken a toll on both sides. My foster father, Lord Maxwell Conwyn, was a wise and brilliant man. He desired nothing more than peace."

As the group continued toward the city's center, the townspeople gave them a wide berth. Belan put a finger to his lips and gestured to their right. A tall man in a cowl was tracking them.

As Lady Durya continued recounting her past, her face appeared serene, yet her reddened cheeks and shifting gaze betrayed her embarrassment. "My foster father proposed a treaty that involved the exchange of hostages between the orcs and humans—my brother and me for Lord Conwyn's young son. And so, I was raised by the Lord and Lady of Marshfield as their own daughter."

"Unfortunately, Lord Conwyn's son didn't survive the harsh Orcish environment he was raised in," Lady Durya explained with a hint of sadness in her voice. "Although I wouldn't be surprised if my birth parents just ate him out of boredom," she added with a shrug.

Kaci couldn't believe what she was hearing.

"It was a tragic end for the Conwyns, but it gave my foster father a significant advantage over the orcs. It was a small sacrifice for the greater good."

"That's cold," Micah remarked, a shudder in his voice, "These your people?"

"Micah!" Kaci cut in sharply, "Have—"

The figure, shrouded in a dark cloak, positioned himself squarely in front of the group, silencing their mounting dissent. Beneath the cowl, a pair of discerning eyes measured them.

"What business do you have here?" he inquired. His voice was cool and hard, and his curt tone seemed to echo in the street, silencing any lingering conversations and demanding undivided attention from the group.

"We are merely passing through to the inner city," The Baroness answered confidently. "We mean you no trouble."

"City is closed to strangers," the man replied. "Duke's orders."

"I am no stranger to the Duke," Lady Durya put her hands on her hips. "I will be most welcome at the gate, I assure you."

"You don't understand. Lord Marcus said no one was to pass. No one." The man placed a firm hand on Lady Durya's forearm. She twisted his arm back and grabbed his throat.

"Who are you?" she hissed, eyes flaring.

Kaci swallowed. They seemed to be drawing a crowd.

"I'm s—ss—sorry. My name is Toran. I am the Mayor!" the man squeaked.

"Well, Toran, I demand you fetch Lord Marcus at once!" Her voice wavered as she said the name, but she did not loosen her grip.

Toran made a choking noise but said nothing further, and Kaci tugged at Lady Durya's sleeve. "I don't think he can talk."

The Baroness blinked. "Oh, pardon me." She stepped back and dusted off her dress. "Please fetch Marcus and tell him his sister is here."

"Sister?" Belan asked, raising an eyebrow. "You mean to say your Orcish brother is in charge here?"

"That is what I would like to find out. He left years ago!"

"You must be living in a hole," Toran interrupted, "Marcus has returned. He is our savior!"

Lady Durya frowned and turned her full attention

to the many. "What is this rubbish? The townspeople always hated my brother and me. He was to be executed!"

"Forgive me, but you must be mistaken," Toran continued. His eyes glazed over as he spoke. "Marcus left us for a while but has returned to us in all his glory. I heard he even rescued the king!"

As the mayor puffed out his chest proudly, his shirt opened slightly to reveal a pendant on a silver chain. He quickly covered it with his hand. "And tonight, Marcus has sent us one of his apprentices to perform a ritual to open a portal to the infinite! We will all be blessed with the power from beyond."

"This is insane! Marcus didn't rescue any king. He went to—" Lady Durya closed her mouth abruptly, looking around. They were drawing a crowd now, and the people looked angry.

Belan laid a hand on Lady Durya's arm and whispered under his breath, "Take a moment and observe."

He turned to the distraught Mayor. "I apologize, Mayor Toran. We have been traveling a long time to reach Marshfield, and we are all tired. Forgive any confusion. Perhaps you can direct us to an inn where we can clean up and rest, and you can inform Lord Marcus that his sister is here."

The mayor gave a slight nod. "I suppose that seems appropriate. But the inn is full, overflowing. Lord Marcus returned home with many apprentices."

Lady Durya opened her mouth to speak again, but Belan hushed her.

"You can use Alma Costgren's home." The mayor smiled. "It has been empty since she went missing. I would not want to anger Lord Marcus by refusing his sister shelter." He gave a slight bow, almost an afterthought.

"Missing?" Micah asked, eyeing the man. "What if she came home?"

"Oh no, I don't think that would happen." Mayor Toran blinked. "She has been missing for nearly a month now. She missed last month's ritual, you know?"

"Last month's ritual? Like the one tonight? How often do you have these things?" Kaci asked.

"Oh my." Toran swallowed. "I believe I have said too much. You are not even initiated yet." He began to pace and tug at the chain around his neck. "Oh, my."

"But I am Lord Marcus's sister!" Lady Durya looked at the others and shrugged. "I'm sure he would want us…" she paused. "Initiated."

"Quite right." The mayor sputtered and turned heel. "This way."

The group followed the strange man through Marshfield's dusty streets, weaving through roads until he stopped in front of a modest wooden home with a thatch roof. He fumbled through his pockets and produced a small key, which he used to unlock the front door.

"I will send a message to Lord Marcus that you are here, and I will fetch you in the morning." He handed the key to Durya. "Do not leave this house tonight. It is dangerous to be about."

"The ceremony?" Micah asked. "When and where is that?"

"Oh, you cannot attend," the mayor smiled. "You are not initiated. The apprentices will not let you near the town hall." The man covered his mouth, eyes darting back and forth. "Stay inside tonight. Please?" His request sounded like a whimper. and looked like

He lingered in the doorway like he wanted to say more, then turned abruptly and walked away, muttering.

The group filed into the home and Belan closed the door behind them.

"Is it just me, or was that really strange?" Kaci asked the others, her eyes wide. "What was that necklace he kept fiddling with? I saw it in my vision."

Micah froze. "Did you get a good look at it?"

"I think so," Kaci nodded. "It had three spirals that were interlinking somehow." She scanned the room until she spotted a small writing desk with an inkpot, pen, and stack of parchment. "Like this." She grabbed the pen, planning to sketch what she had seen, but there, on the paper, was an image exactly matching the symbol.

"Oh, perfect. It was like this!" She pointed to the paper. "Hey guys, look."

Under the sketch was a list of eight names, penned in a sophisticated, yet unceremonious hand. Beside each entry, the word *missing* and a date stood out starkly against the bright paper.

"Something strange is happening here," Belan stated. "And I suspect it has something to do with the crowns. Kaci, tell us everything you remember about your vision."

Kaci cocked her head and closed her eyes as if she could conjure forth the vision again. "The town square was full of people. They were shadowed, so I couldn't see their faces. I'm unsure if they wore cloaks or if the shadows just followed them. There was a woman in charge. She had another crown in my vision."

Kaci chewed on her lip a moment, trying to recall anything else, then jumped to her feet. "Many of them wore a pendant! Like the one the mayor wore! Maybe it's some kind of symbol representing the infinite power he was talking about."

"I know that symbol," Micah spoke quietly. "But I don't understand how there are so many of them, or what this…cult is trying to achieve."

"You said you came from far away, Micah?" Kaci asked. "From across the sea?"

"Not exactly." Micah sighed. "I—well, explaining where I come from is tough. I'm not even sure where to start."

"The beginning is a good place," Belan chimed in and pulled up a chair. Lady Durya folded her arms and frowned.

"I don't even know where that would be," Micah laughed bitterly. "That pendant is a lot like one I had, that I need to get back. But the mayor's necklace was not mine. I'd recognize my disk energy anywhere. This one felt wrong, like some twisted copy."

"And where are you from?" the lady asked with a sneer. "I have certainly never heard your name in royal circles."

"No, not here. I am from what you call *The Wilds*," Micah finally answered. "I call my home Isdralan."

"The home of the gods." Kaci's eyes widened as she took Micah in anew. She tugged excitedly on Belan's cloak. "He is from The Wilds!"

"I heard, child." Belan laughed. "Let him speak."

"He lies," Lady Durya accused, frowning. "He *did* steal the crown from you."

"I'm not lying," Micah's body tensed, visibly bristling with frustration. "I lost my pendant while experimenting. It's not meant to be here, and my mother is going to be angry."

The Baroness burst into a peal of laughter. "You're afraid your mommy is going to be mad?"

"Well, when you put it like that, it sounds pretty stupid," Micah pouted.

"What were you doing that you lost your pendant?" Kaci asked, glancing at Micah.

"I was looking for you." He gave Kaci an impish grin. "Just checking in."

"Me?" Kaci's voice hitched in surprise and her nose crinkled in disbelief. "Are you sure you've got the right person?" she added after a moment's hesitation. Her mind raced. Why would anyone would seek her out? She was just Kaci, after all—a mere blip in the grand scheme of things. Wasn't she?

"I missed you!" He gave a melancholy grin. "I didn't grow up in Isdralan. But I had an adventure there once, as a child, and you helped me. You changed my life, actually."

"Are you feeling okay?" Kaci asked, her voice a mix of disbelief, concern, and a touch of fear. She extended a hand, hesitating, before placing it on Micah's forehead. The contact felt foreign and left her palm tingled with an eerie sensation.

"I have never met you in my life," she added, her words trailing off. A shiver went down her spine. She could not shake the uneasy sensation that pricked at the edges of her consciousness and set her nerves on edge.

"Not yet," he corrected. "But you will, many years from now, assuming I have not messed up your timeline beyond repair." Micah smiled sadly.

"So you are from the future?" Kaci asked, pursing her lips. "And old me was your friend."

"Yeah, sort of. The distinction between the past, present, and future is just an illusion, although we perceive it as a straight line. You once told me, *time flies like an arrow and fruit flies like a banana.*" Micah grinned.

"I don't get it." Kaci scrunched her nose. "What is a banana?"

"Never mind." Micah said, his eyes dropping. "You will someday, I guess."

"Perhaps we should direct our attention to the problem at hand," Belan suggested. "We have two missing crowns, a strange cult, and a ceremony happening tonight that will supposedly touch the infinite. I would say touching the infinite sounds like a horrible idea."

Belan, as usual, was right. The urgency of their current situation demanded immediate attention. Kaci made a mental note to circle back to Micah's strange claim once today's crisis was resolved.

"Look!" Lady Durya gestured out the window. The sun was setting, and most people were hurrying into their homes. The few figures that remained on the street seemed to be draped in mist, as if the darkness followed them. Kaci wondered if their cloaks were actually made of shadows, or if it was just an illusion. Each of the hooded figures traveled toward the center of town.

"We need to follow them," Kaci stated. "Whatever happened in my vision is going to happen tonight. We need to be there. Maybe we even find the crown!"

She swung the door open to step outside and one of the cloaked figures turned to look at her, revealing glassy, empty eyes. Then she turned back to the road without a reaction, continuing her slow progress forward. A hand grabbed Kaci's arm, yanked her back into the house, and slammed the door behind her.

"We can't just go out there," Lady Durya hissed. "We need to think this through. Now sit," she ordered, gesturing to the chair. Kaci plopped down and blinked twice, feeling proud of her friend's take-charge attitude, even if it was harsh.

"Let's start with the facts," Durya stated. "There is some sort of religious movement here."

"Cult," Micah interrupted, and Lady Durya rolled her eyes.

"Perhaps we wait before we label things." The lady was pacing now. "At least some of them wear a pendant with this symbol on it."

"Triskelion!" Micah placed a hand over his mouth and mumbled *sorry* under it. "Please continue."

"If you know so much, why don't you tell us, my dear Micah?" The Baroness's voice was syrupy and sweet, but Kaci sensed danger in her drawn expression.

"Should we interrupt?" Kaci whispered to Belan.

He shook his head. "No, they will have to work this out at some point."

"What are they working out?" Kaci asked.

"They are fighting for dominance." Belan grinned and studied Micah and Lady Durya. "Very fascinating."

"Like wolves in a pack?" Kaci asked, forgetting to whisper.

"Are we interrupting something?" Both Micah and Lady Durya frowned and turned to Belan and Kaci.

Kaci shook her head.

"Indeed," Belan spoke into her ear, and they both stifled a laugh.

"All the people out in the streets wore the same sort of cloak. Everyone else seemed to be trying to get home. Like they were afraid of the dark or something," Kaci contributed.

"Let's stick to the facts, darling." Lady Durya gave a condescending smile. "We do not know that they were afraid."

"Sorry," Kaci's shoulders slumped. "Anyway, they were wearing cloaks."

"Of course," the lady replied in a voice that made Kaci feel like a child.

"Ahem," Belan cleared his throat. "What is the goal of this mission? What are we hoping to gain?"

"The second crown, of course!" Lady Durya replied.

"Perhaps we are getting ahead of ourselves?" Belan suggested. "We don't even know how or why these crowns exist!"

Micah spoke up quietly over the bustle as the group contemplated Belan's question. He reached into his backpack, pulled out the crown, and placed it on the table. He carefully traced his finger over the intricate metalwork, pointing out the symbol at its center.

Kaci sensed waves of darkness and despair emanating from the crown. Unease washed over her. Lady

Durya, however, seemed transfixed by the object, as if she were drawn to it. Belan placed a hand on her shoulder, gently pulling her back from the brink.

"Oh, it's like the mayor's pendant!" Kaci nodded solemnly.

"Like *my* necklace. When I lost it, I hadn't planned to come here. Not yet, anyway. I was just watching. But, somehow, the world pulled it in." Micah sighed and pointed to the focal point of the Earthborn crown. Instead of a jewel or a decoration, the crown was adorned with a scrap of metal. "See this?"

Belan nodded, inspecting the crown.

"It's a chip from my necklace. The one I lost."

"How do you know?" Kaci asked, watching Micah's face. He pressed his lips together and rubbed at the light stubble on his chin in an odd gesture that held a mix of awe and disgust.

"The disk on the necklace was a gift from my mother. Let's just say it's an important family heirloom, and she will be angry that I lost it."

"Parents," Kaci giggled. "Am I right?" She snapped her mouth shut when no one answered.

"The metal is made from—" Micah paused. "Well, in a sense, it's made from my mother herself."

"Eww." The Baroness scrunched her nose. "Like her blood and bones and such?"

"We are not orcs." Micah rolled his eyes, and The Baroness swatted at him.

"Ultimately, everything is the stuff of stars," Micah answered. "You, me, the villagers. Everyone. We are all made of the tiniest atoms. I suppose prions are the smallest, but it's only because we have not looked further. I imagine the possibilities are infinite."

"You lost me." Kaci cocked her head. "Who is Atom?"

Micah laughed and continued. "Isdralan vibrates at a certain frequency, but it surrounds us. It also surrounds the world where I grew up. The disk matched that vibration. It holds great power and, in the wrong hands, could probably cause much chaos."

"Like driving a formerly grand king crazy?" Belan asked.

"Maybe?" Micah tilted his head. "I'm not sure why that happened."

"Then perhaps that is what we need to find out," Belan answered sagely.

"Perhaps," Micah echoed.

Kaci watched Micah's face. He thrived on being the most intelligent person in the room, and Belan's smooth logic was throwing him. Kaci smiled to herself. She had forgotten how good she was at reading people.

"I believe Kaci had the right idea, trying to observe this ceremony," Belan suggested. "But we would do well to blend in."

Lady Durya rose and started pacing around the room, opening doors and poking around the home until she returned with a gray robe that seemed to match those the villagers wore. Micah's eyes widened and he started pulling open drawers.

"Here!" He grinned, pulling a pendant from the dresser. "It looks like our lovely Alma was part of this cult!" He waved the chain around.

Lady Durya was already attempting to put on the robes, which were clearly too small for her. Micah burst into laughter, helping to pull them off the large woman's head.

"Here, you try them on, Kaci." Micah said, still

trying to contain his laughter "Alma seems closest to your size."

"This is only reconnaissance," Belan instructed. "Don't interact with anyone. See what information you can get, then get back here before the ceremony."

"See if they have a crown!" Lady Durya demanded, "and if my brother is there." She added as an afterthought, "Please."

"Be careful, child." Belan hugged her. "You are just watching."

Chapter 7

Dark Revelations

"The dance of light and darkness is eternal—a harmony struck at the heart of all things. True balance is not the absence of light or dark, but the understanding that both are necessary for the world to exist" - Bataku Raama, *The Birth of Magic*

As the sun set, Kaci emerged from the small house into the street, mostly deserted except for a few individuals hurrying indoors. Kaci surmised that the cloaked figures had disappeared toward the town center. What was going on? The question stirred a sense of unease in Kaci.

A small child darted out of a door and crashed into her, falling to the ground. "Eli!" a woman called, fear evident in her voice. "Get back inside! Darkness comes!"

Kaci reached out a hand, helping the small boy up. He looked and her, and yelped, making a beeline for the door. Kaci smiled gently at the woman. "There is nothing to fear in the dark."

The woman slammed the door. Odd. People were not friendly here. Kaci noticed doors slamming shut all along the road. Forgetting for a moment about the ceremony, Kaci approached one of these doors and knocked three times. The door opened just a crack, and a voice called out to her, "Go away! I have already paid my tribute."

"Tribute?" she asked, too surprised to mask her confusion. "I don't need any tribute. I just wanted to know why everyone is in such a hurry to get home!"

"Are you daft?" the voice replied. "Have you just been turned?"

"Turned?" Kaci asked, uncertain.

"Did you steal that pendant?" The door opened another inch, and an elderly man's face peeked out. "You are daft! You best be getting home. The shadows will know!"

"What shadows?" Kaci asked. The door slammed in her face. "Go home!" said the muffled voice inside.

She knocked again but received only silence. A sense of dread built in her stomach as she continued up the street. What were these shadows, and why were the townspeople so afraid of them?

In the town square, the throngs of robed people were overwhelming. Waves of fear pummeled Kaci. Was it the crowd, or did the fear emanate from the center of the square?

As Kaci made her way through the throng, the robed people seemed oblivious to her presence. She scanned the area for clues and spotted a great raised dais at the center of the square, where a wooden cage trapped about four or five people behind its bars. Their skin and clothing were soiled as if they hadn't bathed in weeks. Kaci's heart broke as she watched one woman sitting on the cage floor, tears streaming down her face.

Kaci fought through the crowd and pressed against the cage. "What's wrong?" she whispered.

The woman in the cage wailed loud enough for all to hear, "I didn't do it! I didn't steal from Lord Marcus, I swear!"

One of the robed ones laughed a bitter laugh. "Silence, Marta. Your fate is sealed! Be grateful you will become one with the infinite instead of being executed."

The woman didn't reply. She only wailed again, louder than before.

"There is nothing you can do." Another of the caged people faced Kaci. "Be gone. Your taunting just makes it worse."

Before she could say more, a wave of silence overtook the crowd as a slight woman climbed to the stage. She was different from the rest, and Kaci immediately knew this was the woman from her vision. She shivered, and her belly felt as if it were melting.

When the woman reached the top of the stairs, she pulled down her cowl to reveal a severely disfigured visage, burns, and scars covering what once could have been a beautiful face. The woman scanned the crowd until her gaze landed on Kaci. Did she know?

Then Kaci looked closer. She had seen this woman before. Their last encounter played vividly before Kaci: the flames, the screams, the demands for her banishment.

Listen to this—the squirrel girl has a friend.

Kaci didn't like being called squirrel girl, but at least they were talking to her and not laughing.

"Oh no, Mwezi does not like to stray far from the forest. Owls like to stay in their own territory." She could hear her own voice shaking.

The girl blinked, and her lips curled. "Your friend is an owl?" Again, a low roll of laughter built from the group, and another chimed in, "Aren't you afraid Mwezi will eat you, squirrel girl?"

Pressure gathered slowly, deep in her stomach. A wave of rumbling anger pushed against her insides until she couldn't contain it anymore. The fire exploded around them, flames hungry, black smoke billowing above. The great roaring in her ears drowned out all but the loudest of screams. Hers…

Kaci's mind raced as she recognized the young woman, who had now placed a wooden box on the table at the center of the them dais. It was Arda, Cirden's apprentice from the Terra Clan. Kaci had never meant to burn her. A tear slipped down her face. Was this ghost of her past back to haunt her? To remind her of her failure?

Kaci wrapped her arms around herself and blew out a breath. She had a job to do—observe and report back.

What was Arda doing here? Her people had always kept to themselves. The elves had never desired to spread their influence throughout the continent, hungering for power like the humans. They lived in peace, protecting the forests and the balance of life.

Deep scars formed a maze on Arda's face, which appeared even more sunken than Kaci remembered. The woman placed a rich velvet cloth over the box, and her lips turned up in the hint of a smile. Shadows seemed to swirl in her eyes as she scanned the crowd. Then she turned her head to the sky.

"All is ready," Arda intoned. A hush came over the crowd, cutting off the murmurs and chattering from before. All inclined their heads. Kaci's eyes darted this way and that before she did the same, copying the group.

Darkness descended on the crowd. Was it the dead of the night already? Kaci shuddered. She wanted to get back and tell the others what she had observed, but there was no way she could leave without being seen.

"Nou akeyi fè nwa a, nou ouvè a enfini," Arda chanted in a low tone, almost too quiet to hear. Soon the throng of people raised their voices with her. The people in the wooden cage huddled together in the corner, silent and shaking with fear.

A man stepped up to the dias, his cowl concealing his face. Rich black satin robes draped over his body, and a hood hung loosely over his shoulders. He smiled at the crowd and raised a hand in greeting. Arda lifted the box, holding it up to him. The man nodded briefly, then removed the cloth and opened the wooden box.

Something about him stirred a vague sense of recognition within Kaci. His lean figure and the natural elegance of his movements suggested Elven lineage. However, his aura and energy seemed out of sync—a dissonant note in an otherwise harmonious melody.

Inching closer, Kaci could see that the box was covered in tiny swirls and patterns, much like the crowns.

Nou akeyi fè nwa a, nou ouvè a enfini…

Flickering candles cast long shadows on the walls of the building behind the stage. All around her, figures swathed in dark cloaks chanted rhythmically in a language she couldn't understand. Their voices, low and ominous, rippled across the chilly air, raising goosebumps on her skin.

You shouldn't be here, a voice inside her screamed. But there was no place to escape without being noticed.

The dark man opened the box and lifted a crown, placing it lightly atop his head. Kaci could feel the void emanating from it. An inky black maw of nothingness licked at the edges of her consciousness. This crown differed from King Thorlyn's, and also from the one in her vision. It was smaller perhaps, but richer, more intricate. The bands of metal twisted around themselves, culminating in a grand point that peaked right above the man's forehead. It radiated darkness that comprised far more than the absence of light—it was the absence of life, hope, and warmth. This darkness threatened to swallow Kaci whole.

She strained, searching for a piece of metal similar to the one from Micah's pendant. It was right at the center—three swirls where the rich metals met. As he placed the crown on his head, a sense of dread built in the pit of Kaci's stomach.

Shadows and darkness coalesced around the man, and the chanting grew louder. He traced a circle in the air behind him, and the blackness swirled like a cyclone, faster and faster until it was all inky black, with no light to see.

A shiver run down Kaci's spine as she watched the man manipulate the dark energy around him. This was no ordinary cult gathering. It was much darker, more sinister. She glanced around nervously, but none of the villagers seemed to care. They continued chanting, their eyes closed in fervent devotion. She had to be careful. She couldn't let herself get caught up in their web of darkness. She took a calming breath and prepared to step back, but before she could move, the man suddenly turned and locked eyes with her.

When he stepped toward her, Kaci felt pure dread. The darkness and chanting formed a thick cloak around him. She felt trapped, like an animal caught in head-lights, unable to move or breathe.

A loud whoosh filled the air, and a dark portal opened behind the man. It drew his attention away from her and Kaci stumbled backward, gasping for air. Her heart pounded in her chest as she looked at the swirling vortex of shadows and wondered what was waiting on the other side.

A noise emanated from the portal—something between a wail and a dark, disjointed song. Kaci felt the weight of it crushing her. No one else around her seemed to react. Their eyes were as dark as the gateway in front of her.

Suddenly, great shadows burst from the portal, flooding the square and sweeping across the crowd like hungry predators. A shadow seemed to dive for her, its ragged jaws opening to consume her, perhaps swallow her whole.

The man's hand flicked with a sharp motion, commanding the darkness away from the crowd toward the wooden cage. Kaci held her breath as she peeked from her hood. Dread crept up her spine as she realized how narrowly she had escaped a terrible fate.

The night seemed to swirl around the prisoners, circling hungrily until the cage was consumed by darkness. As the vortex twisted and turned, screams of agony and despair echoed through the air, filling Kaci with dread. She couldn't understand why no one else noticed the sounds of suffering. It wasn't just coming from the cage, either; the portal in front of them radiated an overwhelming sense of pain, loss, and despair that made her heart ache.

She felt a familiar warmth building like a fire within her, and she tried to push it away, remembering the day not long ago when the fire had consumed the apprentices.

Looking at Arda, she cringed. Had she somehow set this into motion? The woman's eyes were black now—as black as the shadow hovering over her—and empty too. As if there was no longer anything inside.

Some optimistic part of Kaci clung to the hope

that any moment now, Arda would shake off this strange trance. She would blink away the blackness, and the warmth of her soul would reignite the spark of life within her eyes.

Chaos dissipated as quickly as it had erupted, leaving an eerie stillness in its wake. Kaci gazed toward the cage, bracing herself for the worst. To her surprise, the door was open, and the prisoners emerged unscathed. As they stepped out into the night, Kaci noticed their eyes, now dark as the night sky.

There was only one exception—the woman Kaci had spoken to earlier. Her eyes remained a natural color, and she seemed to search for something in the darkness. She scanned the crowd as she cried out in terror. "Help me!"

Nou akeyi fè nwa a, nou ouvè a enfini...

The crowd continued to chant, softer now. The man in the crown looked at the terrified woman. "Kill her." He waved a hand, then turned and entered the town hall.

The crowd erupted in a roar and descended on the cage, surging toward the poor woman until Kaci could no longer see her. There were no screams this time, and Kaci did not wait to see the result. She turned and ran as fast as she could.

Tears streamed down her face as she entered the house and collapsed into Belan's arms, sobbing, her shoulders heaving as she struggled to catch her breath.

"Did you see my brother?" Lady Durya asked, receiving a swat from Micah.

The old Earthborn stroked Kaci's hair as she regained control. "Take a moment." Belan's voice was soothing.

"I—" Kaci sniffled. "I don't think so; they were all in hoods. But I saw someone I knew." She took a shaky breath.

"Turn your focus inside, child," Belan instructed. "Find that flame deep within."

Kaci shuddered at the thought of flame that had burned Arda's face. "No. Not flame," she protested.

Belan smiled, but his eyes were sorrowful. "It is your inner light, child, nothing to fear."

She shook her head in protest. "You don't know what I've done." But Kaci felt a warm calm fill her, and she let the light spread through her body. Then she faced the others.

Kaci's mind was a chaotic mess, a storm of emotions and memories crashing against each other. She couldn't control the tears streaming down her face, nor silence the trembling in her limbs. But Belan's voice, steady and gentle, penetrated through the turmoil.

"Turn your focus inside, child," he said, and Kaci tried to push past the storm, searching for the flame that burned within her. It was a struggle. Every memory and fear fought against her, but gradually, the warmth spread through her body, and she felt calm settle over her like a blanket. Finally, she lifted her head, her eyes dry and her breathing even, ready to face the others.

Kaci's heart pounded and she trembled as she recounted what she had seen in front of the town hall. The memory of the swirling darkness and the screams made her feel sick. But Arda's presence sent the biggest shivers down her spine.

"I saw something… something terrible," she said, her voice shaking. "A man, his face was obscured. He had the crown, and he opened a portal. There were prisoners. And then something sinister came out of the portal. It was like a wave of darkness, and it was all I could do not to be consumed by it."

"A portal?" Micah interrupted, suddenly alarmed.

"What did you see? Someone could use my disk to open the door to Isdralan!"

Kaci shook her head. "That place was like nothing I have ever seen, even in my darkest dreams." She turned to face Micah seriously. "It was as if it sucked everything that makes us alive into an emptiness. There was nothing there, only darkness. When the door opened, the emptiness spilled through. It swallowed everything light and good, leaving nothing but an empty shell."

"It killed them?" Lady Durya asked.

"Worse. It *erased* them." Kaci pursed her lips. "You know how every living being has a light? An essence? Well, these prisoners looked the same as ever. But hollow."

The Baroness frowned, pacing back and forth.

"That does not sound like Isdralan at all," Micah replied. "But I have seen that place before, and it's nowhere good." He paused for a moment before turning back to Kaci. "What happened to the crown?"

Kaci rubbed her temples, trying to recall what happened to the crown. "I don't remember," she said, frustration creeping into her voice. "He just…gave his command and then left. I didn't see where he went because I ran."

Part of her wanted to keep running, to go home and beg for Elena's forgiveness. To sit under Arba Vitae again and see the dappled light on her skin as the wind's song passed through its silver leaves. To smile at the sky as the clouds drifted above. She shook herself, letting the image drop from her mind. Whatever this shadow was, she knew it would not stop until it consumed them all.

Kaci rose to her feet and cleared her throat. "Light the fire. It's time I faced my fears."

"What do you mean, light the fire?" Micah blinked. "Are you cold?"

"No, silly. I scry much better using fire." She took a breath. "It just terrifies me."

Across the room, near the fireplace, Lady Durya wrung her hands, whispering every now and again to Belan, who would reach out and offer a comforting hand. After a moment, he met Kaci's eyes. "Are you ready?"

She nodded and inhaled deeply, then joined Belan near the fire. It was warm and inviting, and she shoved away her fear. "Show me what is important," she whispered.

Molten stone dripping. A scream. Belan plummeted into the flames below. A stag stood on the other side of the crevice, watching as the Earthborn fell, then turned and walked away.

Kaci tried not to scream. It had been Belan. This time she knew his face for sure. She kept her eyes glued to the fire in front of her. "Show me more."

Arba Vitae. Its silvery leaves dropped to the ground, withered. Death and decay had a firm grasp on it. The forest was empty. No one remained to tend the tree. She opened her mouth to shout for help, but no one could hear.

Tears built in her eyes. The tree could not be dying. It had lived forever. The Great Mother had trusted her people to tend and watch over it—a symbol that she would always be with them. And now she would be gone. "Why?" she whimpered into the emptiness as the flames shifted again.

A labyrinth, intricate and daunting. Thick fog shroud-ed its center. The entire structure felt alive with struggle, the intense duality of good and evil warring. Amid it all, a familiar figure stood wearing a simple crown. The same one from the square, but darkness consumed him—power and ambition, the desire to rule and conquer, the conviction of his own superiority. He laughed maniacally. Dark orbs seemed to swirl around him. "Help me," he whispered, and the orbs thickened with malevolent energy. One lonely orb remained, bright as day.

Icy fear gripped Kaci's heart. His presence filled her with fear. She was sure this man was at the center of whatever was happening. But who was he? The fire pulled at her. There was more!

Four beings sat whispering, too quiet to hear. A woman tall and regal, with hair like the night and a shimmering blue dress like the crystal sea. Two babes nursed at her breast. A mother, a queen.

The Great Mother! Kaci's eyes widened. Was she somehow spying on the gods?

A man with flowing white hair, a crown of antlers on his head, and a beard to rival the noblest Earthborn. He glanced her way, and something in his eyes looked familiar before he turned away. An intimidating woman, powerful and fierce, emanating wisdom. She wore battle armor, and a large black bird rested on her shoulder. Finally, a muscular being with golden hair. When the light shifted, it looked like flames of fire. He looked directly at Kaci and a glorious grin erupted on his face. She took a step back. How could he see her? "You are powerful, daughter of flames—strong enough to destroy the shadows but not as powerful as me." His voice was like music, drawing her in.

"Kaci, Kaci!" The vision winked out, and Kaci blinked in confusion. Lady Durya was pulling on her arm. "You were gone for a moment, and then the fire flared up and went out." The Orcish woman looked afraid, and Belan's face wore a deep-seated concern.

"Did you learn anything?" Micah asked, ignoring the others' worries and cutting right to the core.

"Too much," Kaci sighed, "and not enough. Visions are hard to decipher. Sometimes, they show us our past or what is happening now, and sometimes they show us what is yet to be."

"And what did these visions show you?" Lady Durya asked. "Can we find the crowns?"

Kaci shivered, remembering the darkness in the man. "I am not sure. But I will try."

"Tell us what you saw, child. We are here to help." Belan gave her a reassuring nod, and once again, Kaci saw him plummeting into the lava.

She told them about the visions, except for that one. It haunted her thoughts and gnawed at the edges of her consciousness. The thought of losing Belan was unbearable—a reality she refused to confront, let alone accept.

"I have no way of knowing what is past, present, or future. I know the tree was safe when I was last home, so it's perhaps a fate we can avoid."

Micah looked at her and she could swear she saw sorrow in his eyes. He sighed and spoke softly, "The four beings in your vision—I know who they are."

She laughed, "That much I know. I saw the gods. I would recognize the Great Mother anywhere!"

"You have spoken with the gods?" Belan sounded impressed. Micah nodded as if he wasn't sure how to proceed. There were secrets behind those eyes. Kaci was sure of it, but she would not press.

"One of them spoke to me." Kaci shared. "I am pretty sure it was the god of the day. I have never had my visions speak to me. I have always been a watcher. It was quite curious."

"Tell me about the gods you worship here," Micah asked, caution in his voice.

"In my clan, we worship the Great Mother," Kaci began. "The goddess of the sea and life. She tasked us with protecting the Tree of Life." Kaci remembered the vision of the tree's silver leaves descending to the ground, and with every blackened leaf that fell, it felt like the Great Mother was receding further into the distance. "The one that was dying in my vision."

Lady Durya chimed in, "My people, both human and Orcish, revere the goddess of war. She is the triple goddess: Mother, Maiden, and Crone. She is the embodiment of both war and wisdom. In our tongue, she is known as Valkyriara. They say that when an orc comes of age, they can feel the power of battle boil within their blood. This power makes them fierce warriors, able to conquer any enemy that stands in their way. I don't believe in that rubbish," Lady Durya scoffed.

"Why rubbish?" Kaci asked.

"It's just superstition. I've felt nothing like that." Durya rolled her eyes.

"But I thought it was a significant part of the Orcish culture," Belan said.

"It is," Durya replied with a shrug. "But that doesn't mean it's real. It's just something they tell their young ones to make them feel brave."

Belan spoke, "The Allfather is the god of the mountains and sky. He is the beginning and end, the creator and destroyer. As Earthborn, we live beneath the mountains, but when the time comes to return to our maker, we ascend to the highest peaks to reunite with him."

"That's beautiful," Kaci replied. "I never knew that."

"The god of the day goes by many names." Belan smiled at Kaci. "He is a bit of a trickster, that one."

"You can say that again," Micah smirked. "He likes to play games."

Lady Durya raised an eyebrow but remained silent.

"I think the vision of the man in the maze held the most important clue," Kaci said. "I am sure he was the man from the town square. They both wore the same crown. I didn't see the pendant, but I felt it."

"First we need to get the crowns. Maybe Marcus knows something," Lady Durya stated. "The mayor was going to send him the message that I was here."

"Perhaps, but just in case he knows nothing," Kaci said with a sigh, "let's have a backup plan."

Micah nodded. "Agreed. We should explore the town and gather any information we can. Maybe we'll find some clues that can lead us to the crowns, or whoever is behind all of this."

Kaci felt a glimmer of hope. Maybe there was a way to find the crowns and stop the force causing so much chaos. They just had to be resourceful and persistent.

"It is well beyond time we retire." Belan smiled. "Let's get some rest and find the mayor in the morning."

Chapter 8

Shadows and Flames

"Darkness, in its ambition to claim dominion, tries to masquerade as light. In such times, we must remember that the purest light shines brightest in the heart of the deepest shadows." - Bataku Raama, *The Birth of Magic*

That night, Kaci found no peace. The moon's fiery glow ignited the windows, and she felt trapped, like a bird in a cage, yearning for the freedom of the sky. Her rest was fleeting, interrupted by jumbled thoughts that cut through her mind like broken glass. Terror-filled screams echoed through the night. Was this suffering caused by the night's ritual, or just a product of her imagination. She clutched the blanket closer, shivering in the darkness. Even when sleep finally overtook her, the dreams pulled her in every direction. All she wanted was to go home, to escape this nightmare.

The woman's terrified face in the town square haunted Kaci as she struggled with the guilt of not intervening. She had merely fled from the scene, leaving the woman to her grim fate. How much of this was because she had burned Arda so badly? The burden of her responsibility was overwhelming and weighed heavily upon her.

Morning arrived with its usual fanfare of birdsong, fresh and ignorant of the previous night's horrors.

"Good morning, sunshine!" Lady Durya looked radiant. She had cleaned herself up from the long journey and looked fit to be queen. Kaci hoped against hope that her friend's reunion with her brother would be one of happiness, but she feared the opposite.

The group was somber as they stepped out into the morning. The streets were abandoned, and the few people they saw rushed back indoors. Down the dusty road, a woman sat on her stoop, rocking back and forth. Her eyes were rimmed in red, and silver hair hung loose against her cheek.

"Excuse me." Lady Durya towered over her, but the woman didn't seem to notice. "Do you know where we can find the mayor's home?"

"They are gone. All gone," the woman whispered as she continued to rock back and forth. "Gone."

"Well, she is useless." Durya sighed and turned away, continuing down the road. Belan shook his head. He sat next to the grieving woman and placed a hand on her arm, quickly removing it when she shuddered.

"Are you okay?" His voice was calm, and he looked at the others.

"Wait!" Kaci called out to their friend, but Durya continued without looking back.

Kaci sat down on the other side. The woman didn't respond, only kept rocking back and forth. Then she let out a heavy sigh. "I don't understand why the shadows passed me by. They should have taken me instead. It would have been better if they had taken me, too. Then I could be with Ami." Kaci felt a shiver run down her spine as she remembered the darkness that had poured out from the portal and engulfed the people in the cage.

"What is your name?" Belan asked the woman.

The woman was silent a time before she answered, "Edith. I am called Edith."

"We are wasting time." Lady Durya had returned and was leaning against the home. "This is useless. There is nothing we can do for her. We need to find my brother. The mayor was supposed to get us an audience."

Belan spoke softly. "It is not about what we can do now, but about understanding what happened. And preventing it from happening again. Please share your story with us, Edith. Who did the shadows take?"

Kaci's chest tightened as she remembered hearing similar words from Elena. She had so much anger toward her old mistress. Perhaps some of it had been misplaced. She wished she could go back and apologize.

Edith shook her head and frowned. "Just go. There is nothing you can do now."

The woman's grief was like a lead weight, dragging Kaci down into a pit of despair. She tried to find that inner flame Belan had taught her about, but it was hard to focus with the overwhelming sadness in the air. She breathed in, trying to calm herself, but the air tasted stale and heavy. When she breathed out, the warmth within her seemed to sputter and dim.

Kaci closed her eyes and delved in once more. In the recesses of her being, she found a fragile spark, the source of her magic. She focused her energy, mentally stoking the tiny flame, urging it to grow and fill her with its light and warmth. Gradually, it responded to her will, expanding and casting a comforting glow throughout her.

The air seemed to shimmer as her body began to radiate. Edith, seeing this, recoiled in fear and scrambled away. Kaci, however, did not allow the energy to overtake the terrified woman. Instead, she carefully channeled it, directing the warmth to fill her limbs and then extend beyond her body, dissipating the heavy despair that hung in the air.

Eventually, Edith's tearful sobbing eased, replaced by a shocked silence as she gazed at Kaci. For a moment, only the two of them existed, not a sound except for the gentle rustle of the wind through the trees. Then, cautiously, Kaci extended a hand and placed it on Edith's shoulder. It was a simple gesture that marked a moment of understanding, shared sorrow, and a first step toward healing. Even the smallest spark of hope can light the path ahead in the face of overwhelming despair.

A look of surprise washed over Durya's face as she observed the power radiating from Kaci. Meanwhile, Belan wore an expression of pride, a hint of a smile dancing at the edges of his lips.

Gradually, the silence began to retreat, making way for the familiar sounds of the village—the distant clatter of utensils, the murmur of villagers, and the occasional barking of dogs. At that moment Durya regained her voice. Her words boomed with a mixture of awe and confusion. "What in the blazes was that?"

Belan turned, a twinkle in his eye. "That, my friend, was Kaci, embracing her inner flame, letting go of fear."

Kaci opened her eyes and the light faded from her body as she looked at the two of them. "I didn't know I could do that," she whispered, still in awe of what she had just experienced.

Belan placed a hand on her shoulder. "There's much you have yet to discover about yourself, Kaci. But with time and a little guidance, you'll unlock powers you never thought possible."

Durya huffed, still unsure. "Well, I'll be. You're full of surprises, girl."

The heavy warm feeling at her center didn't frighten Kaci any more. A new idea bubbled up—maybe she could help. Her memory echoed with the haunting image of the people trapped in the cage. Death had not claimed them—not all of them, at least. A shiver traced its way down Kaci's spine at the recollection.

They seemed as though they had become possessed, ensnared by darkness. It was a different kind of shadow than the one that clung to Edith, yet there was a common thread that wove them together.

Their eyes had been empty. What if she could somehow fill them with her inner light? Could she chase away the shadows that consumed them? The idea both excited and frightened her. It was a risk, but it was the only idea she had. She would have to try.

"Did the ones you lost die?" Kaci blurted out, not remembering to smooth her words. "I mean, did they die, or where they just changed?"

"Go!" Edith frowned and rose to her feet. "I told you there was nothing you can do."

"But maybe I can." Kaci rose, frantic. "Are they in the house with you?"

"Are you hard of hearing?" Edith opened the door to her home and entered, but Kaci grabbed her arm. The old woman ripped it back, entered the home, and slammed the door.

"Wait!" Kaci pleaded, knocking on the door. "I can help, maybe. I can try!" She kept pounding on the door until Belan pulled her away.

"She is not ready," Belan said soothingly. "Come, child. Give Edith time."

"But what if we don't have time?" Kaci pleaded. "I saw what the shadows did last night. I need to do something."

"How do you think you can help her?" Micah asked, raising an eyebrow.

"I don't know," Kaci replied, suddenly feeling bashful. "You know how the light of the midday sun overcomes the shadows? I thought maybe I could be the sunshine."

"I like it," Micah chuckled. "Kaci Sunshine. It suits you."

Kaci rolled her eyes, but she felt a glimmer of pride. "I'm serious, Micah," she said, her voice tinged with determination. "Maybe if I can tap into that, I can use it to chase away the darkness."

Belan nodded. "It's possible," he said, looking at Kaci. "If shadows are a manifestation of darkness and fear, perhaps you can focus on the light within you."

Durya looked skeptical. "How do you know it will work?" she asked.

Kaci shrugged. "I don't know," she admitted. "But I have to try. I can't sit here and do nothing while people suffer."

Micah placed a hand on her shoulder. "We'll help you, Kaci," he said, his voice soft. "Whatever you need, we're here for you."

"Look." Belan pointed toward a group of people purposefully making their way toward the town center. "Let's follow them."

"Finally!" Lady Durya huffed and turned to follow the villagers.

The town center was bustling with movement, but eerily silent. The townsfolk were building a stone wall around the raised dais. On the wooden platform sat Arda, hood pulled tight around her scarred face, in a quiet conversation with the mayor. The portal hovered behind them, darkness still spilling out. Kaci felt waves of torment emanating from within. Did the others notice? Belan and Lady Durya seemed oblivious, but Micah was as white as a sheet. He backed up and glanced around.

"Does that portal lead to The Wilds?" Kaci whispered to him.

Micah shook his head, licking his lips. "No." He swallowed hard. "This is not good at all. I need to get home," he breathed. "I think I—we—need help."

"You think?" Durya spat, then pushed through the crowd until she stood in front of the mayor and Arda. "I demand to see my brother. You said you would get him a message."

The mayor's eyes widened as if he were afraid, then flared brightly before darkening once again. "I don't know what you are talking about," the mayor answered calmly. "I don't even know who you are."

"Of course, you do, you idiot." Lady Durya frowned. "You told me you would get a message to Marcus."

"I do not know what you are talking about," the man insisted, looking at Arda.

Kaci sensed a dull energy emanating from the man, but a flicker of fear occasionally pierced through. As she studied him, she sensed not an essence but an absence—a void that seemed to consume everything around him.

Arda's sharp gaze interrupted her thoughts. Kaci was suddenly aware of it fixed on her. "You," the woman hissed. "I thought I felt your presence last night."

A heavy blanket of guilt draped over Kaci as she met Arda's eyes. They swirled with darkness like the mayor's, but they were less empty, as though this woman had more control. The elders would have trained her in the deeper magics, like Elena had with Kaci.

As Arda approached her now, Kaci could feel the fear and anger radiating. She tried to push the memories away, but Arda's scarred face screamed pain and fire. "Arda, I'm sorry about what happened. It was an accident."

Arda's expression remained cold and unforgiving. "You and your untamed power are a danger to everyone around you."

Kaci felt the familiar sting of Cirden's words echoed in Arda's, and she fought to control her rising anger. "I have learned to control my power since then," she said, glancing at Belan, questioning. Had she learned to control it? Days of training during travel did not make a master.

Arda was unyielding. "You burned me, squirrel girl. Then you and Elena disappeared back to your home."

Kaci felt a surge of frustration and helplessness. She couldn't change what happened with Arda but knew she had to prove herself. She took a calming breath, focusing on the warmth within her. "Why are you here?" Kaci asked Arda. "I mean, how?"

"I should ask the same of you," Arda hissed. "Clearly, Elena came to her senses and finally banished you."

Kaci was about to speak when a shadow exploded from the portal above. It circled the crowd, then disappeared into town.

"Now, see what you've made me do." Arda frowned. "My job is to control it!"

"Control what?" Belan asked. "What is this?"

"Cirden," Arda began. Her gaze turned toward Kaci and her body language betrayed an internal struggle. "Cirden bargained with the Great Mother to rescue Arba Vitae."

"What?" Kaci asked, blinking in confusion. "Why would Arba Vitae require saving? Elena is still with us, isn't she?"

A hollow laugh escaped Arda. "You have no idea, do you?"

"Tell me, then!" Kaci pleaded. "What's happening?"

"Following the conclave—the one you missed because you chose running away over facing the truth—" Arda's hand traced the network of scars on her face.

"The council of elders convened to determine your destiny. You were viewed as a danger, and they suggested you be stripped of your abilities and exiled."

As Arda's words sunk in, Kaci's shoulders sagged. "I didn't mean for it to happen, I swear! I don't even understand how it happened!"

Arda just shook her head. "The others were in favor of banishment. But Elena resisted. She told the council that she foresaw Arba Vitae's demise upon your birth, and that you were its only hope."

Kaci shifted uneasily under the woman's gaze, feeling as though she were being dissected. Memories of her former mentor flooded her mind. Elena had not always been a gentle teacher, yet in times of challenge, she had been the one to step forward and defend Kaci. Why? Kaci's question hung in the air, unspoken but deeply felt.

Elena had held an unwavering faith in Kaci. Once again, she had shown her conviction that there was something within Kaci worth protecting. What had Elena seen in her? Could Kaci truly be the last hope for the survival of Arba Vitae?

Arda's hand absently grazed her cheek again. The subtle movement drew Kaci's attention back. Underneath Arda's hardened exterior, Kaci could sense the fear and anger that simmered. The scarred woman held a grudge against her. She needed to be careful—she had already caused the woman enough pain, and she didn't want to make it worse.

Still, Kaci's mind was a tempest, roiling with Arda's revelations, and she craved answers. "When did Arba Vitae begin to die?"

"It was after—" Arda's voice was laced with bitterness as it cut off. "As I was healing, Elena was…preoccupied. The tree began to wither. Only Cirden took action."

Kaci's memory churned with the events of that fateful summer. After the fire, Elena had rushed Kaci away to their cabin, leaving the others to care for Arda. Aside from that, her recollection of the events was hazy.

"In the remains of the fire," Arda continued, "Cirden discovered a disk on a golden chain in the ashes. It radiated with power—a gift from the Great Mother."

Kaci's eyes widened and she glanced at Micah. Could it be the same amulet he had misplaced?

A note of pride seeped into Arda's voice as she resumed her tale, "Cirden took me from my sickbed and laid me under the tree, using the artifact to summon a window to speak to the Great Mother herself. She was disoriented at first but agreed to heal the tree and to save me."

As Arda glared at her, Kaci couldn't help but feel a twinge of guilt. "Through the portal, I could tell her world was as black as night," Arda continued. "It was strange; I always imagined The Wilds would be green. The Great Mother said it was because the tree was dying. She and my master spoke at great length, then she entrusted the pendant to Cirden and went back to The Wilds. When she went through, that world looked exactly as I had pictured it: beautiful flowing hills, no longer filled with darkness."

"What did you say the Great Mother looked like?" Micah interrupted. "Can you describe her?"

"Yes," Arda replied. "She had high cheekbones and almond-shaped eyes. Her hair was the color of wheat, almost white in some places, and it hung in loose waves down her back. Her skin was smooth and flawless, with a warm golden hue, and her eyes were as dark as a moonless night."

Arda appeared to lose herself in the recollection, her gaze unfocused and her body swaying as if caught in the grip of some unseen current. She was not just reciting a memory but reliving it.

"Her dress was a rich red, bold like a ripe berry—a color that commanded attention and seemed to demand respect," she continued, her voice dreamy and distant. "It was as if that dress was alive! It pulsed with energy, and I could feel its intensity and passion. It was a symbol of power and authority that could not be ignored."

Kaci frowned. None of this made sense. Why would the Great Mother come to Aeloria, and what was wrong with Arda?

Then the woman seemed to snap out of her trance, and her eyes came back into focus. "But the tree wasn't healed. It started to die again after you left, and Elena continued to protect you. She wouldn't tell us where you had gone. So Cirden summoned the Great Mother again. This time only her shade appeared."

"What do you mean, shade?" Belan asked, raising a bushy eyebrow.

"And what did the world look like?" Micah added.

"A projection of herself. Like a shadow. She is a god, and we are, well, we are just us. We didn't question her choice of communication," Arda scoffed.

Kaci rolled her eyes. Cirden couldn't have been that stupid. Elena was harsh, but she had always taught Kaci to question everything. Belan seemed to shake his head, too.

"Her shade instructed Cirden that healing the tree had failed, that he needed to give the tree the life of the land," Arda continued. "She instructed him to craft three crowns with pieces of the pendant to represent the three great powers on earth—the elves, the humans, and the Earthborn. She showed him how to infuse the pieces with the shadows that came from the portal. The shadows were fragments of the Great Mother herself. With these crowns, the leaders of earth could feed the tree with the essence of the land."

"What do you mean, the essence?" Durya interrupted, "Were these crowns going to kill their wearers? Are you an idiot, girl?"

Arda rolled her eyes, ignoring Durya's harshness. "Of course not. It is a uniting force. The wearers become one with the tree." She continued, "Once I recovered, I was responsible for distributing the crowns. Cirden sent me to bring one to King Thorlyn of the Earthborn and one to King Robert of the humans. I gave that one to Lord Marcus to pass along. Cirden kept the final crown for himself."

"Wait—Marcus?" Lady Durya echoed, her brow furrowing. "Tell me more."

"Marcus," Arda began, a scowl of distaste marring her features, "was an orc who came under Elder Cirden's guidance to learn about the Great Mother. He had *somehow* established connections with the human king, a circumstance that Cirden sought to leverage."

Despite her outward stoicism, disdain threaded its way through Arda's voice. Marcus's inclusion in the sacred tutelage of Cirden had obviously been a source of irritation for her.

"Elder Cirden entrusted Marcus with an important assignment," she continued. "He was to deliver one crown to the human king. Yet Marcus failed. Seduced by power, he chose self-interest over his duty and took the crown to his own father instead."

Her lips twisted in a bitter frown as she added, "And now I find myself here to rectify his blunder."

Durya blinked in shock, her disbelief manifesting in a sharp gasp. "My brother, consorting with elves?" The revelation was evidently a difficult pill to swallow.

Darkness flared in her eyes. Arda's mouth clamped shut, and she hunched over in pain.

"Are you okay?" Kaci asked. She reached out a hand.

Arda shoved it away. Her eyes were now completely black. The woman straightened her shoulders and inspected the group with a frown before speaking in a strange tongue that Kaci didn't recognize.

"Arda?" Kaci approached the girl. "What's going on?"

The portal flared and shadows began pouring out of it, circling above them like birds of prey at hunt. All around, the townsfolk turned to the dais and moved toward them.

"I don't like this," Lady Durya murmured. She drew a dagger from her heeled boot and flung it at a shadow above. It passed completely through and clattered onto the cobblestone. "Not one bit."

The villagers were closing in on them now and Kaci froze with fear, remembering the people that devoured the woman in the cage. Every eye in the crowd was as dark as night. Durya drew a second dagger from her boot and threw it at the head of an encroaching villager. He dropped to the ground in a heap and a dark shadow rose from the body to circle above with the others.

"No, no!" Kaci wailed, rushing to the motionless body. Her heart hammered as she knelt beside the lifeless form. "He's gone," she murmured, dread knotting in her stomach. She turned a wide-eyed gaze on Arda. "The shadows have claimed them."

Belan looked thoughtful. "It seems their true selves are still in there somehow. This Arda—she spoke with genuine concern for Arba Vitae."

The shadows were circling faster now, and one dived at Micah, missing his body and swooping back into the air in another attempt. He dropped to his knees as if in pain and shouted, "Kaci, this would be a good time to test your sunshine theory."

Before Kaci could even take a step, chaos unfurled. A villager, a ghost of his former self, came barreling from behind, grounding Belan with a tackle that seemed to reverberate through the air. Kaci watched as Belan's features morphed from surprise to worry. His body was pinned helplessly under the weight of the attacker. The villager held an axe aloft, its icy gleam a promise of the strike to come.

A fresh wave of terror washed over Kaci as she noticed Durya and Micah, too, caught off-guard by sudden attacks. A group of villagers had pulled Durya away. Micah was still on the ground, his face white with shock.

Time seemed to freeze, suspended in the moment as the axe hovered above Belan. Even the air seemed to hold its breath. Kaci reached inside, willing the light but finding only emptiness. Her eyes were on Belan. She could never make it to him in time.

Then a bright red light burst forth from behind Belan, and her heart swelled with joy. A miracle in the form of three nimble silhouettes broke free from the enveloping shadows, one proudly sporting a red plume in his hat. Its bright color shone like a beacon of hope against the turmoil.

"Smeadon!"

"Goblins?!" Lady Durya sneered, but stepped deeper into the protective circle they formed. "I thought they would have been long gone.

The goblins were on high alert, spears raised as they circled around Kaci and her companions, guarding them against the angry villagers.

Kaci's heart pounded in her chest, and the air was so thick with anticipation that it was hard for her to breathe. As she closed her eyes, attempting to shut out the chaos around her, she sought the comforting warmth at her core.

A sudden rush of energy shocked her system, jolting her back to the present. It felt as if a dam had burst within, releasing a wave of heat that flooded her veins. The sensation was both bewildering and invigorating, and she gasped as her eyes flew open.

Her hands, held in front of her defensively, were radiating a golden light. She blinked. They were glowing!

A gasp echoed through the square, and Kaci saw Smeadon's eyes widen. The villagers, mid-attack, came to a sudden halt. Their assault faltered as they stared at Kaci, expressions a mix of fear, shock, and confusion. The tide of battle, for the moment, seemed to pause. All eyes fixed on her luminous form.

Belan pushed himself up from the ground. "You can do this. We are all here with you!" he shouted, his voice barely audible over the surrounding chaos.

Another villager shoved him as he spoke, pinning him back to the ground as shadows encroached, swirling closer to the circle.

Kaci felt time slowing down as she summoned every ounce of energy within her. Suddenly, she was a beacon, brighter than the sun above. Kaci experienced a familiar feeling as the light within her burst forth, radiating outwards in a terrifying explosion that consumed the encroaching darkness. What had she done? As the beams washed over them, the villagers around them fell to the ground in little piles. Kaci struggled to hold herself together.

Kaci's glow intensified and the portal above them flickered, its tendrils of shadow recoiling from the brilliant gleam. With a last surge of power, Kaci directed her light at the portal, willing it to close. The shadows dissipated, and the portal turned a dull gray, lifeless and inert.

She collapsed to the ground in exhaustion. The heat melted away as her skin returned to its normal paleness. Only the spattering of freckles across her nose still glowed with a slight tingle. She pushed herself to her knee, panting in exhaustion, and as time returned to its usual speed, Kaci noticed the others staring at her.

"Did I—kill them?" she asked, eyes brimming with unshed tears as she looked around at the crowd. No one moved. "Are they okay?" She forced herself to stand, panic beginning to rise as she remembered the charred bodies that surrounded the bonfire many seasons ago. "Arda?" her voice shook as she made her way to the woman.

Arda's eyes were open, but she lay in a heap on the ground. Her breathing was labored. Kaci inspected the slight woman, touching the scars on her face and looking into her blue eyes. Arda's eyes were blue, not black! The shadow was gone!

Arda was fading fast. Her breaths came in ragged gasps. "We were wrong," she whispered. "You must tell Cirden how wrong we were." Her grip on Kaci's arm tightened and then suddenly slackened as Arda collapsed against her.

Kaci caught the woman, cradling her in her arms. "Arda, no!" she cried, desperation creeping into her voice. "You didn't survive the bonfire only to die now."

Arda's eyes fluttered open and she coughed up blood. "It was never the Great Mother," she choked out just before the light left her eyes.

Kaci's heart sank. She had failed again. Big fat tears streamed down her face as she held onto the girl.

Micah raised a hand. "It's not your fault, Kaci. You didn't cause any of this. Cirden and his followers made their own choices."

"Marcus couldn't have been among them," Lady

Durya spoke up. She was pacing, her fists balled. "He is better than that. He has never cared about power."

Belan nodded. "We can't know for certain what Marcus may or may not have done. But we have to find out. The crowns change people. They could be the key to stopping all of this."

Durya stopped and looked at Belan, panic showing in her eyes. "And if Marcus is corrupted, what then? How do we help him?"

"I don't know." Belan sighed. "We may find that Marcus is as corrupted and paranoid as my brother, and I couldn't help him."

"You do not know that!" Lady Durya retorted.

"You are right. We know nothing. We must go and find out."

Her friends' voices came to Kaci as if from a great distance. All she could see was Arda's lifeless body beside her. "I am so sorry for everything," she whispered. "You didn't deserve any of this, and it's all my fault. This would have never happened if I hadn't caused the fire." A silver tear trailed down Kaci's cheek as she stroked the woman's hair, rocking her as she would an infant. "I'm sorry," she whispered again and again.

Chapter 9

Flames of Farewell

"In the ashes of death, we find the seeds of new life. It is through this eternal cycle that we uncover the essence of existence." - Bataku Raama, *The Birth of Magic*

The square was strewn with bodies, each one like a husk. After Kaci ripped the shadows from them, the spark within seemed to have been replaced by emptiness. A few still clung to life, but their vitality was fleeting, their grip on the mortal world wavering like a flickering flame in the night.

Lady Durya stepped over the body of an elderly man, her cold gaze barely acknowledging him. His eyes were cloudy in his pallid face, evidence of the shadow entity that had possessed him. He reached out a trembling hand as she passed, then collapsed to the ground.

"Help him!" Kaci implored, her heart aching with

the man's plea. Kneeling beside him, she held his cold hand. She had always tried to follow Elena's lessons about compassion, viewing each person as an individual life, not a pawn in a larger game. This was no exception.

"What good will it do?" Lady Durya countered, her tone harsh. She seemed very much like human nobility at that moment. "We need to get to the manor and ensure Marcus's safety."

Kaci looked up at Durya and found herself at a loss for words. How could she make Durya understand that this was her fault and her responsibility?

"Every life matters, Durya," she retorted. Kaci didn't understand how her friend could be so callous, but then again, Durya always seemed to hide her emotions beneath a veneer of duty and authority.

Yes, they had a task at hand. Marcus's safety was important, but Kaci couldn't ignore the suffering. As the light retreated from the old man's eyes, she felt his life force ebbing away. Her heart sank. Would it have been kinder to leave these people possessed?

Belan kneeled beside her and whispered a few words over the man. Kaci's shoulders trembled with suppressed sobs, but no tears remained to be shed.

"I did this!" she cried out. "I don't know what to do. We have to stop the shadows, but I can't abandon these people."

"Your heart is filled with light, child," Belan said tenderly. "Don't let the darkness triumph."

"Kaci, they're dead or soon will be," Lady Durya said, her voice gentler. "It's time to let them go."

"You don't understand. It's like the bonfire all over again. We can't just leave them here. Someone must watch over them as they transition from this realm to the next."

Lady Durya sighed and pushed up her sleeves. In an effortless heave, she picked up one body and placed it gently on the stage, then turned to find the next.

"What are you doing?" Kaci asked, blinking.

"That stage is made from wood. It will be a lovely base for a funeral pyre." She lifted another load as Kaci walked next to her. "I grew up here. Most of the townsfolk's customs are intertwined with the nearby orc tribes. They worship the Valkyriara. This is how we honor our dead and send them home."

The goblins were helping now, working as a team to lug the corpses toward the stage. They worked with surprising efficiency, stacking the bodies on top of one another into a rough pyramid. Smeadon stopped before Lady Durya and Kaci and spoke in his low, grave voice. Lady Durya narrowed her eyes, then shook her head and sighed.

"We help." He barred his teeth in a smile. "Make a pyre so you can fix." He gestured at the gray, inert portal. "We help people too."

Belan stepped in. "This is a sacred task. We must honor those who have passed and send them on to the next life with dignity."

The goblins nodded in understanding, their gruff voices murmuring in agreement.

"Thank you, Smeadon," Kaci reached out to touch his shoulder but instead wrapped him in a warm embrace. "And thank you for helping us. I don't think we would have survived the shadows without you." The large goblin looked uncomfortable in the hug but finally relaxed and petted the girl's head awkwardly. As she pulled away, her hand brushed against his pack. It was heavy, filled with treasures likely pilfered from the fallen.

"That was strange." Lady Durya said in a soft voice. "Goblins rarely do anything without an ulterior motive."

Kaci glanced at Smeadon's bulging pack and suppressed a giggle. "Perhaps Smeadon and the others are different." She shrugged.

"Where is Micah?" Lady Durya's sharp gaze scanned the crowd, suspicion evident in her voice.

Kaci followed her gaze, finding Micah at the edge of the scene, his demeanor distant and detached. She moved to go to him, but Durya held her back.

As they observed, Belan took Micah's hands and murmured in quiet conversation. After a moment, Micah's demeanor changed, his shoulders straightened, and together they approached Kaci and Durya.

"We will help Smeadon and his crew with the Pyre," Belan said with authority. "Perhaps the two of you can go to the manor?"

"Thank you!" Lady Durya breathed. "I've been trying to do this all day!"

"But—" Kaci protested.

"This is what is needed," Belan interrupted. "It is good to admit mistakes and then seek to restore honor. But it takes time. We will wait for your return at sunset to light the pyre. "

Kaci nodded. She forgot that the old Earthborn was also a high priest. This was one of those moments she needed to defer to his wisdom.

She clasped Durya's hand, and The Baroness did not pull away. "Let's go meet your brother."

Marshfield Estates was a towering stone residence that resembled the great human castles to the north. In a typical castle manner, there was a moat surrounding the residence, with a drawbridge. Across the moat, a single guard stood watch. He was tall, with dark gray skin, but lacked Lady Durya's prominent tusks. He raised a hand in greeting.

"The family is in mourning; there is no admittance today," he shouted.

"It's Durya, Sharn," The Baroness called. "You can let down the bridge."

"Lady!" The guard rushed to the winch, gripping the handle firmly and turning it with practiced ease. The heavy chains rattled and clanked, and the drawbridge gradually lowered, creaking with the strain. "We weren't sure if you would make it in time. Where is Lord Barclay?"

"That doesn't matter right now," Lady Durya stiffened. "Is Marcus okay?"

"Aye, he is, but he rambles and blames himself for your father's death." The man returned and touched a thumb to his forehead. "He will be pleased to see you."

"I know," was all Lady Durya replied.

Both the guard and Lady Durya seemed uncomfortable speaking of Marcus. Kaci looked from one to another before whispering. "Why does everyone seem strange about your brother?"

"That's none of your concern!" the lady snapped before letting out a breath. "I am sorry, Kaci." She looked at the bridge, which seemed to move at a snail's pace, and gave a half smile. "That is a job for two people, yet Sharn insists on doing it himself."

"I'm sorry for pressing you on your family. I know you dislike it," Kaci replied to her friend.

"No, it's okay. You are different." Lady Durya smiled as Kaci cringed. "In a good way!" she added.

"I love my family, but it has some…" She paused. "Disfunction. Orcish families are straightforward. Everyone is the same. The strongest is the leader. At the time of the wars, my birth father led our clan. Children belonged to the clan, rather than the parents. I was very young when I came to live here. Though my history teachers told me about my culture of birth, that is all I know."

Kaci remained silent, listening intently. Durya had never shared so much of herself before. The drawbridge was now a quarter of the way down, and Durya continued, "As you've probably noticed, the surrounding towns boast a diverse mix of people and cultures. Around here, Marcus and I are accepted. But further north, we were a curiosity at best and an aberration on most days. Mother and Father often left us at home when traveling to the capital. However, they took us with them occasionally to Etharion. After all, we were their only living children."

The bridge was halfway down now, and Kaci glanced at it nervously, knowing as soon as it was down, Durya's story would be done.

"I never cared for Etharion. I could never compete with those pretty human girls. But Marcus loved it. He loved the grandeur of the city and the balls and prestige. Marcus had a gift with magic, as well." Lady Durya smiled and glanced at Kaci. "Not as strong as you, though. Don't forget, I have a room in my employ as a lady-in-waiting." She winked.

"On one particular trip, Marcus was going to visit the Arcanum Academy. Father planned to use his influence to secure him a place there."

As the drawbridge lowered further, Kaci hoped that Lady Durya would have time to finish her story. The Baroness glanced at the bridge, then at Kaci, and chuckled.

"Long story short, the mages tested Marcus, and he unintentionally killed another noble son during the process. Incidents like this frequently occur at Arcanum Academy—magic is risky business—and the consequences are usually minimal. The boys receive a slap on the wrist, and their families handle the political fallout. But Marcus's case was different. The other noble families were already uneasy about his Orcish heritage. After that tragic incident, they deemed him too dangerous, and he was sentenced to death."

Lady Durya glanced at the bridge and continued faster. "My father—he wouldn't stand by and let Marcus suffer. He aided in Marcus's escape and gave him a chance at freedom."

Her voice had a heaviness as she spoke. "Marcus had always wanted to study magic. Just before he escaped, I overheard him and my father speaking of plans to learn magic in Aeloria. That was about two summers ago. He vanished shortly after. Just disappeared. We never heard what became of him."

Her face hardened, the ghost of pain flickering in her eyes. "Not long after Marcus disappeared, my father married me off."

Kaci's eyes widened. "I am so sorry, Durya!"

As the drawbridge clicked into place, Kaci found her mind wandering back to the night of the bonfire incident. She tried to recall if Marcus had been there. She remembered a large, hooded figure looming in the backdrop of her memories. Could it have been him?

Sharn's leather boots pounded across the bridge as he ran to greet them. He bowed deeply to Lady Durya. "It's lovely to see you, Milady!"

Lady Durya blushed and inclined her head. "You too, Sharn."

"Lady Evelyn and Lord Marcus are awaiting you in the anteroom." Kaci noticed that Sharn couldn't keep his eyes off the lady. "I'll take you there." He gave another bow and turned, waving them along. Lady Durya's gray skin had taken a rosy tone, and Kaci grinned to herself.

The anteroom of Marshfield Estates was cozy and bright. Large windows overlooked an elaborate garden. A small table was set with steaming tea and delicate pastries. Lady Evelyn looked frail, her long, dark hair plaited and peppered in gray. Marcus sat next to her, holding his mother's hand. He was huge, with skin a darker gray than Durya's. His tusks were longer, too, curling upward to almost meet his nose. Kaci watched as Durya's face transformed, the lined tightness melting into something else. Sorrow? Regret. A tear formed in the woman's eye but still refused to be shed.

"Sister." Marcus clasped Lady Durya's arms formally before drawing her into a tight hug. Everything about the lady seemed to change at that moment. She melted into her brother's arms, sobbing, and he held her as one would hold a child. Lady Evelyn sat sipping tea, ever the picture of properness, but Kaci could see in the elder's eyes that she, too, was moved by the scene in front of them.

"I see you have somehow convinced an Elven lass to be your lady-in-waiting," Lady Evelyn commented, ignoring Kaci. "I assumed that was all you. Edward would never have the wits to do that."

"Oh, I'm—" Kaci started, but Durya glared in her direction. "I'm—er—honored."

Lady Durya stepped away from her brother, brushing off her skirts and clearing her throat. "Yes, this is Kaci."

Kaci watched as Lady Durya nodded her head repeatedly. Was she okay? Finally, the woman mouthed, *curtsy*. Kaci's mouth formed an oh as she gave an awkward little bob. Human traditions were so strange!

"Mother told me you had married," Marcus commented, his voice dry. "And where is that little bespawler? I am surprised he did not accompany you here."

"He was drowning in work." Lady Durya shifted and her skin paled.

"Hmm…" Marcus ran a finger along a tusk. "I thought he would drop everything at the chance of inheritance."

"Enough!" Lady Evelyn's tiny fist pounded on the table, and Marcus stepped back, dropping his head.

"I'm sorry, Mother," he mumbled, pulling a chair from the table and lowering himself into it.

"Now," Evelyn continued. "I dismissed Hannah for the day. Would your lady fetch us some more tea?"

"Kaci can stay," Lady Durya gestured to a chair.

"She does not know the household. If your girl is away, then Sharn will fetch something."

Sharn gave the nod. "Of course, Lady Durya."

The silence was thick as Marcus nibbled on a small biscuit, looking chastised. It was as if no one wanted to be the first to speak. Kaci glanced out the window. The sun had passed midday and was making its descent. Lady Durya finally broke the silence. "What happened to Father?"

Lady Evelyn's eyes narrowed, and she blinked back tears.

"It was around the time when Marcus finally came home that your father's health took a turn for the worse. Not so much his physical health but his mental state. He was no longer himself."

Marcus watched silently, his face full of regret.

"Maxwell was overjoyed to see his boy, and Marcus had brought his father the most beautiful crown, a gift from the elves. But the joy didn't last. By the dark of the moon, my husband was gone."

Lady Evelyn dabbed her eyes with a handkerchief. "He went out riding one afternoon and never returned. We sent Sharn and a few others to search for him that evening. They found him on the side of the road, his neck broken, and his horse grazing nearby." She fought back the tears.

"Wait," Lady Durya's face grew red. "Marcus came home, and you didn't tell me?" She turned to her brother. "Why didn't you write? I thought the worst!" She rose, anger plain on her face, and let out a gut-wrenching roar.

"Darling," Lady Evelyn chided. "Calm your emotions. This behavior is unbecoming of a woman of your rank. Marshfield Estates and the Dukedom will be given to Edward after—" She bit her lip and didn't finish her sentence. "And your children shall inherit. This should be a joyous day."

"Marshfield Estates should go to Marcus." Durya stomped a foot. "We all know that."

"You've never been one to refuse power, Sister." Marcus chuckled. "We all know it cannot be me," he added ruefully.

Lady Durya's shoulders slumped and she looked frail. "Why? Why does it have to be Edward?"

She was trying not to cry now as Marcus gave her an embrace.

Sharn returned with tea just in time to watch the lady of the house rise to her feet.

"Enough of this outburst," Lady Evelyn interrupted. "You should go visit your father's memorial and pay your respects." The lady rose, but Marcus interrupted.

"I will take her, Mother. You rest." Lady Evelyn nodded and shut her eyes to the world around her.

Marcus led Kaci, Durya, and Sharn up a set of spiral stairs and down a long hall, stopping in front of a set of double doors. He looked at Lady Durya and paused. "I'll be in my quarters if you need me." Then he turned without a word.

Durya sighed. "You stay here, Kaci. I would like to say goodbye to my father alone. You too, Sharn. "

"I'll be *waiting*," Kaci said with a wink. "Get it? I'm a lady-in-waiting."

Sharn let out a snort of laughter, and Lady Durya raised an eyebrow. "You are so strange, Kaci," but she paused and hugged her friend. "I'm glad it was you who came up here with me." With that, she turned and entered the room.

The guard stood outside the door, stoic and strong, but every now and again, he would turn his head as if he could peek inside. Kaci paced with boredom, wishing she could be outside under the trees. A great window at the end of the hall showed the sun sinking ever lower, and she longed to be back, helping the lost souls find their ways to the next life.

"You love her, don't you?" she blurted out to Sharn, forgetting to think before she spoke.

He blinked in surprise but answered quickly. "Of course I do. She is a daughter of this household, and I am duty-bound to love them."

Kaci burst out into laughter. "You can't be duty-bound to love something." She giggled again. "You can be duty-bound to protect them, perhaps. But love is not something to be forced. I can see it, though, in your eyes when you look at her."

"Oh, no," he disagreed. "She could never love me; she is married to a baron. I am a lowly household guard. I have never even fought in a battle."

"But you admit you love her?" Kaci ignored the way Sharn kept his lips glued shut. "I think she loves you, too."

Sharn remained silent, his gaze fixed straight ahead. Perhaps she should have held her tongue. Human society was peculiar about love, especially its noble families. They had so many rules regarding marriage. Elena had explained to her that human marriage wasn't primarily about love. Power seemed to take precedence. Her thoughtless words wouldn't help Sharn. He had buried his feelings beneath a sense of duty to the family; perhaps that was all he could hope for. But it didn't seem fair.

Kaci was determined to find out more about Lady Durya's husband. She rarely spoke of him, but it was clear that the lady held little affection for her spouse. Why would her parents force their daughter into a marriage like that? Humans were so perplexing.

"Where did you grow up?" Kaci asked Sharn. He clearly had Orcish blood. At least orcs made sense.

"I grew up here. My mother worked in the kitchen, and I was lucky enough to be taken into service as a page relatively young. Then—"

The door opened and Lady Durya entered, carrying a large leather box with intricate designs all around it.

"Time to go," she whispered. Her eyes were rimmed in red, but Kaci could see from her fixed expression that she had shoved all her emotions down. "I will fetch Marcus. He will come with us to Marshfield and put things right."

"What about the—" Kaci gestured to her head, and Lady Durya rolled her eyes and shook the box, then turned to Sharn.

"Keep my mother and brother safe when I leave," Durya whispered to the large man, pain obvious in her eyes.

"Yes, Milady." Sharn complied with a slight nod of his head. "When will you and Lord Edward take over the Estate?"

Lady Durya didn't answer. She just turned, straightened her shoulders, and walked purposefully down the hall.

"I guess that's me, too," Kaci grinned at Sharn. "Next time you see her, tell her,"she said before jogging off to catch up with the others.

Chapter 10

Echoes of Eternity

"In the depths of darkness, the smallest spark of hope ignites the path to greatness." - Bataku Raama, *The Birth of Magic*

As the sun dipped below the horizon, the last rays of daylight bathed the remaining few villagers in its warm glow. The woman who had closed the door on them sat alone on a bench, close to Belan and the others. Kaci approached and quietly took a seat beside her.

"What were their names?" Kaci whispered.

The woman gazed into the distance, her eyes glassy. For a moment she did not respond. "Ani," she finally started. "She was my daughter. And her husband, Poul. They had a little one, my grandchild. Gabi." Tears streamed down the woman's cheeks. "Why did they have to go?"

"They all went to join that ceremony?" Kaci asked gently, not wanting to pry into the wound, yet knowing that she needed the information. The elder woman nodded, a tremor running through her frail shoulders.

"Yes. Ani first. She said it was the right thing to do. Poul and Gabi followed her." The old woman's voice cracked as she continued. "The orcs had started attacking shortly after Lord Maxwell's death—may Valkyriara keep him safe. Things improved when the Elven priestess arrived with young Lord Marcus. The Orcish raids ceased, and we were overjoyed at the blessing. Each week, the priestess claimed people for various reasons, and when they returned, they were transformed. Not all returned. We all chose to ignore it, just turn our heads the other way.

Kaci sighed, placing a comforting hand on the elderly woman's shoulder, then turned to look at Belan and the fire. He assessed their work, nodding in satisfaction. The funeral pyre was nearly complete, a testament to the day's hard work.

Belan turned to the woman and whispered. "The pyre is ready. We will light it soon." She nodded, her face etched with grief and fatigue. Kaci squeezed her hand, offering comfort.

Belan met Kaci's eyes and waved her over, handing her a burning torch. The goblins, Micah, and the townsfolk had packed the base of the stage tight with hay and wood shavings. Someone had found some ash and sandalwood to mix with the fuel so the souls would be protected. All had been coated with a sticky resin to help the flames burn hot.

Kaci placed the torch at the bottom of the pyre but instead summoned the fire within and directed the flames from her fingertips. The pyre roared to life. The flames pulsed like a living, breathing thing, preparing to bring these people home. In Earthborn tradition, the smoke from the pyre would escort the souls of the deceased to the sky, allowing them to touch the heavens on their final journey.

Belan's rich voice chanted, causing Kaci to shiver involuntarily. Few beings from outside the Earthborn ever got to hear their funeral chant. Though Kaci knew he would not speak all the words aloud in this mixed crowd, she was sure he sang them in his heart.

Through the burning bier

Be but an empty shell

Tonight I shall be one with the sky above

On the great mount of Theral's Peak

Yet, my memory lives on

In the minds of all.

The flames grew voracious, eager to consume. Kaci wrapped herself in a comforting squeeze. In nature, when flames swept through a forest, it spelled the end for some, but the nutrients released gave life to the young. This situation was not natural. There was no way to make it right; they could only show the dead the path home.

She glanced at the portal still hanging in the air, gray and inert. What if it were to flare to life suddenly? She shuddered as its gaping eye stared at her.

From the eerie silence, a whisper seeped out, a mere breath. "It is you. Come closer," it urged. The voice was hypnotic, lacing her fear with a strange intrigue. Its tone was much like a siren's call, pulling her in while her instincts screamed *flee.*

The flames had reached their peak, dancing, leaping, and singing, and Kaci was sure she could see the light within the shells of the dead rise. They appeared above as though tiny, bright orbs that swirled, then disappeared into the night. Now and again, a shadowed orb would emerge, only to be quickly consumed by the ravenous flames. Kaci found herself transfixed, caught in the spectacle, until one shadow orb detached itself from the fire's depths. This orb was different—darker and larger—and instead of succumbing to the flames, it arched high into the air, etching a silhouette against the night sky. It circled once then dove straight at Kaci.

The vision engulfed her suddenly and she stiffened, unprepared for its intensity.

An older man and a younger woman stood side by side. A teacher and student? A kaleidoscope of colors enveloped them—tiny spheres like the bright souls that had floated skyward, but these spheres swirled with various hues and luminosity. They formed halos around the pair, creating a tempest of power.

The voice of the elder echoed everywhere. "Please, my ma'chien. Please forgo this path and come back to me."

"*Thank you for the gift, General Katan'Raama. Now, the secrets of the portals, please,*" *the younger replied.*

The elder's profound sigh resonated through the air. It spoke volumes of despair, a mournful testament of endured pain, silent sacrifices, and unspoken regrets. "*No.*"

"*Then my armies shall combine our might, break through your protective barrier, and coerce it from you! You have earned this with your acts of rebellion against our throne!*"

The man shook his head, "*No, Javina, my lovely daughter whom I cherished, it is you who have brought this upon us all.*"

He stood at the center of the vortex. Shadowed orbs began drawing toward the pair, each darker orb seeming to attract another until all of the orbs flowed together into a large void, then flattened to create a massive sphere around the pair.

"*Shadow of spirit shall bind you to this place. It shall keep you from death, but also life. People will know this place as Kashara, Darkness Eternal.*"

The colorful orbs danced around as if resisting the darkness until the man, straining under an aura of self-control, glanced at the woman before clenching his fist. All the orbs rushed at him at once, exploding outward.

Kaci collapsed to the ground in agony; thousands of screams echoed in her ears. The place became devoid of light. Nothing remained but looming darkness, pain, and torment.

Kaci wondered, if one died in a vision, would they die in the world outside as well? "Help me!" she cried, but no one could hear her. She ran, pumping her legs until her lungs screamed and she could go no further. She collapsed, letting the night swallow her whole.

The screams persisted, unrelenting. But they kept her alive, sane. Without them, there was nothing. No one.

She tried to focus inward, to find that light within. Where was it? She felt empty! She laid down to wait. For what, she was unsure. Was there an end? Was this eternity? How long had she been here? Time seemed to have no meaning in this place.

In the darkness, a force stirred. It was a presence so corrupt and powerful that it seemed to seep into the very air around her. The darkness pulsed with hatred, a rage that had been festering for eons, and Kaci felt it grow more potent with each passing moment.

The dark presence turned its attention toward her, and the sensation sent a bone-chilling terror down her spine, like an icy finger had traced a path along her soul. As the presence took notice of her, its malevolence became a palpable force that threatened to crush her spirit.

"You are my path out," the woman whispered, her voice reverberating all around.

The darkness swirled, and the twisted presence emerged as a monstrous, shadowy figure, barely discernible in the inky blackness. Its eyes glowed with a sinister crimson light, burrowing into Kaci's being, searching for the weakest point at which to strike. The surrounding air grew colder, suffocating as if it was drawing light from her body.

Kaci's heart pounded in her chest and her breaths came in short, desperate gasps. The darkness, the hatred, and the sheer power of the presence were overwhelming—an ocean of malice and despair that threatened to drown Kaci. She had to escape before it consumed her entirely. But the figure's gaze held her fast.

Finally, a tiny flicker of light. Kaci rose, moving toward it like a moth to a flame. In its faint light stood two men. The younger held a candle. Micah? No, this man was too old to be her friend. The other man she recognized clearly. He had visited her dreams since childhood. His face had always been hidden like an artist's sketch left incomplete, yet there was no mistaking his essence. It was as unique to him as her own soul was to her. "You must first learn the rules before you play the game, child of flames." What games? She tried to speak, but nothing came out. Then he snapped his fingers, and the darkness collapsed around her.

Kaci woke with a heavy blanket draped over her, and she could feel the warmth of a fire. Nearby, Micah and Belan spoke softly. She cracked an eye, not moving a muscle as she listened to the conversation unfolding.

"I understand. We all make mistakes, but it's how we respond to them that matters. It's how we grow and learn." Kaci could sense Belan's comforting presence as he placed a hand on Micah's shoulder.

Micah's voice was contemplative as he continued, "I can't help but feel responsible for all of this. The portals, the danger we're facing—what if it's my fault?"

Belan's pause lingered long before his reply. "Micah, we can't know for sure what caused the portals. It's easy to blame ourselves when things go wrong, but we must focus on finding a solution rather than dwelling on guilt. Remember, we're in this together."

Micah took a deep breath, and Kaci could hear the weight of his thoughts in his voice. "I can't help feeling that I've put Kaci and everyone else in danger. I just want to make things right again."

Belan's voice was reassuring as he squeezed Micah's shoulder. "And we will, Micah. We'll work together to find the answers and put an end to this threat. But you mustn't shoulder all the blame. No one could have foreseen what's happening."

"I should have foreseen it."

What mistake had Micah made? The men were silent now, and Kaci gave a small cough, sitting up. She was indeed in a bed. Belan sat next to it, a look of concern on his face.

"Welcome back to the land of the living, child." He smiled warmly, but she could tell he was terrified. "The sun is rising on the second day." He patted her shoulder as she pushed herself up to a sitting position. "Micah and Lady Durya were ready to leave without you. What happened, child?"

"I had a vision," she said with a sigh. "But somehow, this one found me. It was connected to the portal somehow. I'm sure." She shuddered. "All those people, lost in the dark, just wanting to escape."

"What people?" Belan asked, raising an eyebrow.

"I am pretty sure the shadows that came from the portal were once living beings. They were imprisoned. Now there is nothing left but anger and hatred. It's as if all the good has gone, leaving only the darkness. Somehow I was trapped with them." She shivered. "I didn't think I would ever be able to leave, but then—" A violent bout of coughs racked her frail body.

"Take your time," Belan's voice was soothing. "You have been through an ordeal we can't understand."

"They rescued me…" Her voice trailed off.

"Who rescued you?" Belan asked, giving one braid in his beard a tug.

"It—" Kaci pursed her lips. "I'm pretty sure it was Micah, and—"she grappled to put into words the mystery of the man whose face she had never seen yet whose essence felt as familiar as her own. "The Micah in my vision was much older. When I saw him, I was sure I had been trapped for decades! The other one spoke to me." She shook her head.

The door to the room flew open with a bang, interrupting their conversation. Lady Durya stormed in, her expression a mixture of relief and reproach. "You promised to tell us when she woke!" she exclaimed, her voice booming in the room.

"She only just opened her eyes," Belan gave a warm chuckle. "Give her a moment."

"What were you thinking?" Lady Durya ignored the Earthborn and plopped herself down on the other side of Kaci, her face scrunched into some unreadable emotion. "I—I was concerned."

"I didn't intend to do anything!" Kaci apologized, patting the large woman's shoulder. "Like the rest of you, I was helping the souls on their way. But the shadows are still out there, at least some of them. I saw them."

"I knew it!" Lady Durya glared at Belan. "We should have left sooner. There is no time to waste. Let us be on our way!"

The woman rose from the bedside and stomped her foot. Belan remained seated, calmly looking her up and down. "This mission will fail without Kaci."

Durya balled her fists. "I *still* don't understand how you reached that conclusion. Who put you in charge, anyway?"

Belan chuckled, then caught Micah's eye in the doorway. "Come in. Don't just hover."

Micah approached Kaci in disarray, his cheeks

rough with stubble. He brushed a flop of dark hair from his eyes.

"Come," Belan eyed Lady Durya and indicated the door. "Let's give them a moment."

"I'm not leaving her alone with him!" Durya's eyes flared. "No way."

Why were they being so odd? No one had *ever* been this concerned for her. "It's okay, Durya. I will be fine." She gave the large woman a tired smile.

Grumbling the whole way, Durya exited the room, and Belan closed the door behind them.

The silence was thick, and Micah stared at her, shadows under his eyes. The rich smell of stew cooking in the next room made Kaci's stomach rumble as she realized how hungry she was. Micah followed her eyes, and his widened in realization.

"Oh!" he exclaimed, "Do you want me to get you some food?"

"It's alright," Kaci giggled. "Something seems to be on your mind."

He froze, his mouth opening and closing a few times before he finally spoke. "This is all my fault."

The door blasted open, and Lady Durya barged in once more, grabbing Micah by the throat and lifting him into the air. "I knew it!"

The young man didn't struggle; he merely succumbed to her violence.

"Durya!" Kaci exclaimed. "You're hurting him!"

The Orcish woman released her grip and blinked a few times in surprise, then lowered him back to the ground.

"Please," Kaci turned to Durya. "Give him a moment. I promise I am okay." Durya gave a curt nod and walked toward the door again. "Durya?" Kaci insisted. "Please give us a moment."

Turning, the lady left without a word, clicking the door shut.

"She has frightened me since I was a kid," Micah said with a nervous chuckle. He seemed unable to look away from the door.

"As a kid?" Kaci was confused. "We have only just been acquainted. And, though I feel like I have known you forever… Did you know Lady Durya before?"

"Sort of," Micah took a deep breath. "That's what I

wanted to explain. To you, at least. *She* obviously hates me."

"Lady Durya is certainly full of passion." Kaci laughed out loud. "But hate is just another side of the coin. I would fear indifference from her more."

"You have always been wise." Micah smiled fondly at her.

Kaci grinned back. "You had better say what you are going to say because I am getting more and more confused!"

"This whole thing was my fault." Micah sighed and paced. "I was separated from my sister and birth mother for many years but met them when I was twelve. I had just moved to Maine. I followed my birth sister to Isdralan, The Wilds, but could not stay. I went home, went to university, and lived a normal life, you know?"

"No," Kaci giggled, "but I get what you are saying."

"I would see my sister every year on the solstice. Sometimes even Mir. Then I would go home and live my life." He sighed. "Mir intended me to stay in my realm much longer. But, like it or not, Isdralan was a part of me. Life outside seemed pointless."

"Who is Mir?" Kaci asked, raising an eyebrow.

"The woman that gave birth to me," Micah replied.

The fire cracked and released a puff of black smoke into the air, and Kaci was transported back to the funeral pyre. The shadow diving for her—

"*No!*" she cried, trying to duck beneath the blanket.

Micah jogged over to her and clasped her hand. "Are you okay? What can I do?"

The walls were closing in, and shadows were everywhere. Great globes seemed to spin around Micah like those in her vision, colorful and bright. But there were shadowed ones, too. She squeezed her eyes shut and breathed in and out before opening them again. It was only Micah now. No shadows, no color. Just him.

"I'm okay," she whispered. "The fire just startled me. Please, continue."

"After I set foot in Isdralan, I never fit in anywhere else." He smiled sadly and brushed the hair from his eyes. "Eventually, my younger human sister, Bethany, graduated from high school. She was moving to New York to study the arts, and Mom and Dad bought a place in Florida. By then, I'd made something of a life for myself. I had my job and my studies, but without my family, they were not enough of a reason for me to stay any longer, so I finally returned."

"To The Wilds!" Kaci gave him an encouraging smile and pushed herself upright. Her arm almost gave out, but she caught herself before anything embarrassing happened.

"The first time I was in Isdralan, I was just a kid. I had shunned magic and fantasy. I thought I was too old for it, but that world was full of it. Going there changed my life. I had some of the most meaningful friendships I had ever made, and getting to know my sister was magical." He gave Kaci a bashful grin and took a deep breath. "You were one of those friends."

Kaci stared at him for a moment before finding the words. "I feel as if I have always known you." She remembered the vision she'd seen in the fire with Elena. The tall, regal woman she now knew as Durya, and the boy who'd looked like Micah. "But I don't understand."

"I figured if I could explain it to anyone, it would be you." Micah sighed. "We perceive time as moving forward, like an arrow."

"I like that," Kaci nodded to herself, repeating it. "The arrow of time. Time flies like an arrow."

"And fruit flies like banana," Micah replied with a

grin.

"Huh?" Kaci scrunched her nose. "You lost me there."

"Never mind." He trailed off for a moment, staring up at the ceiling. "Time doesn't *move* at all. That is a construct. Everything that has happened, or will happen, or could be possible—it all just *is*. It exists simultaneously. When you see visions in the fire or the scrying bowl, you are not looking at some distant future or a possibility. You are looking at something that exists."

"No!" Kaci shook her head. In her mind's eye, she saw the flames swallowing Belan again. "That can't be right. There must be a way to change what I see in my visions. They don't exist. Yet."

"There is a way to change it for *this Kaci*." Micah smiled sadly. "You can change your perception path. But somewhere, in some alternate universe, what you see is still happening. If not to you, then another version of yourself."

"I don't like that at all, Micah," Kaci replied, frowning. "Why even tell me this? If I can't do anything about it."

"I guess that's the point. Our perception is important to us, and I needed to tell you this to explain how I know you." Micah sighed. "I met both you and Lady Durya when I was a kid. But it is in your perceived future. Make sense?"

"I am not sure I get it," Kaci answered. "But I will try."

"Everything is really about gravity. If you take the relationship between mass and the curvature of space and dilation of time—"

"I am going to stop you right there. You are moving further away from my understanding instead of closer." Kaci ginned.

"Exactly!" Micah bounced on his toes a little. "After I returned home from Isdralan, I majored in physics, so I could quantify Isdralan and everything I had seen."

"Still lost." Kaci shrugged. "But I get the concept that my visions are happening. I just don't like it."

"Fair enough," Micah replied. "It's a hard pill to swallow."

"There you go, saying strange things yet again." Kaci giggled. "So how does this make everything your fault?"

Micah's bouncing slowed, and his shoulders slumped. "Well, when I returned to Isdralan, I wanted to show off to my sister. She grew up there and understands her powers better than I do. I had only studied the *science* of things. The two of us are stronger together, and I could never explain that with math. But she would sit by my side during my practice sessions. We would often watch what could have been." He sighed. "The tricky part is, the more of my possibilities I touched, the more I could remember them. It's as though I've lived thousands of lives."

He stood and began pacing again, and Kaci tried to ignore the rumbling in her stomach. Micah obviously needed to get this off his chest.

"Muirenn is great at creating portals to connect the different worlds and universes," Micah continued without looking at Kaci. "Me, not so much. But I had an amulet, a gift from Mir—a pendant. If I used that, I could focus on pinpointing the people I was connected to. It was something. I would see my dad's many paths and my grandfather's. I even looked in on my little sister Bethany a few times. It was easy to connect Isdralan and Earth, where I grew up."

He glanced at Kaci. "One time, I was looking in on an old friend, and somehow my pendant got sucked through the portal. I promised Muirenn I would re-trieve it." He gave a half smile that didn't meet his eyes. But when I came to your world, it was the wrong time. Many months had passed. I tried to get back to Muirenn so we could find the right time."

"You are trapped here, aren't you?" Kaci interrupted. "You need that amulet of power to return home."

Yep," Micah sighed.

Kaci was silent for a long time, studying Micah's face. He looked at her like she was some wise, all-know-ing being that could fix everything. But she was barely out of girlhood. Not some hero of the ages. Who was he, anyway, to toy with the stuff of gods? Any help from her would probably mess things up even further. She shook her head and gave Micah a sad smile. "I can't help you—"

A soft knock at the door interrupted them, and Belan entered, carrying a steaming bowl of stew. Kaci's stomach rumbled so loud they all heard it.

"I figured you would be starving." Belan smiled as he placed the bowl on the table next to the bed. "Old family recipe." He winked.

The two men waited as Kaci thanked the Great

Mother, then slurped down the meal. "Where is Lady Durya?" she asked, mouth half full.

"Marcus sent word he needed to speak with her this morning. She went to Marshfield Estates." He walked to the corner of the room and gently laid a hand on the intricate wooden box. "We have two of the crowns now. Arda told us that the third resides with Cirden in Aeloria."

"Have you heard anything of King Thorlyn?" Kaci asked.

Belan shook his head sorrowfully. "It is unlikely that I will see my brother any time soon. The Allfather wishes I see this through to the end."

The Earthborn tugged at his beard and turned to her. "And now, child, I must ask a great sacrifice of you."

Sinking back into her bed, Kaci already knew what was coming. Why did everyone seem to need her? She had left her home and Arba Vitae to escape her destiny and live her life the way she chose. Now, destiny seemed to chase her down.

"I will go after the third crown, and I could use your guidance in Aeloria," Belan said with a sad smile at Kaci, as if he were privy to the *same* secrets she was.

Molten fire swallowed him as he fell, and she could not reach him. Death's shadow surrounded him, and they both knew it.

"Please?" Belan added.

Kaci turned to Micah, her eyes pleading. The thought of confronting Cirden terrified her. "Do you think perhaps you can reach home with just the two crowns? Maybe your sister or your Mir could help Belan's brother?" As she voiced the idea, a spark of confidence ignited within her. If Micah's family could help, Cirden would have to respect her.

"Mir is her name." Micah giggled uncomfortably and shrugged. "I will try."

Chapter 11

The Hidden Path

"Through veils of enigma and shadows of uncertainty, the heart's compass steers the seeker toward the light that awaits." - Bataku Raama, *The Birth of Magic*

Micah spent the afternoon working on the crowns with Belan's help. They removed the pieces of his amulet and Belan, experienced with a forge, attempted to weld them back together. Oddly, the pendant's intricate pattern of swirls seemed to maintain its shape in defiance of the intense heat.

After hours of tinkering, Micah sighed and stared at the pieces of the amulet in his hands, exasperated. "This is driving me mad! The amulet is our only hope for help, and I can't seem to fix it."

Observing Micah's frustration, Belan knelt beside him. "What's bothering you, Micah?"

Micah hesitated, as if unsure whether he should share his thoughts. Finally, he admitted, "I feel useless. I thought I could repair it, but it's beyond my abilities. I don't know what to do now."

Belan placed a reassuring hand on Micah's shoulder. "Don't lose hope just yet. We'll either fix it or come up with something else. Remember, we're a team."

Kaci chimed in, nodding. "Belan's right. We'll work this out."

Micah, eyes downcast, resumed his work. He removed a small piece of metal from the crown and carefully placed it onto the amulet. As he muttered a few words, the amulet glowed brightly.

Belan and Kaci gasped in surprise as power radiated from the pendant. A sense of urgency built in Kaci. "What did you say?" she inquired. "Was that some kind of incantation?"

Micah laughed, shaking his head. "I was just repeating, *please work, please work*! Normally, I don't need any words."

Belan nodded approvingly. "Excellent work, Micah! We'll need all the help we can muster."

It was at that moment Lady Durya burst through

the door in a swirl of skirts, and the light emanating from the amulet went dark. She flipped her dark hair over a shoulder and began breathlessly, "Marcus reported that the portals are opening across the lands on their own now." She narrowed her eyes in Micah's direction. "What are you doing?"

"I was trying to use *my* amulet to call for help." He took a menacing step toward her. "But you just screwed it up!"

Kaci shook her head. What was it with these two? It was Belan that spoke the thoughts out loud. "It's rain that grows the flower, not thunder. Imagine what you two would grow if you worked with each other instead of against."

Micah and Lady Durya each stomped a foot in unison, almost as though it was choreographed. Kaci laughed so hard her ribs hurt, reminding her that she'd not quite recovered from her ordeal.

"Take a breath and tell us your news." Belan was all business now as he turned to Durya. "What has Marcus shared?"

A few hairs had sprung loose from Lady Durya's neatly plaited hair, and she tried unsuccessfully to tame them. "Marcus received word from nearby cities that strange portals are opening and closing at will. Monsters a spewing forth and possessing anyone around." She sighed. "They sound exactly like the portals that the woman Arda called forth in the dark of the moon."

"I fear its opening has produced a chain of events that is now out of our control," Belan said. "Any more luck, Micah?"

Micah shook his head, dejected.

"Then we must attempt to retrieve the third crown," Belan stated. He turned to Kaci. "I do not think we can stop this on our own. Will you help me find Cirden, child?"

Kaci wanted to say no. Her heart and soul pleaded with her to find a quiet corner of the world and live out her life in peace. She inspected Micah, thinking about their conversation earlier. Was there some version of herself that did that? In some instances of her life, she had run away and found happiness. What would have happened if she hadn't sheltered in the cave on that rainy day not so long ago?

From where she sat now, she could only make one choice and still live with herself. If these portals continued, there would be nowhere safe in all the lands. She gave a quick nod at Belan. "I will go."

"I will as well," Micah added. "You will need me to use the amulet when we have the last piece. I can summon help."

"I will come as well." Lady Durya threw her shoulders back, looking more like a warrior than an aristocrat. "There is no way I am leaving him with you two." Her eyes narrowed at Micah.

"What did I do?!" was the man's reply.

Lady Durya pulled out a neatly folded piece of parchment. She opened it to reveal a map, which she gently placed on the table. "This was among Arda's belongings."

A circle stood out in the middle of the map. Kaci noted the flowing hand-written script: *return here when the task is complete. Beware the traps of which I informed you.*

This is where we need to go,"Durya said, pointing with authority.

"Your family needs you, Lady Durya," Belan spoke in a voice of reason. "And your husband is still missing." The lady's eyes flitted back and forth, and she seemed to shrink into herself for a moment before standing tall again.

"Marcus will handle Westerfield, and my mother is not afraid to lead." Lady Durya sighed. "Something tells me…" She shook her head and started again, "I am going."

"So be it," Belan nodded. "If you are feeling well enough, Kaci, we'll ride at dawn."

This was her path. Kaci shivered, remembering Elena's last words. *You have a duty to fulfill.* Why did that woman always have to get the final say?

Marcus generously supplied them with horses and provisions sufficient for a year-long battle. Kaci chuckled awkwardly, hoping that all these resources would prove excessive. She couldn't imagine the world enduring a full year of shadow attacks.

As they traveled, Belan and Kaci's bond grew even stronger. Kaci had never experienced a parental figure growing up. Although Elena had been a role model in her life, Belan felt like the father figure she had longed for.

In the evenings, as the group settled down to camp for the night, Belan captivated Kaci with stories of the Allfather and the Earthborn's ultimate dream of touching the sky. One particular story, about the Allfather's amazing creation of the world, caught Kaci's interest, spurring more and more questions about Earthborn beliefs and traditions.

Even though she was drawn to these new ideas, Kaci still loved The Great Mother and everything she stood for. She held onto the essence of what that embodied—the intertwining cycle of life, the symbiotic relationship of all creatures, and the everlasting pact between earth and the heavens. She shared her own tales of Arba Vitae and how it connected her people to The Great Mother.

Each conversation, each shared story, helped her grow and blossom like the tree herself! But this spiritual growth carried with it a shadow of fear. What if Arda had been telling the truth and Arba Vitae was unwell? A dreadful question began to take root in her heart; if Arba Vitae was ill, did it mean The Great Mother was ill, too? Or was it simply that their route to her, their spiritual link, was weakening? Wrapped in these dilemmas, Kaci found herself in a maelstrom of fear and responsibility.

Despite the crushing weight she was feeling, something was different. She wasn't alone anymore. She had friends who believed in her. The stronger these connections became, the more at ease Kaci felt. She would help her friends and, in doing so, help her people, Arba Vitae, and the Great Mother herself! The fear that once loomed in her heart had gradually started to recede, replaced by a quiet confidence. Shared laughter, open dialogue, and unfaltering support had all combined to make Kaci feel more grounded and less isolated. She was prepared to face whatever may come her way.

Occasionally, Micah would join them, claiming to have met the great gods in his childhood. But when they asked him to share more of his youth, he would close up tighter than a clam.

Lady Durya would sit apart from them, pretending not to listen. She probably would have pulled it off until the derisive snort at Micah's claims escaped her lips.

New portals manifested along their path as the group journeyed. With each encounter, Kaci sharpened her skills in vanishing the emerging dark creatures, though she remained unable to fully seal the portals. After her interventions, the once-active gateways became gray and lifeless—vacant eyes with no souls lurking behind them.

Whenever Kaci approached these portals, a chilling sensation crept over her skin, like swarms of tiny ants biting relentlessly. The discomfort only intensified her desire to distance herself from these eerie voids.

As the group approached the destination Cirden had indicated on the map, the once-lively conversations dwindled, and the silence grew heavier with each passing day. It was as if they could all sense the impending doom and their thoughts turned inward, consumed by their individual fears and worries.

One evening, after sharing a quiet meal, Kaci found herself entranced by the fire. Her eyes followed the flames as they danced and leaped in a mesmerizing display of light and shadow. The flickering flames, dancing almost joyfully, contrasted starkly with the oppressive silence surrounding the group.

Through her conversations with Belan, Kaci had learned to see the light of creation within the fire, rather than solely focusing on its destructive power. This new perspective brought solace, helping her to find beauty and hope in their circumstances. As she watched the fire, she felt a sense of connection to its vibrant energy, a reminder that life and growth could still exist amid the darkness.

It had been a while since Kaci had allowed herself the simple pleasure of observing the flames, and she now found comfort in their hypnotic dance. This moment of tranquility provided her with a brief respite from the weight of their journey.

She let the fire draw her in tonight, and the visions envelop her.

She was a child again, dancing barefoot under Arba Vitae, an owl watching over her serenely from above. Pure joy washed over her. A melody wafted on the breeze, a sweet song so vivid its colors seemed to dance through the air. She danced after the musical notes, following them down a path.

In front of her was a great circle of light that made it hard to see. A ring of fire opened into a vast, verdant field brimming with wildflowers, but nothing was burning. The colors and musical notes led right into the ring, and she followed them without hesitation.

Inside the ring, she saw the source of the emanating light. There was a man with golden hair, powerful muscles, and a gentle smile. He picked her up and swung her around, and she giggled with delight. Together, they picked flowers and wove them into beautiful crowns. He placed one on her head and called her the queen of the fairies.

He taught her to conjure a tiny flame in her palm and

to play a game with figurines on an intricate board, designed with intersecting lines and patterns. In the distance, the circle of fire remained open. Kaci couldn't recall how long they stayed in the field, laughing and playing, but eventually, Elena's shouts interrupted their joy.

Elena stood at the edge of the circle, careful not to step beyond its bounds. The man looked up, a twinkle in his eyes. "Come, my darling. Join us!" Elena held herself firm at the entrance. "I will not be fooled twice."

"Oh, but she is so sad and lonely. Come share in the love!" When Elena still didn't budge, the man sighed and rose to his feet, tenderly taking Kaci's hand and leading her back to the portal.

Time seemed to shift. Elena, the field, and the memory melted away, leaving only the man and her standing in a void.

"Nothing can dim the light that burns within," he whispered. "Hold this memory close, and you will find it when you need it. Go well, Child of Flame."

"Kaci?" Lady Durya's voice interrupted her reverie.

"Sorry, I must have been in the stars for a moment," Kaci answered. She did not want to share what she had seen. It was hers, and it was precious. Her vision was more like a memory than a possible future. These events had not existed before, but now Kaci could clearly remember that day. She remembered Elena scolding her for running off, and that she had heard Elena fighting later that night. Her combatant, someone with an unfamiliar voice, had assured her mistress that the child would not remember a thing.

She knew the man and the voice well, for he had invaded her visions thrice now. He had been the one to rescue her from the darkness. This new vision had been meant especially for Kaci.

"How long is left of our journey?" Lady Durya asked. "You, out of everyone, would know best."

"We will arrive before the midday sun if we leave at dawn," Kaci replied.

Cirden's map was guiding them to a sacred place steeped in Aeloria's ancestral lore and customs—a place profoundly interwoven with Elven history and mythology. However, this was a side of Aeloria she had scarcely seen. The old magics had been nearly forgotten, replaced by more modern ways of thinking. These once-hallowed barrows, pulsating with ancient wisdom and mystical power, were no longer frequented. They were a relic of a bygone era, their memories and purpose preserved only in tales and folklore.

No one spoke after that. As they turned down their beds in silence, anticipation loomed like an ominous cloud. The fire crackled in the night, the only sound to break the stillness.

Eventually, the forest thinned and the underbrush receded. It gave way to a vast, open field that stretched before them as far as the eye could see. Throughout the field were countless ancient barrows rising from the ground like low, gentle hills. Mounds of earth and stone, scattered across the landscape in an irregular pattern, concealed the ancient mysteries of the past beneath. Their round and elongated shapes disrupted the flat expanses of the surrounding land like waves on a calm sea. This was where Cirden's map had led them.

Lady Durya, scanning the landscape with a mix of confusion and frustration, let out a great sigh. "There is nothing here!" she exclaimed, her voice tinged with disappointment.

Cocking his head, Micah gazed ahead. "Such a strange landscape. I have never seen so many tiny hills."

"They are grave sites." Kaci laughed as Micah choked and sputtered. "It was the burial rites of our ancestors. The Earthborn mausoleum did not seem to bother you so much. Why this?"

"I was just surprised," Micah pouted. "That's all."

"It doesn't change the fact that there is nothing here!" Durya was pacing, clearly agitated.

"Now what?"

"Relax, Durya." Belan smiled as if this was what he had expected all along. "You don't expect a corrupted Elven elder to lead you right to his front door, now do you?"

She shook her head, clearly annoyed.

The group fanned out, carefully exploring the barrows for any signs or clues that might lead them to Cirden. The wind rustled the tall grass, casting eerie shadows across the mounds as the sun began its descent toward the horizon.

The field held no immediate answers or solutions. It seemed nothing more than a vast graveyard, a ghostly reminder of lives long past. Disheartened but not defeated, they regrouped.

"Shut your eyes," Belan instructed, "and listen for a moment."

Kaci squeezed her eyes shut, expecting to hear the sweet song of the birds and the chattering of forest life in the distance. Oddly, there was nothing—not a sound. More than that, the air was still and empty. Not a hint of a breeze, just pure silence.

"I don't hear anything," Lady Durya complained. Kaci opened an eyelid to peek at her friend. The lady was clearly not following instructions. Her eyes were wide open, and she bounced on her heels and swished her dress. Was it odd that Kaci could not hear the swish of her dress?

She retreated into the darkness of her mind again and assessed. It was as though everything within the boundary of the field had paused. She peeked out at the world again. Belan was lost in concentration, like he was trying to solve a tough puzzle. Micah's eyes were closed, but his face was twisted in a mix of horror and curiosity. Suddenly, he blinked his eyes open as if in surprise. He took a few steps back before composing himself.

"Do you hear the ocean?" he asked. "In the distance?"

Lady Durya shook her head and Belan, concentration broken, opened his eyes. "I hear nothing, and that frightens me."

"What did you see?" Kaci asked Micah.

"Nothing," he answered too quickly. "Why would I see anything?"

"Your eyes. They tracked as if you were following multiple things," Kaci answered. "I just assumed you saw something we didn't."

"Well, that would be strange." Micah's tortured expression had smoothed into a smile again. "Of course I didn't see anything."

Lady Durya glared at him but remained silent.

"Indeed," Belan answered with a wink.

"What are you trying to get from us?" Micah frowned at the man. "Perhaps instead of making everything a teaching moment, you just tell us straight."

"When you are in a dark tunnel, are your eyes leading the way?" Belan questioned. "Teaching moment or no, before we give up, we must look at the full picture. Even if we cannot see the way, we must keep moving."

Kaci shut her eyes again, and a gentle lilt of a harp floated in the back of her mind. She was not sure if it was all in her head, like a memory, or if it was really playing. It seemed to come from the northeast, but the sound disappeared when she opened her eyes.

"This way!" She pointed and closed her eyes again. She reached a hand out to Belan. "Keep me from falling?"

"Of course." He clasped her hand and guided her as she moved toward the music. As others followed, Durya muttered under her breath. Micah was quiet now, probably considering Belan's words but pretending he wasn't.

The music grew louder until it rose in a crescendo and halted, leaving behind an unsettling silence. "Here!" Kaci exclaimed.

When she opened her eyes, she found herself standing in front of a medium-sized mound with freshly dug earth in front of it. An inexplicable urge tugged at her. She moved toward the mound and began to scoop the dirt aside. She needed to dig, to explore, to discover. Something about this particular barrow called to her, a voice from beneath the earth that beckoned her to reveal its secrets (hopefully not some wraith from the past!).

Belan and Micah remained at a distance, watching Kaci. For a few heartbeats, they merely stood there, spectators to Kaci's sudden actions. Then, as if reaching an unspoken agreement, their hesitation melted away. They strode toward her, movements mirroring Kaci's, their hands reaching to join hers.

"Are you going to help?" Micah asked Durya. "Or just stand there watching."

"I am supervising," she sniffed. "Dirt is so…dirty!"

They continued working for several more minutes, moving large piles of dirt until Belan's boot struck something solid. Underneath the soil was a large, concealed trapdoor. Kaci and Micah cleared away the remaining dirt while Lady Durya, with some effort, pulled open the heavy door.

"There, I contributed," she declared with a hint of pride.

Beneath the trapdoor, a long ladder descended into the dark depths below.

"It might only lead to the bodies interred beneath these mounds," Lady Durya said, wrinkling her nose in distaste. "I've seen enough corpses in recent weeks to last a lifetime."

"Or it could lead to Cirden," Belan suggested.

"There's only one way to find out!"

Chapter 12

Library of Forgotten Knowledge

"The Caves of Chaos guard the origins of magic. Those who dare to venture within may unearth ancient wisdom and untold power. Yet caution must guide each step, for unseen perils abound: shadows weave and secrets slumber, and one false move could seal an eternal fate." Bataku Raama, *The Birth of Magic*

Upon reaching the bottom of the old ladder, the group paused, adjusting to the dimly lit surroundings. The floor was clean, considering it lay beneath a burial mound. Sconces lined a long hallway, their small flickering tapers providing just enough light to see by. The passage stretched out in either direction from where the group stood.

Lady Durya shivered as she glanced down each end of the seemingly endless hallway. She filled her lungs with stale, dusty air. "Well?" she asked the others. "Which way should we go?"

Micah inspected both paths and shrugged noncommittally as if waiting for Durya to suggest some-thing so he could disagree. Belan, uncharacteristically quiet, offered no words of wisdom or lessons on deci-sion-making.

"Something feels off about this place," Kaci said, shaking her head to clear the fog and cobwebs clouding her thoughts. "I—" Closing her eyes, she sniffed the air, recalling Belan's earlier advice. The scent held a floral hint, like the memory of a long-faded bloom.

Micah poked at the walls, using an index finger as if he were writing messages in the air. "I don't under-stand…" he muttered to himself.

"*What* don't you understand?" Lady Durya snapped. "Perhaps you can share with the rest of us?"

"Not yet," Micah replied. "Not until I understand."

"Well!" Durya flipped her hair. "That will be never!"

"Are you okay?" Kaci whispered to Belan as Micah and Durya continued to bicker. She fully expected him to say he was fine. The elders always seemed to be *fine*, even when Kaci could sense they were not. But Belan surprised her.

"I knew this day would come." He sighed, shaking his head. "Now that it is here, I am afraid."

"Afraid?" Kaci was worried now. She had never seen her friend and mentor act this way. "What could you be afraid of?"

A vision invaded her mind. *A flash of molten lava, Belan falling as she watched.*

No, that was irrational thinking. This strange place was likely affecting their minds, amplifying Micah's and Durya's bickering. If she had learned anything on the journey, it was the extraordinary things that made the people she traveled with unique.

Durya thrived on arguing, using dissent to project strength when she felt vulnerable. Micah, on the other hand, always needed to be right, reveling in the attention his knowledge brought him. They were two sides of the same coin. Kaci smiled faintly as she looked at Belan, the person she aspired to emulate with his wisdom and gentle demeanor. She briefly wondered how her companions perceived her. Was she just a child fleeing responsibility? Micah seemed to adore her, but she suspected he saw her as the person she would become. Lady Durya appeared to view her as a dazzling trinket capable of wielding fire and magic. Neither seemed to care about her truly, only the image they had created.

The candles flickered as these thoughts swirled, and

the walls seemed to close in on Kaci. They were at least fifty feet underground. There was no sunshine to draw hope and light from, no trees to offer solace beneath their boughs. The realization sent a shiver down her spine and her breath grew shallow.

A warm hand clasped hers. "Breathe, child," Belan spoke. "Look for the light."

"But there is none!" Kaci cried out, panic consuming her. "All I see is the darkness!"

The others had stopped their bickering and were now watching her with evident concern. Belan tightened his grip on her hand, and she focused on the rough texture of his skin. "If you look for the dark, that's all you will see. But if you search for the light within you, you will find it."

Kaci exhaled a long, shuddering breath and inhaled deeply. Micah was there now, his offering his crooked smile. "Count to five," he suggested gently.

"You are the best of us," Lady Durya declared with uncharacteristic sentiment. "You can't afford to be weighed down by despair now."

Kaci nearly giggled at Lady Durya's statement. How it must have chafed her pride to admit someone else was better. The laughter bubbled warmly within her, and she took another steadying breath.

One, two, three, four, five.

Belan was right. She *did* have a light within. She had used it during the past week of travel to defeat the shadows, and she could draw on it again to push back her own darkness. All of their darkness, if needed! She straightened her shoulders and smiled widely.

"We have a misguided Elven elder to find before he destroys the world!" she exclaimed. "Let's get moving!"

"Okay then." Micah smiled, and Lady Durya nodded her assent.

"The question still begs to be answered," Lady Durya sniffed. "Which way?"

They all laughed. Kaci pulled her pack from her shoulder and, rummaging through it, pulled out a small piece of charcoal. She kneeled on the ground and drew a thick arrow pointing north. At least, she thought it was north. There was no sky or landmark to confirm.

"This way," she said, attempting to sound confident. Belan smiled, but the shadow of doubt still clung to him.

The emptiness of the tunnel was eerie. It seemed almost as if deliberately designed to disorient and discourage intruders. The monotonous walls seemed to consume any sound, leaving the space hollow.

As they ventured further, the air grew colder and heavier, pressing down on them like an unseen burden. Shadows seemed to gather in the corners of Kaci's vision, playing tricks on her mind and sowing seeds of doubt. How long had they traveled, and how much time had they wasted here? What if Cirden wasn't even in this place? Each step felt heavier, and the silence grew louder, amplifying the uncertainty that gnawed at her resolve.

Just a little further, Kaci thought, *and then we can turn back*. She placed a hand on the stone wall and was surprised by its warmth. "Feel this," she instructed Lady Durya excitedly.

The lady touched the wall and raised an eyebrow. "It feels like—" her eyes widened and her hands spread in a flourish—"a wall!"

"I know, I know," Kaci said through a sigh. "But does it feel warm to you?"

"It feels wall temperature." Lady Durya shrugged. "I'm afraid you are grasping at straws."

Kaci scrunched her face. "Micah, Belan, what do you think?"

They both placed a palm on the wall. Micah gave a sad smile. "I hate to say it, but Lady Durya is right. It just feels wall temperature." Belan remained silent. He had been sinking deeper and deeper into himself.

"Okay then, just a bit further," Kaci suggested. "If we don't find anything, we will turn back."

"Look! There is something on the floor ahead!" Lady Durya, suddenly excited, strode with purpose, her long legs giving her an advantage. Micah had to jog to keep up with her. Kaci hung back with Belan, not wanting to leave him behind. By the time they caught up, Durya's excitement had wilted as she stared at a charcoal arrow drawn carefully on the floor.

"Is that the same one you drew?" Micah asked.

Kaci kneeled next to it, inspecting the black smudge. It was most definitely her arrow. They had wasted hours on nothing!

She needed to think. Kaci sighed and slumped to the ground. She shifted her weight to lean against the wall, but the wall did not catch her. She continued falling backward. The solid rock that surrounded the hallway was not solid at all. It was not even there. It had all been an illusion!

Leaping to her feet, she grabbed Belan's hands and spun him in her dance of joy. This brought a tiny smile to his morose face. "The answer was in front of us all along!" she exclaimed.

She raised a hand and placed it against where the wall should have been, and it sank right through. "Let's see where this leads."

The entry opened into a grand, circular library that seemed to defy the bounds of the underground space. Shelf upon shelf, stack upon stack spiraled higher and higher, creating a dizzying labyrinth of literature. The vibrant bindings and dusty old tomes climbed the walls to the ceiling and stretched into infinite darkness above.

Warm, diffused lantern light cast a golden glow over the countless volumes. As Kaci wandered through the library, she felt a sense of excitement and wonder. She had always been drawn to the books on Elena's shelves, and to the modest collections in each village, but this library surpassed anything she had ever seen. It was as if the shelves were alive, filled with stories waiting to be discovered and knowledge yearning to be revealed.

She ran her fingers over the spines, marveling at their embossed lettering and intricate designs. Some books appeared ancient, their pages yellowed and fragile, while others seemed fresh off the press, their ink still vibrant and crisp. She could feel the energy of the library, the collective wisdom and imagination contained within its walls. Someday, when this was all over, she would return and spend months down here just reading, absorbing the centuries of knowledge and the worlds hidden within these pages.

Micah watched her with a smile. "I used to go to the library all the time," he said, his voice quiet. "Many years ago, someone I knew talked about all the books she had read from all the different worlds. It inspired me to love the library. I would sneak in there and hide out for hours when I was lonely. There, I had shelves upon shelves of friends."

Lady Durya gawked at the vast expanse of shelves, which she perused, running her gray fingertips along the spine of a book. She turned back to them, flashing the most childlike smile Kaci had ever seen on this woman's face. "I could stay here forever!" she giggled. *Lady Durya giggled!*

Kaci jogged over to join her and pulled out a book with a blue spine. *A Wrinkle in Time by Madeleine L'En-*

gle. She opened the tome and thumbed through a few pages. "Curious. This seems to be written in some sort of ancient text, but I can read every word on the page!"

"Let me see." Micah wandered over to Kaci, and she handed him the book. "This is a story my dad read to me after I returned from my first trip to Isdralan." His voice was soft, tender almost. "It isn't an ancient language at all. It is from my world."

"I am intrigued." Kaci smiled, tucking the story into her backpack.

"You can't steal that!" Lady Durya frowned. "Put it back!"

"Knowledge belongs to everyone. But if it makes you feel better, I will ask permission when we find Cirden." Kaci gave a wink and turned to inspect the rest of the room.

At the center was a massive wooden desk with stacks of paper, a few sheets scattered as if someone had left in a hurry. Belan stood at the desk and as he read through the papers, a look of concern spread across his face.

Lady Durya's nose was so deep in a dusty tome that she didn't even notice as the others left her side.

Kaci joined Belan at the desk, and after a moment, Micah peeled himself away from the great shelves as well to inspect the papers Belan was studying.

"It appears Cirden has been gone for some time," Belan stated. He looked like a child, seated in an oversized chair. "Years even, judging by these notes."

"How is that possible?" Kaci asked. "The bonfire accident happened only one summer ago."

Micah's eyebrows furrowed in concern. "I think this place exists outside of time. I was worried about that the moment we entered the field full of barrows."

"If you were worried," Kaci grinned, "then why didn't you say something? Of course this place exists outside of time. It's a well-known secret among the elves—one of those ancient enigmas passed down in whispers. These places are safeguarded, and one must understand profound mysteries to locate them."

It made sense why Cirden would go here. He could have taken all the time in the world to create the crowns and perfect them, and not more than a minute would have passed in real life.

"I couldn't quite comprehend how it was possible, and I didn't want to say anything until I had a better understanding. It's sort of like Isdralan." Micah scanned the room with a look of intense concentration. "I still can't make out the how or why."

"The ancient Elven elders used to be required to journey through the tunnels beneath the barrows to the roots of the Arba Vitae. It was said that they could commune directly with the Great Mother there," Kaci explained. "Those traditions faded long ago and, after a time, we stopped burying our elders in the barrows. The place has been mostly forgotten, relegated to the realm of myths and stories that everyone knows but no longer practices. Fortunately, Elena insisted on my understanding the ancient knowledge. Honestly, I hadn't thought about it until you mentioned the place is outside of time. It makes more sense now."

"Maybe this will help?" Belan pushed a tome that looked older than time itself toward Micah and Kaci— *The Birth of Magic by Bataku Raama.* Someone had tucked sheets of parchment with notes throughout the book.

"It looks like Cirden used this tome extensively in his studies." Belan opened it to one of the places marked by a sheet of paper—a chapter titled "The Caves of Chaos." Small, neat writing noted that one entrance to the caves lay at the root of Arba Vitae, and the only way to reach it was through the barrows. Kaci read the passage:

These caves are mysteriously linked to Isdralan, the land of magic and wonder. Only a handful have ever dared to enter their dark depths, as they are rife with danger and deception. However, for those fools courageous enough to seek them out, the rewards are immense.

Numerous entrances to the Caves of Chaos are dispersed throughout various lands. That of Arba Vitae is perhaps the most captivating. By legend, the tree is a portal to the Otherworld, a gateway to the realm of spirits and gods.

I have never visited the Arba Vitae, but I have heard accounts from those who have. They speak of a magnificent tree with roots that delve deep into the earth and branches that extend toward the heavens. At its base lies a hidden entrance, shrouded by magic and protected by an enigma. Only those pure of heart and resolute can hope to pass, but even they must pay a price.

The Caves of Chaos are not to be underestimated. They are a place of darkness and danger, teeming with traps and pitfalls. Even the strongest, most skilled, and most knowledgeable can fall victim to their snares. If you choose to seek them out, proceed with caution and vigilance.

Cirden's pages noted the perils and gave suggestions on how to prepare.

After hours poring over the diagrams and notes tucked into the tome, Kaci's eyes began to burn with the strain. She blinked rapidly, trying to clear her vision as a dull throb pounded at the base of her skull. She glanced away from the table strewn with musty, yellowed papers, searching for something to rest her gaze upon. That's when she noticed a small, unassuming journal lying apart from the rest.

Kaci's breath hitched, and her heart pounded like a frantic drummer. *Cirden, Elder of the Terra Clan,* was inscribed in the upper corner of the book. Was it his journal? Cirden was the one person in the world who looked at her with such disdain that it was like a physical blow. After the fire, he had been open about his loathing for Kaci, but the thought of finding out exactly how keen that hatred was sent chills down her spine.

Reluctantly, she turned the page and began her reading. The penmanship was tidy, featuring elegant, swirling loops.

Third Moon, First Cycle

Today marks the first day of my service to the Great Mother. I have been chosen as a vessel for her divine power. I feel honored and humbled by this sacred duty. The Great Mother is benevolent and wise and watches over her followers, providing guidance in their times of need. I am eager to experience the blessings she will bestow upon me.

My Apprentice continues to improve. Her injuries were grave, and she will always bear the scars of her ordeal, but she will survive. The Great Mother was true to her word. Why, then, does my fear persist?

I always believed meeting The Great Mother would feel like a return to childhood—like being wrapped in a mother's arms. Instead, I feel fear and confusion. Is she angry that I did not fight harder to banish Elena's girl? It was almost as if the Great Mother was afraid of the child. Who am I to question?

I lost time again today. Arda inquired why I was asking so many strange questions earlier, but I do not recall any of them. Perhaps I am suffering from Leth'Valan? Or perhaps it is merely due to my troubled soul. I have begun this journal to note my health.

Kaci felt the sting of being reduced to *Elena's girl,* but it was tempered by the lack of malice in Cirden's words.

"Lethallen?" Micah's question cut through the silence.

"Leth'Valan," Kaci clarified, her voice holding a note of gravity, "is a condition that effects some of my people as they age, especially those with magic. Memory erodes, and time becomes muddled." She paused and shuddered. "Imagine being adrift in your own mind, the present and the past intertwining until they're indistinguishable."

With a shake of her head, Kaci pushed the thoughts aside and returned her focus to the journal.

Third Moon, Third Cycle

Serving the Great Mother has been a complex mixture of wonder and terror. Her immense power courses through my veins, enabling me to perform feats of magic I never thought possible. However, there are moments when I feel as though I am losing myself to her influence. My thoughts no longer feel like my own, and I struggle to maintain control over my actions. Shadows seem to encroach upon my mind, casting doubt and confusion where once there was clarity. I pray that this is simply a temporary side effect of the Great Mother's power and not a more sinister consequence.

As the Great Mother promised, the improvements to Arda's health have been exponential, but her demeanor is changed. It seems as if darkness has taken root within her, threatening to consume the light that once shone so brightly. Our relationship used to be one of closeness, as I am the only parent she has ever known. Now I feel an unsettling distance between us.

I cannot help but worry about the Great Mother's influence on Arda and myself. I hope we can harness the gifts we have been given without losing ourselves to the shadows that seem to lurk ever closer.

Kaci read the entry aloud, her voice faltering slightly as she finished. She looked up from the journal, her gaze meeting the solemn faces of her companions.

For a moment, no one spoke. The room felt cold, the air heavy with the weight of Cirden's words.

Finally, Micah cleared his throat. "Sounds like he was struggling," he murmured, his jovial demeanor replaced with uncharacteristic seriousness.

"Power at a cost," Belan whispered as Kaci turned the page.

Third Moon, Fifth Cycle

Javina. This name rings continually in my ears. Another presence seems to have taken root within me. It feels as if this presence, which I have come to call Raelon, is attempting to control my thoughts and actions. It whispers the name to me: Javina.

My doubts about the Great Mother continue to grow. There are moments when I feel as though I am not serving a deity at all, but a sinister force that manipulates my mind. I fear the entity I am serving is a shadow of something much darker than she claims to be.

I do not want to doubt the Great Mother, but I cannot ignore the unease that has settled in my heart. Does the Great Mother have a name, as deities often do? Is it possible that I actually serve the Empress Javina?

The crowns are more than halfway completed now. I struggle to maintain control and understanding. As the shadows continue to encroach upon my thoughts, I find more and more time is lost. I must find answers for the sake of

both Arda and myself. If we are unwittingly serving a malevolent entity, the consequences could be dire. I pray we will
find the truth and that we can rid ourselves of the darkness
that threatens to consume us.

The name *Javina* sent a jolt of recognition through Kaci. She had heard it before—in her vision after the funeral pyre. *Javina, my lovely daughter whom I cherished...* And now here it was, written out on the parchment before her.

She could feel the gaze of her companions, and the tension in the room was palpable. No one spoke. Only the rustling of the parchment broke the silence as Kaci continued to read.

Third Moon, Seventh Cycle

It is too late. I have been fooled by her false promises, and have allowed her to take control of my soul. In my times of wakefulness I have tried to warn Arda, but Raelon is always there, always watching and reporting back to Empress

Javina. By luck or the will of the Mother, Raelon is absent for the moment, as though he has been ripped from my mind. I feel him fighting to return, so I must write quickly in the hope that someone finds my account.

The three crowns that Javina demanded of me are complete. Arda and Marcus have gone to deliver them and, with Raelon, I will soon follow to ensure their success. The world is doomed if the curse spreads with them.

I fear that Arda and I are both lost. Perhaps there is still hope for her. If she can break free from this creature's grasp, maybe she can find redemption and prevent others from suffering our fate. I fear what the orc will do. He has seemed so far resistant to the darkness has overtaken Arda and me, but I believe he has his own agenda.

In a last effort to save us all, I have taken the burden of the final crown upon myself. It is a dangerous gamble. I have become a living player in Javina's great game of Fidchell. Perhaps this crown will expand her hold on me, but if I can bear its weight, I may still have the power to save Arda, and everyone who has unknowingly become a pawn in Empress Javina's twisted game.

I will allow the darkness to consume me. Perhaps it will provide the strength and knowledge I need to overcome this evil force. I must sacrifice myself so our savior can reach freedom before I am consumed. It is a heavy burden, but I will carry it to protect my people, for the chance however slim to save the world from the darkness that threatens to engulf it.

Kaci's scanned over the rushed scrawl that seemed to embody Cirden's growing desperation. She shivered as she pieced together the fragments of her vision. The dark entity that had nearly trapped her—the sinister presence that had threatened to consume her—had been the same Empress Javina. Kaci was sure of it.

The group sat in silence following the end of the entry. Lady Durya finally spoke, breaking the tension. "What is Fidchell?"

Both Kaci and Micah started to respond. "A game—" Micah began.

"It's more than a game," Kaci corrected, her tone thoughtful. "Fidchell means *wisdom of the wood*. It's an ancient game our elders would play when they had important decisions to make. It's said to hold a kind of magic, and it can almost play itself. The elders' game pieces were carved out of wood from Arba Vitae, but kids would also play versions made of stone or other materials for fun."

She glanced at Micah, curiosity burning. "How do you know of it, Micah?"

With a nonchalant shrug, Micah replied, "A friend taught me the rules of the game."

A realization sent a shudder down her spine as she recalled the words of the older man in her vision: *You must first learn the rules before you play the game, child of flames.*

Those words now resonated in her mind, and Kaci believed they held the key to understanding and ultimately defeating Javina.

Chapter 13

Sacrifice Unseen

"In the realm of magic, to be severed from existence is a fate more harrowing than death itself. The soul is left to wander the abyss without rest, seeking solace in the echoes of what once was." —Bataku Raama, *The Birth of Magic*

Belan held up the tome where Cirden's notes had been tucked. "Perhaps there is more here," he said, gently flipping through the pages and searching for any further details. As he did so, something slipped from the book and fell to the ground.

"What is it?" Micah asked, peering over Kaci's shoulder.

Kaci reached down to pick up a scrap of paper and felt something wrapped inside. She carefully unraveled it, revealing a small map center around the library, and a tiny key concealed at its heart. The key's delicate craftsmanship suggested great importance. Kaci examined the hand-drawn map, on which a marked path seemed to lead to the roots of Arba Vitae.

"It looks like it leads to the entrance the book describes—to the Caves of Chaos," Kaci said. "Cirden must have tucked it away for safekeeping before—"

"Do you know how far it is?" Lady Durya had abandoned her reading and joined the others.

Belan shrugged. "It's a sketch. We cannot know if it is accurate. Perhaps we should study the book further."

Belan's shrug stung, and Kaci's heart felt heavy. Didn't he trust her judgment? As she started to challenge his doubt, she paused to look at him. His face was taut, not like the usual wise and stoic Belan she knew. Was he trying to dodge this mission? This new concern pushed aside her hurt. This wasn't like him at all.

As they huddled back around the ancient tome, Kaci's finger traced a passage that seemed to glow in her mind, as if magic embedded in the old words pulsed through her, guiding her, enticing her. She began to recite,

Prodigy of Flame

In Arba Vite's sacred shadow, where her roots entwine,

A portal lies, its secrets locked, a challenge to devine.

Earthborn iron adorns the door, an entrance vast and round,

Its landing lined with colored stones, five mysteries to be found.

The first a hue of vibrant blood, cerise as dawn's full light,

The second deep as emeralds' gleam, a green as dark as night.

The stones repeat a pattern that all travelers must discern.

A sacrifice must be embraced for passage to be earned.

Two must pay a heavy price for progress to be given:

One is lost from memory's gaze, and one to sorrow driven.

The sacrifice is dire, yes—for one a fate that's worse than death,

And one must bear the mark—Leth'Valan till their final breath.

The group was silent, pondering the words of the poem. "It continues," Kaci said.

"Deeper into the Caves of Chaos, those who dare

to venture will encounter myriad trials, unpredictable and seemingly without reason. Some may pass unscathed, while others meet their demise. Some will solve puzzles, and some may live lost in time for eons. Many ancient cultures used these caves as rites of passage, although their true nature has been obscured by the mists of time."

"Perhaps the caves are part of the old Elven traditions," Kaci pondered aloud as she pushed the map in front of the group again.

Everyone gathered around Cirden's sketch this time, taking in intricacies they'd originally overlooked. The sting of their earlier dismissal faded as Belan, Micah, and Lady Durya studied the map, faces rapt with a focused intent.

They agreed to follow the map's guidance and moved with renewed purpose as they left the library. Casting a longing glance back, Kaci made a vow to herself. She would return someday to lose herself among its endless shelves.

The marked path lead the group through the ancient vault's labyrinth of corridors. After a short while, they stood before a passage, just as the map had shown. The smell of earth permeated the surrounding space, and Kaci could feel the moisture in the air as if it were a living thing. The ground had changed from a stone floor to packed earth.

"I can't help but think that we abandoned these practices for a reason," Kaci said with a shiver.

Ahead, an immense, rounded door, gilded with Earthborn, iron blocked their way. Five colored stone tiles lined the entrance, just as the poem had described. The first was a shade of pink, the next a deep green, then red, then green, and the last was pink. Micah dug around in his pocket until he found the key. His face was full of hope, and Kaci latched on to that. Could it be so simple? Belan, on the other hand, had seemed to shrink even further into himself. The whites of his eyes seemed to glow in the darkness as he took in the massive door.

"Hey," Kaci whispered to him. "Are you okay?

"I will be." He breathed. "This adventure, being able to teach and to learn again—has been an unexpected gift." He tugged at his beard. "Before I met you—all of you…" He smiled tenderly at Micah and Durya, now arguing about who would turn the key. "I was well prepared to meet my fate. But now, I find myself afraid."

"It's going to be okay," Kaci reassured the old man,

embracing him. "You've taught me something that no one else could. Because of you, I will lead with my light instead of cowering from it. You have nothing to fear on this journey!"

Belan returned her hug and took out a tattered piece of parchment from his belt pouch. "Take this. You'll need it to understand. Never let the darkness overcome you, Kaci. There will be challenging times ahead. Remember your light—it will always guide you home." With that, he walked toward the door.

"Let me." He held out a calloused hand. Micah and Durya looked at each other and shrugged. Their eyes met for a moment, and it must have been an acceptable solution, for Micah handed Belan the key without question.

"You two stand here." Belan pointed to the emerald green tile to the left of the door. "And Kaci, you here." He pointed to the green tile to his right, then he stood on the deep red tile directly under the lock mechanism. Belan drew a ragged breath and placed the key into the hole.

A great groaning filled the air, and time seemed to both speed up and stop simultaneously. Further down the hall, the rumbling grew in the direction from which they had come. Then she could see it. The floor was giving way to a gaping chasm. The sulfur hit her nose in a blast, and she coughed and sputtered. The rift spread toward them, and there was nowhere to run.

"Hold fast." Belan was calm now. Whatever morose feeling had consumed him before was gone. "We will be safe if you stay on the tile."

"How do you know?" Kaci cried, her voice shaking with terror. "What are you keeping from us?" The chasm was encroaching quickly, and soon it would engulf them. Then she saw it—molten lava pouring down the crumbling walls. She looked at Belan's face and, at that moment, she knew exactly what would happen. She had seen it before so many times. It had ripped her apart in a way she could not share with Belan. Now it was so clear. He had known all along and had borne it alone. What a curse to know the day of your demise!

But Micah had told her that her visions were only a possible future. She was in control of the destiny she perceived, and she would not let Belan die. There was plenty of room on the green tile for them both. Why had he chosen the red one?

The chasm was upon them now, a burning lake of fire below, and the heat was unbearable. Yet the gilded door still stood in front of them, unchanged. The two outside tiles of red crumbled and dropped away. She watched Lady Durya and Micah huddle closer together. The green tiles remained untouched.

She didn't need anyone to spell it out for her: the emerald tiles were the only safe place to stand. Kaci turned to Belan and reached out her hand. She would not let him die. She was in control of her light.

He was engrossed in prayer, and both fists went to his forehead in reverence. "From fire we are forged, and by fire, we are destroyed."

Molten steel dripped from the newly created cliffs, pouring into the basin below, streaming out and filling every crack and crevice.

Kaci reached out a hand to clasp Belan's wrist and pull him to her tile, but he was too quick. He shifted and pushed away her hand just as the tile below him fell away. Kaci screamed, clasping at the empty air in front of her as he plunged into the fire below.

"Noooo!"

A peaceful aura surrounded him, like the tranquility of an infant before it drifts to sleep. Then Belan's body hit the molten lake.

Silence. That strange moment between moments when everything is still. She could hear the blood pumping in her ears, like the roar of that disastrous bonfire. Standing on the precipice, she wondered—should she go on? Jump in after him? She turned her hand front and back, staring at its smooth skin. He had been right here. *Right next to her.*

Suddenly, time seemed to resume its normal pace. Kaci could hear Micah and Durya shouting at her, but their words were muffled and distant. The door in front of them vanished, revealing a tunnel between two enormous tree roots. Were they beneath Arba Vitae? Was this the pilgrimage the texts had described? She looked back at where the lake of fire had been, but now there was only a long hallway with an earthen floor. Belan was gone, as if he had never existed.

"Come on!" Lady Durya shouted at her. "We have to go before it all resets." She grabbed Kaci's hand, which still floated in front of her face, and yanked her through the entrance.

Kaci followed in a daze, her gaze traveling back to the hallway behind them as it slowly faded from view. "What..." she summoned all the courage she could find. "What about Belan?"

It hurt to say his name. She wanted to scream and cry and rage. Her insides felt like they had been raked across coals. It was too raw, too empty.

"Who?" Lady Durya asked.

Kaci wanted to slap her. How dare she say that? It's one thing to shove your emotions down, but to pretend nothing happened? "Micah, help me!"

His eyes were soft, and his face showed no trace of his usual flippant grin. He shook his head and shrugged his shoulders. "Kaci," he whispered, "how about you sit down a moment and take a breath? That was terrifying. I know you have issues with fire."

"It's not about *fire*," she screamed. "Can we take a minute and mourn?"

Lady Durya opened her mouth until Micah laid a hand on her harm. Surprisingly, she didn't bark back. She just snapped her lips closed and gave a curt nod.

"Come on."

Micah took Kaci's hand and led her up a dirt tunnel that wound through the roots of the tree. It resembled a fresh animal burrow. As they traipsed through it, the path split in two.

"Which way? Left or right?" Micah asked the group.

Kaci was silent, still lost in her pain.

"Left," Lady Durya said after a moment.

"Why left?" asked Micah.

The lady shrugged. "I don't know, I was just being decisive."

"Fair enough," Micah replied. "Let's just agree to take the left path each time it splits. Does that work for you, Kaci?"

She shrugged and followed.

"Well, this is fun," Lady Durya huffed. "The only person with anything interesting to say is silent." Nobody replied, and the lady shut her mouth.

The earthen tunnels split a few more times, and the group chose the left fork each time until the path opened to a dark cavern damp with moisture.

As they moved through the entrance, the dirt walls seemed to groan with effort as enormous stones rolled into place, blocking their exit. Micah sucked in a breath and tried to push the stone away.

"Durya, Kaci, help!" They tried to push the great

wall away, but it would not budge.

"The only way is forward," Kaci sighed, her face void of emotion. Why was nobody talking about what happened to Belan? He was the sacrifice, and he had known it all along! Then she remembered the note he had given her. She pulled it out of her pocket and read.

Kaci,

When I was a young child, I saw my fate and I knew that one day I would make this sacrifice. I chose this path willingly, knowing that it would lead to the greater good. Always remember the light within you is stronger than any darkness you may face. Trust in your own strength and the love of those around you. Never lose hope, for hope is the beacon that guides us through our darkest moments.

I believe in you and know you will lead with courage and wisdom. My sacrifice was made of love and belief in your ability to make a difference. Please, do not squander the opportunity that my sacrifice has given you. Carry my memory with you and continue to shine your light upon the world. Stay true to yourself and the path you walk.

With all my love and faith in you,

Belan

She clutched the note to her chest, tears pouring down her face.

"What is it now?" Lady Durya sighed, attempting to smooth her harsh expression.

"Proof," Kaci sniffled, "That Belan was here!" She handed Lady Durya the note and watched as the woman shook her head.

"I'm sorry, Kaci. There is nothing on this paper."

Kaci snatched it back, the words still clear as day. Then she handed it to Micah, who shook his head without examining it. Her heart shattered into a million pieces as she realized that nobody else seemed to remember Belan. It was as if he had been erased from existence, and his sacrifice had gone unnoticed. She desperately tried to hold on to his memory, grasping for pieces of his presence, but the more she tried to share her grief, the more it felt like she was mourning a ghost. It felt like a part of her soul had been ripped away along with Belan. The weight of his sacrifice bore down on her, threatening to extinguish her light, but she refused to let it. For his sake, she would carry on and make sure that his sacrifice was not in vain.

As the trio pressed on, the sounds of their footsteps echoed louder against the walls and the air grew increasingly frigid, until Kaci could feel the chill seeping into her bones. The further they went, the colder it became until their breaths were visible in the air and they shivered uncontrollably.

The three huddled together, teeth chattering, and brainstormed ideas to get warm. There was no wood to make a fire, and they considered using their own body heat, but knew it wouldn't be enough to stave off the biting cold. So they walked on at a brisk pace, hoping it would be enough.

The minutes ticked by, and the temperature continued to drop. Just as they were about to lose hope, Kaci noticed a faint glow in the distance. As they drew closer, they saw it was a pinprick of an opening in the rock through which warm air emanated. Around it was a spiral pattern with an inscription carved above it. The words were ancient and cryptic.

Micah scanned the writing, his expression serious, and Durya read the inscription aloud:

"I am always hungry. I must always be fed. The finger I touch will soon turn red. What am I?"

Kaci, Durya and Micah exchanged looks. After a few moments of thought, Micah spoke up. "It's fire."

Kaci gasped in realization, and she could hear Belan's voice echo in her mind.

"Breathe, child. Look for the light."

"You're right, Micah!" How could she be so stupid? The answer had been right there, and she couldn't get past her grief long enough to help. Kaci felt her insides warm as she directed a stream of fire at the tiny hole.

A satisfying click sounded, and the stone wall began to grind open, revealing a path forward. Durya and Micah exchanged a relieved smile and continued on. Kaci plastered a fake smile on her face and followed behind them.

The air was a comfortable temperature now, and they continued choosing left until the pathway widened again, opening to a large marble chamber filled with bubbles of all shapes and sizes. As they made their way into the pristine room, the tiny globes floated in front of them.

One bubble in particular caught Kaci's eye. "Micah, come here! Is that you?" He joined her side and his face went pale. In the tiny scene, he was sitting next to a woman who looked very similar to him.

"My twin," he breathed. "Muirenn."

Kaci, curious, reached a finger out to touch the tiny scene, but the moment her finger contacted the bubble, it burst. The room seemed to collapse around them and she felt her stomach lurch as she was falling, falling, never stopping, until it all screeched to a halt. The alternate Micah and his sister were right in front of her, close enough to touch. "Micah?" she called. But they didn't seem to see her. She looked around for *her* Micah, but he was nowhere.

Then she looked up and scanned the horizon. The curve of the globe was obvious, and she could see Micah's and Durya's giant faces hovering above her.

"Micah! Lady Durya!" she screamed, but no one seemed to hear her. She pounded on the wall of her prison, trying to burst through and free herself, with no luck.

Inside the bubble, Micah and his twin spoke softly to each other and she turned to listen. She was a ghost to them, but she could observe them.

"What could go wrong?" the Micah in the vision asked. "We both know time is an illusion, persistent though it may be."

"You still shouldn't mess with it." His twin's voice was urgent as she tugged at his sleeve. "Not until you know a bit more about what you're doing. You just got back to Isdralan. Sit, relax, and break bread with us like a normal person."

The portal in front of them was about the size of a large boulder. The young woman glared accusingly. "You are trying to find them, aren't you?"

Micah nodded, a familiar grin on his face. "I haven't quite figured out the formula to go forward yet, but I seem to have no problem looking backward."

"What do you mean formula?" the woman questioned.

"That's just it, Muirenn—it's not magic; it's math. Everything is math. It's all about the flow of energy. This little portal? It's the same as when Kaci used to scry. But it's not earth magic. It's time."

"Hmm," Muirenn frowned, "I think you have it wrong. There are no formulas or spells, or whatever you are rambling about. Now that you are back, your magic is more potent, that's all. It's Isdralan."

"You're wrong. Throughout history, we haven't understood magic, but there are always rules. It's science. Take this, for example." He ran a thumb over the broken disk he wore around his neck. "Someone created these objects of power that are so important."

"Yes," Muirenn interrupted, "the past guardians who created them had plenty of time to understand the power of the universe. You just got here. When you over-analyze this magic and try to document it, you take away its beauty."

"Who cares about its beauty?" Micah rolled his eyes and continued. "We are saying the same thing, anyway. Plus, there is beauty in patterns and logic. The building blocks of energy can be broken down into smaller pieces and rebuilt. Chemists use high temperatures, pressures, and catalysts to change elements. These objects of power are no different. You can call it magic or science, but it does what it does."

"Micah, you are being careless and I think you should stop messing with this stuff until you have been here longer." Muirenn sniffed. "Someone could get hurt."

"No one is going to get hurt," Micah scoffed. "This portal is like a window to the past. We are watching something that happened long ago. Like a movie."

"A movie?" Muirenn raised an eyebrow. "You realize you are contradicting yourself. If time is an illusion, then what is happening here—" Muirenn waved her hand at the tiny portal, "is just as real as what's happening now."

"Have you always been so stodgy?"

Muirenn ignored his jab as she leaned in.

"So we couldn't enter if the portal were big enough to climb through?"

"Well, I didn't say that." Micah grinned. "But I'm worried about how long I can keep it open. I need more time to fine-tune my calculations before I take any chances."

"Micah! I told you this isn't safe. At least wait until Mother is here."

Micah glanced at his sister's furrowed brow. "Fine. I'll stop for now." He lowered his hand, but Muirenn clasped his wrist.

"Wait," she breathed. "That's her. It's Kaci. I know it!"

Kaci's ears perked up at the sound of her name.

"Oh, now you're curious." Micah chuckled, but his gaze intensified as he turned to the scene in front of them.

Still invisible to Micah and Muirenn, Kaci stood between them and peered into the portal.

She could see her own face, the smattering of bright freckles contrasting her pale skin.

Leaning forward next to Micah and peering into the portal, Kaci watched as a great bonfire crackled. Scattered around the fire was a group of teens—all with pointed ears and bright faces like Kaci's. Behind them was the silhouette of a massive tree. She wanted to look away, knowing the worst moment of her life was about to play forth, but she couldn't.

"Elves," Micah whispered. "Her world is full of elves."

"Maybe." Muirenn shrugged and peered closer. "I wonder what they are doing down there."

Micah tapped a pen against his chin and jotted a few things on his pad of paper, then turned back to watch the tiny portal.

Kaci watched her younger self stand apart from the group of young elves, her hands fidgeting like she had to say something meaningful but could not find her voice. Now and then, she would open her mouth and shut it again.

"Hello, fellow apprentices. I am Kaci, the girl of the forest," she said, smiling. But Kaci could see now that her hands were shaking.

The raven-haired girl closest to her, Arda, looked up and snorted. "Well, aren't you a strange one?" She nudged a boy and snickered. "She is Kaci, the girl of the forest." Then she turned back toward Kaci. "Do you not have a proper home?"

"No—Well, I live here. It is just…" Kaci froze. All the faces turned in her direction as everyone waited for her to say more. She opened her mouth, and all that came out was a strange noise, halfway between a chirp and a squeak.

"Oh! Maybe she is a squirrel!" The mean girl smirked and the others broke into peals of laughter. Horrified, young Kaci glanced toward the great tree line as if she could escape into the forest.

The raven-haired girl scooted toward her. "What does a girl of the forest mean, anyway?"

"Oh, my best friend gave me that title! It describes me to the others in the forest."

"You have a friend?" The girl smirked. "I would have pegged you for a loner."

"Oh, I have lots of friends. I speak with the forest creatures all the time," Kaci said.

"You don't say," the girl said, her lips turning up in a smile that did not reach her eyes. She leaned into the others and whispered, "Listen to this. The squirrel girl is friends with the forest creatures. "

"Muirenn, look—something is wrong," Micah said. "That girl is being cruel!"

Micah garbled a disk from around his neck and ripped it away as if it were burning his skin. Then the necklace moved toward the portal like a magnet.

"What are you doing?" Muirenn hissed. "Look at her!"

In the scene, fire exploded into hungry flames and black smoke billowed. The bonfire twisted and changed, growing and devouring until its flames consumed the group. Screams of fear and terror echoed in the night.

Kaci wanted to turn away, but something caught her attention. The disk suspended from Micah's neck had transformed. The bright red was swallowed by darkness, shadows cascading over it like a tidal wave. The energy she felt was the all-too-familiar surge she experienced in Marshfield and at the other portals, a pulsating force eager to be unleashed. Javina's whisper seemed to intermingle with the undercurrents of energy.

"Stop it!" Muirenn lunged at Micah, breaking his concentration. The portal shifted and spun, sucking the disk from his hand into the portal. A trail of shadows followed it until the portal snapped shut.

"Muirenn, NO!" Micah shouted. "My necklace. I don't know if I can get it back!"

"You were killing her!" Muirenn screamed at her brother.

"You don't know that!" Micah yelled back. "I contained it. What happened?"

"Get it back! Bring the portal back," Muirenn demanded, her eyes darting nervously around the bubble.

"I'm not sure if I can." Micah scratched on his notepad, trying to rework his math while his sister paced back and forth. "My pendant was the catalyst for my calculations. I don't know how to make the portals work without it." He jumped to his feet and took two giant steps toward his twin. "Let me use yours."

"No way!" Muirenn covered the disk around her neck with both hands. "You'll lose mine too. We should get Mother."

She spun on her heels and Micah grabbed her wrist. "Wait! Mir will send me away." His eyes pleaded.

She inhaled slowly, blew the air out between her lips, and composed herself. "I'm sorry, Brother."

"It's okay—you were right. I went too far. But my necklace. It's gone."

"We need to tell Mother." Muirenn sighed but made no move.

"No. I just got back to Isdralan. Mir already thought I wasn't ready. She wanted me to stay on earth until I reached my middle years. But I can figure it out! Just give me time."

"This is a bad idea, Micah," Muirenn cautioned. "We should ask for help. Bad things happen when you meddle with the timeline. You could get trapped, lost in the vortex of moments and events. I would never be able to find you, not even with Mother's guidance. To us, you would be as good as dead. Please, think this through."

"Give me a chance. Wait until dusk. If I am not back, go get Mir and show her my notes. I'm sure she can figure out the correct place in space and time."

Muirenn sighed. "Alright, but if you are not back, you're the one who will be accountable to Mother!"

Kaci's gaze lingered on Muirenn's retreating figure before snapping back to Micah. Understanding crashed into her with all the subtlety of a sledgehammer. It was Micah who'd brought in the shadows and Javina into her world. His mistake may have been unintentional, but her world paid the price. Anger rose, fierce and burning. Betrayal, she realized, had a particularly bitter taste.

Micah tinkered with his sister's amulet for a moment until a new portal opened. A storm raged in the background, and Kaci recognized exactly when and where he was. The portal grew until it was big enough to step through. Micah steeled himself with a breath and went in, and she followed him.

The world was falling again, and Kaci felt her body crash to the ground. She expected to wake up in the storm. Instead, she was in the cave, with Durya's face peering down at her.

Chapter 14

Sunken Past

"In the ever-winding path of existence, the echoes of our past are never fully silenced. They lie in wait, destined to resurface and shape our fates." - Bataku Raama, *The Birth of Magic*

What just happened?" Kaci pushed herself up to a seated position, her gaze darting around the room. The space was still filled with bizarre bubbles. "And where is Micah? Did he touch one of these things?!"

Lady Durya's face flushed with anger. "We saw everything," she spat out, her voice heavy with anger and accusation. "This entire disaster was his fault!"

A low, resigned sigh escaped from Kaci's lips as she absorbed the harsh reality. "I know," she admitted, her voice carrying a dull echo of Durya's rage. "I—"

"Are you not furious?" Durya interrupted. "He's

torn apart our world!"

Kaci felt a surge of indignation, but it was tempered like a fire burning beneath a layer of ash. Yes, Micah had set their lives ablaze with his reckless actions. But the fact remained that he was no different from them – too young and inexperienced, charging headlong into risks they were ill-prepared to handle.

An unexpected chuckle welled up within her at the irony of their situation. "He's no wiser than us, Durya," Kaci responded, the edges of her mouth tugged up in a rueful smile. "We're all stumbling through this together."

The room stilled momentarily, the shadows seeming to hesitate at her words. A flash of grief sliced through her as she thought of Belan. This pang did not fuel her anger. Rather, it grounded her, reminding her of the reality of their circumstances. She was tired. So tired, but they needed to keep moving, or all of their sacrifice would be for nothing.

"We can talk about it later. Let's get out of here, find Micah, and go."

"That might be a problem." Lady Durya's face darkened further. "He ran off."

"What? Why?"

"Because he's a coward," the lady muttered, staring at her feet before raising her eyes to meet Kaci's.

Kaci buried her face in her hands, shaking her head before standing up. "He wouldn't leave me here. It doesn't seem like him."

"But he caused these shadows! Of course, he would do the cowardly thing and run. Unless—"

"Unless what?" Kaci tried to be patient, but she felt a strong urge to shake the information from Lady Durya.

"We were searching for a way out when a hooded man appeared. We couldn't make out his features. Micah tried to speak to him, muttering something. But the stranger merely turned, conjured a door, and stepped through it. Micah might have followed him. I was so angry I couldn't see straight."

"Was it Cirden?" Kaci blinked. "Where is this doorway?"

"It was there." Lady Durya pointed to the south end of the chamber. "But it's gone now."

"It—"

The echoes of crying interrupted the two women. Kaci tilted her head, listening.

"That sounds like a child."

As they followed the noise, Kaci held a small light in front of her that cast eerie shadows on the cave walls. Its beams revealed a young girl sitting on a rock. Her long hair was draped over her face, and when she looked up, her eyes were as fathomless as the sea, with tiny white flecks that swirled round and round.

"Are you okay?" Kaci asked, approaching her with caution.

The girl startled. "I'm lost," she whispered. "I don't know how to get back home."

Kaci and Durya exchanged a worried glance.

"She could be another puzzle or a trap," Durya whispered.

"Trap or not, she is alone and afraid," Kaci said.

Kaci's heart skipped a beat when she turned back to the child. The realization hit her like a tidal wave— this young girl was Micah's sister, only much younger than she had appeared in the bubble. Remembering that the Caves of Chaos existed outside of time, she knew that anything was possible, including different versions of people.

She exchanged a glance with Lady Durya, who seemed to share the same thoughts. "Muirenn, we're friends of your brother, Micah. We're trying to find him and another man that looks like me, with pointy ears. We could use your help."

A puzzled expression crossed Muirenn's face. "Brother? I don't have a brother Micah."

Kaci and Lady Durya exchanged worried looks. In this version of reality, Muirenn did not know of her twin. Kaci decided to tread carefully, not wanting to cause the young girl any distress.

"Perhaps we were mistaken," Kaci said gently. "It's okay. We will work together to get you home, but we could use your help to navigate these caves."

Muirenn hesitated for a moment but then nodded. "Alright, I'll help you."

As three of them ventured deeper into the caverns, Muirenn recounted her path to the best of her ability. She had a good sense of direction. Kaci and Durya led the way, noting their route and anticipating danger around every corner.

As they walked, Muirenn shared about her life with her mother in Isdralan, their studies of the mysteries within a seaside cave, and how she had gotten lost.

Kaci listened intently, her heart going out to the girl. Muirenn's mother reminded her of Elena. "Do you know anything about Arba Vitae?" Kaci asked. "It's a massive tree."

As she waited for Muirenn's response, Kaci's thoughts wandered to the cryptic passages she'd read in the ancient tome. Arba Vitae had a twin. If she understood correctly, this would be the entrance to Isdralan. The book suggested that the tree existed in two places at once, linked by the Caves of Chaos. This was a concept Kaci found paradoxical. Was it physically split, with half its existence rooted in another location? Or was it more metaphysical, the tree's spirit split between two realms? The writing had been vague and poetic, shrouded in layers of metaphor that made it difficult for her to grasp the concept.

Muirenn nodded. "Of course I've heard of it. It goes by many names, but I'm sure it's what you're looking for!" she declared. "However, it's a day's sail through perilous waters. If we manage to find our way back, my mother will help you!"

Kaci felt a crease forming between her brows. "I'm not sure we can spare that much time. Our world is in danger and our friend is missing. We were supposed to uncover the path through the caves, like a trial of sorts."

Muirenn tilted her head, her gaze thoughtful. "These caves lead to many places, not all of them safe. That's why I'm not supposed to wander alone. But I'm certain there is a way."

Kaci's thoughts began to swirl. If Muirenn's mother was indeed Mir, the one Micah was desperately searching for to fix their reality, it added a new layer to their task. She wondered if approaching from a different entry point would somehow alter their quest's outcome. Did they need to access the right door to reach the correct timeline? Did it matter which version of Mir they sought assistance from? Would she be able to help them find Cirden and the third crown?

The questions gnawed at her and made her long for Belan's wisdom. His insightful counsel could have provided clarity. Kaci shook her head, pulling herself back from the edge of despair. She realized they needed to pay attention, for their chosen path could alter their destiny.

Kaci and Durya shared a glance, and Durya responded with a noncommittal shrug.

"Do you have any idea how to get there?" Kaci asked the child, making one last effort to find the tree entrance.

Muirenn shook her head, a small frown tugging her lips downward. "I can't. My mother would be very upset with me," she said.

Finally, they arrived at the entrance to Muirenn's cave, which opened to a spectacular view of a vast sea. It was a breathtaking sight, the sapphire-blue expanse stretching as far as the eye could see, sparkling under the sun's caress.

"Thank you so much for your help," Muirenn cried, wrapping her arms around Lady Durya. The orc woman stiffened and patted the child on the head.

"I couldn't have done it without you." Muirenn smiled shyly. "I'll never forget your kindness," she said. Then the child's eyes lit up, and she ran to the corner of the cavern.

"Here! Take this." She handed Kaci a small wooden carving of a fox. "It's carved from the wood of Arba Vitae. Perhaps it will guide your way!"

Kaci turned the smooth wood over in her hands

and smiled at the girl. She wasn't sure how the trinket would help, but she had faith. "Thank you, Muirenn."

Kaci and Durya stood at the entrance of the cave, taking in the view of the sea and contemplating their options. They had reached Isdralan, but it clearly wasn't the right time or place, and Micah was still missing.

"What do we do now?" Kaci asked. "Do we stay and try to find *this* Mir and ask for help, or go back to the caves and find Micah and the correct path?"

Durya's expression tightened in contemplation. "I'm sure Micah will be just fine wherever he is. Staying here might have its advantages. We could learn more about Isdralan and its secrets. It's a sure thing."

Kaci nodded, torn. "I know, but I doubt Cirden is up here. We're so close, and yet so far. Micah needs us, and Be—" she breathed before continuing. "We need to reach the right place in Isdralan. We can't risk wasting time here when we don't even know where or when we are."

After pondering further, Kaci and Durya decided to go back. They recognized that their likelihood of crossing paths with Micah was greater within the cave. More importantly, they understood they needed Cirden to get the third crown and, hopefully, close the portals for good.

As they walked, Kaci almost smiled thinking how excited Belan would be. Then she remembered, and her heart broke all over again.

The two women searched the caves for what felt like months without encountering another soul. They scoured every nook and cranny, calling out Micah's name and shining their torches into the darkness. Yet Micah remained elusive. Strangely, there were no more tests or puzzles, just an eerie emptiness.

Eventually, they had to give up on Micah and focus on finding the correct entrance to Isdralan. They retraced their steps to the chasm that had once held the strange bubbles, only to find it empty. Feeling defeated, Kaci wondered if they should turn back and find the young Muirenn. They could always wait in Isdralan until the right time. Would that even work?

A movement from her pack commanded Kaci's attention. She reached in to find the tiny fox carving that Muirenn gave her had sprung to life. It jumped out of her hands and pointed its paw decisively. Deciding to trust it, Kaci followed its lead, with Durya right behind.

To their amazement, the fox carving led them straight to a small dirt-covered tunnel.

As they pressed on, the stone walls changed to soil, interwoven with an intricate pattern of plant life. Gnarled and strong roots, tendrils of a great tree ancient and robust, formed a dense canopy that arched over them, their shadows dancing on the path ahead as stray beams of light pierced through. It seemed they were moving through a living tunnel, carved by the passage of time itself.

A familiar hum resonated through the air. It echoed the voice of Arba Vitae but held a slightly different note, like a mirror's reflection distorting the original image. Kaci's heart surged with anticipation. The tunnel concluded, surrendering to the brilliant embrace of daylight. This was it!

"I hope you find your way, Micah." Kaci sighed and leaned down next to the little fox. "Find our friend and lead him here," she whispered.

The tiny creature dashed away, and Kaci could only hope it was following her instructions.

When they surfaced, the sky was a brilliant shade of cerulean. The green and silver leaves shifted and sighed with the breeze, singing a song of lament. It would have been beautiful if she were not still so heartbroken. She felt the warmth of the great tree, like a mother welcoming home a prodigal child. This was most certainly The Wilds, Isdralan. They had made it. She laughed as she removed her shoes, feeling the lush grass on her bare feet.

"Here," Lady Durya gave a smile and exposed her long tusks, then patted a patch of ground. "Have a seat, and we will talk about whatever is ailing you."

Kaci knew Micah's disappearance was hurting Durya more than the rough woman let on, but she couldn't bring herself to care. A good friend would sit on that stupid piece of grass, talk, listen, and console, but all she wanted to do now was run and hide away.

"Would prefer to be alone for a moment," Kaci replied quietly. Lady Durya shrugged and pulled a small book from her pack.

"Did you take that from the library?" Kaci raised an eyebrow.

Lady Durya shrugged. "I thought you wanted to be alone?" She buried her face in the book.

Sighing, Kaci scanned the area until she spotted the tree. She was on her feet in a flash, scaling the majestic beauty. She found a branch and sat on it, leaning her head against the solid trunk. The bark felt rough and strong and reminded her of Belan's hands. The hands that had pushed her away in those last moments. *Why, Belan?* And why did no one seem to remember him?

As Kaci pressed her forehead against the rough bark, her consciousness seemed to intertwine with the tree's essence. She communicated through a cascade of emotions and images, like painting a picture on the canvas of her mind. It was a wordless, intimate dialogue, Arba Vitae, embracing her with its ancient wisdom.

A question formed within her. Was her world's Arba Vitae okay? Its struggle for survival appeared in her mind's eye. The response from the tree flowed back to her in a wave of sorrow, an empathetic mirroring of her pain. The sadness was deep and resonant, like a well echoing with the hollow notes of a mournful melody. It was as though this tree felt every moment of the disease that consumed its twin, the tree in her world. *When will the sorrow end*, Kaci thought.

An undercurrent of solace flowed from the tree, acknowledging her heartache over Belan's death. It was a quiet acceptance of grief woven into a blanket of tranquility. The tree seemed to mourn its dying twin. It was grief shared and understood, a bond formed in this quiet sanctuary of nature.

A fat tear cut a path down her cheek, pooling at her chin and falling to the branch beneath her. It flashed with a silver light before being absorbed into the bark. Belan would have loved that. The Wilds had a sort of beauty that he would have been able to appreciate. It was as though the land radiated wisdom and peace, but there was also a sense of sorrow and something that she could not put her finger on. Perhaps urgency? It sang to her as colorful orbs of all different shades, radiant and shimmering like precious gems, moved through the land. The orbs glided effortlessly in a harmony that made Kaci want to join them, casting vibrant hues of azure, emerald, amethyst, and sun-kissed gold onto the surrounding landscape.

Then she remembered her friend was gone. The realization weighed heavily on her heart, causing the once vivid colors to lose their luster and melt from her vision. The enchanting music, which had seemed so alive moments ago, now dulled and faded into the background.

She remembered the letter Belan had given her. Rummaging in the pockets of her smock, she pulled it out and gently unfolded it. At the top was the image that he had sketched of Arba Vitae. She wondered how she had missed this the first time she had read the page, and when he had found the time to draw this. The tree's branches were reaching the sky, thirsty for the sun's light. Below, the roots tangled together, forming intricate patterns. She could see how their twists and turns formed. They had to be the same symbol Micah told her about—a triskelion. Under Arba Vitae, the tree continued, growing into its twin, connected at the center. Two trees, two worlds.

Belan had known Arba Vitae grew in both directions. Elena had always taught her that the tree led to The Wilds, but she had thought of it as a story—old lore passed along for generations, embellished and changed. Now here she was, on the other side.

Belan had known all along. She wanted to be angry, yell and scream and rage at the tree until her knuckles were battered and bloody. Instead, she sat quietly, breathing in and out, until she felt ready to move once more. *Never lose hope, for hope is the beacon that guides us through our darkest moments.*

Oh, Belan. Wise, sweet, and kind. He was the sacrifice. Would the Great Mother welcome him into her bosom? She sighed, hugging the parchment close before tucking it back into her pocket. There would be time to grieve later. Now it was time to do what they came to accomplish. She would not let Belan's sacrifice be in vain. She descended the tree, letting her hand rest on it for another moment, drawing from its power, and pausing in reverence before turning to join the others.

Lady Durya had moved to the base of the tree and was leaning against it as she continued to read.

Kaci cleared her throat. "Let's find Cirden," was all she could muster.

"Glad you could join me," Lady Durya chided, but her expression was concerned. "In all seriousness, are you all right?" She rose to her feet, standing in front of Kaci, and then she patted the friend's head awkwardly.

"I'm okay now." Kaci tried to giggle but failed. "My mind is a bit jumbled."

"Yes, mine too. I imagine it has something to do with being in The Wilds," Durya said.

"So you think we made it?" Kaci asked, raising an eyebrow.

Lady Durya nodded. "Any idea on where we should go next?"

"Cirden's notes, in the beginning, seemed to show he was looking for the real Great Mother. Perhaps we find her?"

"Do you know where we are?" Lady Durya asked.

"And where would we even go to find Cirden?"

Arba Vitae sat in the center of a vast field of green, surrounded by thick forests in every direction. To the east was a massive mountain that touched the sky. Kaci's heart tightened as she thought of Belan touching the sky. She hoped with all she was that he could still become one with the Allfather. She closed her eyes, letting her other senses guide her. Turning to the West, she could hear the gentle crash of waves and smell the sea air.

"What are you doing?" Lady Durya asked, tilting her head and trying to sniff the air.

"I am trying to use all my senses." Kaci giggled for real this time as her friend sniffed and snorted. "Like Belan taught us."

"You seem to keep forgetting that I was not raised with you. I am not sure who this Belan is you keep talking about."

"Sorry," Kaci shrugged, "It must be the fog this place is putting in my brain." The strange thing was her brain no longer felt coated in spiderwebs. She felt clearer than she had ever been.

Facing south, she attempted again to see through

the thick forest, to no avail. When she closed her eyes and listened, playful notes floated in through the air, shifting until they were filled with a passion that made her want to weep. She could feel the light inside respond, and her body followed. Bare feet padded through the thick grass until Lady Durya's hand stilled her.

"Where are you going?"

"Nowhere," Kaci blushed and turned in the last direction, not bothering to explain the music to her friend. Lady Durya was already facing north, shoulders square and standing tall. If you ignored the velvet dress and heeled shoes, she looked like the picture of a warrior queen. A trail of a tear ran down her silver cheek. A single black bird lifted from one tree in the distance, circled the lady once as if in reverence, then continued until it disappeared over the horizon.

"The great battle," Lady Durya whispered as her face slackened in awe. "I can sense it. I feel it boiling in my blood. This has never happened." She looked at Kaci with joy.

"I don't know what that is," Kaci said with a smile, "but I am happy for you."

"I may look like an orc." Lady Durya sighed. "But human life is all I have ever known. Truth be told, I have always been human, through and through. Only, I was never accepted into the society of my family because of the color of my skin, and these." She pointed to her tusks.

Kaci wrapped her arms around her large friend, squeezing tight, and surprisingly, the lady did not pull away.

"When I came of age, I traveled to my clan with my father's blessing. He said I always had a place in his home, but accepted my need to understand my past."

"Your father seems wise for a human." Kaci gave a half grin. "They tend to lack empathy."

"Well, orcs are much like humans in that regard." Lady Durya gave a sad smile. "My clan shunned me. They said my blood would never feel the heat of the battle. They said I was corrupted and would never be a true orc."

"I'm sorry."

"It's not your fault." Lady Durya shrugged. "I went home after that and shoved it away, pretending it didn't matter. You may have noticed that sometimes I act a bit…aloof."

"No!" Kaci covered her mouth with a hand, and

Durya gave her a playful swat.

"I have only talked about this with one other. With Sharn." Lady Durya gave Kaci an intense stare. "So keep it to yourself!"

Kaci's smiled and gave a nod. "Sharn is in love with you. You know this, right?"

"I am a married woman, remember?" The lady stiffened, sinking back into her typical Durya demeanor. "Enough of the chatter. We were trying to figure out where to find Cirden." Instead of facing Kaci, she turned back to the North and inhaled deeply.

"Micah mentioned the four guardians of Isdralan. That's where we are, right?" Kaci gave a circle, looking in each direction. "He said one of them might help."

"You realize these beings are gods to us, right?" Lady Durya gritted her teeth, exposing her tusks. "What about Muirenn? She may remember us helping her. Perhaps it is best to head toward the sea."

"Seems as good as any choice we have," Kaci agreed. "West it is. To Muirenn or Mir."

Nodding in agreement, Lady Durya tucked the book in her pack, slung it over her shoulder, and walked to the west.

Ahead was a thick forest, and as they drew closer, Kaci could make out a path that meandered through the tall evergreens. She reached out with her senses and felt the forest thrum with life. All was in harmony.

The trail was hidden and overgrown, but taking it would certainly be faster than trying to navigate around the edge of the forest. Kaci pushed a branch aside and stepped into the woods, her bare feet sinking on the soft pine needles that blanketed the path. Lady Durya high-stepped through the layers, and with each step, her heels sank into the accumulation.

"It may be easier if you took those fancy shoes off." Kaci giggled. "The path is soft and will be gentle on your delicate feet."

"That's the problem, "Lady Durya rolled her eyes. "My feet are far from delicate. I don't want to see them."

Glancing back at her friend, Kaci felt a warmth overtake her. Durya had changed during their journey. More and more, she was showing the little vulnerable pieces of herself, and was becoming stronger for it, Kaci was sure.

"I know what you are thinking." Durya glared at her and continued with a growl. "Stop right now. I will not hesitate to end you if you ever share any of this!"

"I don't believe you." Kaci laughed at her friend. It felt strange to laugh, knowing that Belan was dead. Was it disrespectful to him to be so happy? He would have welcomed her smile, but somehow it still felt wrong.

"Where did you just go?" Lady Durya cocked her head. "Your mind. It was somewhere else for a moment."

"Nowhere," Kaci lied.

"You're right, you know." Durya's voice was soft. "I wouldn't end you. I've never had a proper friend. One that accepted me for who I am—every part of me. I would never end you. Just—" Durya paused a moment before continuing. "Don't tell anyone."

"That were friends?" Kaci teased, then turned to Durya, as serious as she could be. "Your secrets are safe with me."

"What about Sharn?" Kaci asked as they walked on. "He seemed to understand you pretty well."

"He was close, once." Lady Durya's face softened briefly, then darkened. "But that ship has sailed. Quite literally, when I left Marshfield and sailed across the sea with my husband-to-be."

"Oh, I forgot you were married."

"Indeed."

The lady was silent again, lost in a faraway world she wasn't ready to share. This time Kaci didn't push. She just clasped Durya's hand and gave it a squeeze. She had never had many friends either, aside from the forest creatures.

While they sat in quiet companionship, an ethereal mist began to unfurl around them. The air held a tangible expectancy and gently coaxed forth a narrative that yearned to be shared. Each atom of air, each speck of dust, each blade of grass and drop of dew seemed to conspire, nudging the lady to unravel her tale. This was a story shaped by the magic woven into the fabric of the land, a tale that Isdralan itself was eager to manifest.

When she finally spoke, Lady Durya's voice was different, amplified by the mists that surrounded them.

"Edward was a cruel and abusive man who married me for status and money. I was nothing more than a possession. He—" Durya shook her head. "Suffice to say, I lived in fear of him. This was not a fitting state for an orc. He wanted a child and an heir, but I would not let that be. No child of mine would be treated with respect in that world. For years I endured his abuse until, one day, I took matters into my own hands."

Kaci let her friend continue.

"We were on the ship, sailing home to Westerfield, and one night, when my husband was in a drunken stupor, I poisoned him. Before we left for Westerfield, I had purchased some toxins—to kill vermin. Ships are notorious for rats and, if you recall, I despise them. But this poison was never meant for the rats." She let out a shaky breath. "Before his body was even cold, the storm hit. It was most certainly my punishment for murder."

Kaci struggled to process the information. A whirlwind of emotions swept through her—shock, disbelief. Yet, despite the revelation, she tried her best not to judge her friend too harshly.

"As the waves grew taller and more violent," Durya continued, "the ship creaked and groaned under the strain. I heard the scream of wood splitting apart as the hull gave way. The crew frantically worked on deck to keep the vessel afloat, but it was a losing battle. So I returned to my cabin, intending to meet my fate.

"Water rushed into the lower decks, extinguishing the lanterns, and the ship plunged into darkness. Panicked screams of other passengers echoed through my head, and all I could think was, *this is my way out*."

"The ship leaned to one side. The wind howled

through the rigging, and the sails flapped in the squall. The wood cracking was the worst sound. When the ship tilted even further, it made a sickening crunch and finally began to sink."

Durya's eyes glazed over.

"I watched Edward's body slip below the waves, believing I would join him soon. I felt the water rising to my chest and I didn't fight as I sunk into the depths and out of consciousness."

Durya paused for a moment, collecting her thoughts before continuing. "Somehow, I awoke, gasping for air as the storm raged on. Drenched and disoriented, I stumbled onshore and through the downpour, desperately seeking shelter. Eventually, I found myself at the entrance of a cave, exhausted and chilled to the bone. You know the rest."

The air grew heavy with silence, and the mists that surrounded them sank back into the earth as Kaci tried to wrap her mind around Durya's story. She felt the weight of the revelation, the sorrow that seemed to envelop her friend. She imagined Durya journeying through the storm, cold and alone, haunted by the memory of her actions.

Kaci searched for the right words but found nothing. Instead, she simply reached out and placed a comforting hand on Durya's shoulder in a gesture of understanding and support.

The sound of a trickling brook pulled Kaci out of her dark thoughts. A small wooden bridge spanned the stream, and sitting on it was a peculiar old man, muttering to himself while stitching a pair of tattered trousers. As they neared, he looked up with a sly grin.

"Oi, will y'lassies help a fellow out?"

Kaci's face lit up in a wide smile as she approached the old man. Of course she would help him. It was what she did best! As she drew near, she noticed colored orbs rapidly circling his head. These were dull and shadowy, unlike the vibrant orbs she had seen earlier.

The old man's appearance flickered for a moment, transforming into a dark figure with wild red eyes and the hooves of a gigantic horse. Then, in a flash, his appearance snapped back to the old man's form. Kaci blinked a few times, uncertain if what she had seen was real.

The man's cunning grin disappeared, replaced by a grimace of fear. "Your 'is bairn," he whispered before scuttling off deeper into the forest.

Lady Durya had caught up now, picking her way down the dirt path in her heeled shoes.

"What was that all about?" she asked.

"Not sure," Kaci replied, still processing all that had happened. Why would anyone be afraid of her? Especially someone who clearly had power. She was nothing here. "I was going to help that man. And he just ran away."

"Peculiar," Durya said with a shrug, but she was already looking past the small bridge at the break in the trees.

A powerful gust of ocean air stung Kaci's face, and she turned to inspect her friend.

"Seems like we have almost reached the sea," Durya said. "We have made it as far west as we are going to get."

"That seemed quick." Kaci tossed her braid over her shoulder. "I always thought Arba Vitae would be in the center of the Wilds. Isdralan couldn't be this small, could it?"

As they emerged from the forest, they found themselves at the edge of a high cliff. Durya's face was ashen, her body rigid as if held captive by an invisible, menacing force. Kaci caught up and stood beside her friend. Something had changed in Lady Durya, and Kaci could sense the fear gripping her companion.

Down the cliff, Kaci followed her friend's gaze to where a majestic ship had washed ashore. The vessel's golden figurehead depicted a magnificent seabird with its wings outstretched, ready for flight.

Lady Durya inhaled sharply. "That ship—" she stammered, "it shouldn't be here. It sank along with my husband."

Chapter 15

Shadows of Uncertainty

"As I beheld the resurrection of the Golden
Gull, I knew the possibilities were great and not to
be taken lightly. With the aid of Aion, I sought to
undo my mistakes and harness time for good. But re-
gret proved my undoing, and now my fate is forever
bound to the ship. Let this serve as a warning to all
who seek to change its course, for the consequences are
as inescapable as they are dire." - Bataku Raama,
The Birth of Magic

The galleon below appeared eerily deserted, yet remarkably intact from their vantage point high on the cliff. It lay half submerged in the shallow waters, surrounded by a shroud of mist that seemed to guard its secrets. To uncover the truth, Kaci and Durya would need to find a way down to the ship and examine it up close.

"It sank," Lady Durya whispered, her voice trembling. "That cannot be."

"What cannot be?" Kaci asked, her confusion

growing. "What is going on?"

"There is no doubt in my mind. That is the Golden Gull, my husband's ship. The one that sank."

"Are you sure?" Kaci studied Lady Durya's face, which had now turned ghostly pale. "Perhaps it survived the storm? Do you think your husband is alive?"

"No. I was there, Kaci. I watched it go down, and I was the only survivor."

Lady Durya shook her head and sat down at the cliff's edge, gesturing for Kaci to join her. "He is not alive. He was dead well before the storm. I am sure of that." Her voice cracked with emotion, and Kaci imagined the crushing weight of her memories.

"Could it be…?" Kaci's voice trailed off as a thought crept into her mind. The memory of old tales she had read resurfaced—stories of living ships imbued with the souls of ancient seafarers forever bound to the material realm.

"Could it be what?" Lady Durya asked, her eyes fixed on the ship, her face ashen.

"Well," Kaci hesitated, "there are old legends, stories of ships—haunted, or maybe even alive—bound by magic or cursed."

Durya turned to her, a quizzical expression on her face. "Are you suggesting that Edward, my husband, is haunting the ship?"

"I don't know," Kaci confessed, shrugging. "But the tales speak of ships that refuse to sink, trapped in their final moments, forever reliving their tragedies. Maybe it is haunted."

"No." Lady Durya's gaze never left the ship. She was frozen in the throes of memory. "The ship hated my husband."

A quizzical expression crossed Kaci's face as she raised an eyebrow.

Durya sighed. "Sometimes," she began, her voice shaky, "when I was sad, I would stand at the bow, near the figurehead. I would talk to it. Pour out my heart. In its own way, it seemed to listen."

Kaci turned to look at her companion, surprised. "You talked to the ship?" she asked.

"Not the ship," Lady Durya said, casting a sidelong glance at Kaci. "To the figurehead. I felt a connection. Some kind of...resonance, as though it could understand."

"I understand," Kaci said. "That was Arba Vitae for

me."

Lady Durya's lips curled into a weak smile, exposing her tusks. "Then you know what I mean."

Kaci pondered the ship below, her gaze sweeping across its vacant decks. Could the Golden Gull somehow be imbued with a living essence, and how did it find its way to Isdralan? "Maybe the ship is alive somehow?"

"If that's true," Lady Durya said, her voice barely above a whisper, "then the storm—could the gull have created it?"

The sound of light footsteps interrupted them, and Kaci looked up to see a tall woman walking toward them. As she approached, Kaci could see the orbs swirling around her head. That sight seemed almost commonplace in this strange land. The woman's pale hair cascaded down her back like a silken waterfall, seamlessly blending with her gossamer gown. The energy that encircled her was muted, and the vibrant hues faded. Yet at their centers, tiny flecks of light darted about as though yearning to break free from the dim orbs that contained them.

Raising a hand in greeting, the stranger stopped about six feet away. Her eyebrow arched as she looked at Durya, who had risen to her full height. The lady emitted a menacing growl and took a step forward, but Kaci reached out a hand to stop her.

"I apologize for bothering you and approaching unannounced," the woman said sweetly as she studied Kaci and Durya intently. I can't help but notice that you are…not native here."

Lady Durya let out a breath, relaxing, but Kaci could see she was still ready to pounce. Her friend's emotions had been bottled up tight for so long that anyone who disturbed this uneasy peace would feel her wrath.

"It's no bother." Kaci stepped in front of Durya, shielding both her friend and the stranger. "We could use help from someone who knows the lay of the land."

"But of course," the woman's voice sounded of sweets laced with poison, sending a shiver down Kaci's spine. Something was off. Kaci wished she could warn Lady Durya to be careful without words. The elders of the ancient clans were said to have been able to talk to each other without speaking. Perhaps she could some-day as well, but today, words and actions were all she had. "I would be happy to help with anything you need."

What did they need? Perhaps they should have

discussed this before a stranger approached them.

"We are looking for a man." Durya blinked and shook her head as her cheeks reddened. "Actually, the guardians of this realm. Or a young girl named Muirenn."

The woman seemed unfazed at the mention of the guardians, but her dark eyes widened at the mention of Muirenn.

"Do you know Muirenn?" Kaci asked, "Or Micah?"

Any look of surprise Kaci may have detected had disappeared from the woman's face as she let out a tinkling laugh. "Oh goodness, how rude of me not to introduce myself! You may call me Keres." She stepped back in expectation. "Who do I have the pleasure of conversing with?"

"I am the Lady Durya Conwyn Barclay, Baroness of Marshfield Estates and Westerfield. You may address me as Baroness, Lady Durya, or my lady. This is my lady-in-waiting, Kaci"— Durya paused—"of Aeloria."

"Oh my," Keres bowed deeply without a hint of mockery, but Kaci could sense a burning anger in this woman. The shadow and light that encircled her seemed to flare a bright red.

Kaci gave an awkward bob, not knowing what someone at her station was supposed to do in human society. Was this even considered human territory? No one seemed to react, so she assumed it was okay. "We should go, Lady Durya." She tried to convey her urgency to her friend without being obvious, but her voice just squeaked.

"Oh," Keres exclaimed, "don't go! If you need to speak to all four guardians, you must be in dire need. Most Isdralan guests seek only the deity they worship in their homelands. They're unaware of The Four." Kaci could detect a hint of disdain in Keres's voice, but it was so covered in honey she wondered if she imagined it. "Tell me more of this Muirenn, or Micah. Do they live in Isdralan, or are they guests?"

"This is their home," Durya replied. "At least Muirenn's."

Keres nodded, a slight smile spreading as if she were plotting and planning in her head. "I have not heard of Micah or Muirenn," she finally answered, the lie plain on her face. "The only twins I know of in these parts are newborn babes. Mir's progeny. She calls them Aion and Ananke."

"Interesting." Kaci pondered a moment. "I didn't

know gods had so many children."

The air seemed to grow colder as Keres chuckled, not a tinkling laugh this time, but the hollow sound of the bells after a funeral march. "The word *god* is a construct of those with lesser understanding. Mir has many children, as do all the guardians—as do many other entities. Unlike others, however, we have an unbounded lifespan."

"Are you a—" Lady Durya paused, clearly not wanting to use the word *god*.

"I am not one of the guardians." Keres gave a sly smile. "However, Mir is my mother."

"Then you may be able to help us!" Lady Durya beamed, clearly impressed that this woman was of some importance. "Have you lived in Isdralan your whole life?"

Kaci observed her friend's recognition of the local term for The Wilds and her apparent respect for this woman's status. The woman ha appeared seemingly out of nowhere just when they needed help. Kaci, however, was not so quick to trust. She stepped back and let Lady Durya take the lead in this conversation. She had far more experience dealing with royalty, formality, and the intricacies of such encounters.

As Kaci watched the exchange, a thought struck her. If Mir was Micah's mother, then it was entirely possible that Keres was another sister. There was little resemblance, but Kaci couldn't shake the feeling that it connected them. She kept this revelation to herself for the moment, remaining cautious as she tried to piece together the puzzle before her.

"I was born here," Keres answered, and the colors around her head darkened. "But, raised in the world of my father."

"What part of Elyndris is that?" Lady Durya asked.

"Oh, child," Keres answered, voice all honey again. "Do you think your realm is the only one that exists outside Isdralan?"

"Of course not." Lady Durya's face reddened. "You just looked very *human*."

"I see." Keres raised an eyebrow as if wondering whether she had misjudged this pair's usefulness. "What do you need help with?"

"Well—" Lady Durya started and stopped. How could one explain their ordeal?

Kaci realized that the only way to get answers was to share information, so she intervened to help her friend. "On Elyndris, a man named Cirden opened a portal to communicate with the Great Mother in The Wilds. We've since discovered that the gateway didn't reach Mir, but something much darker, and it is causing havoc in our world. We just want to find him so we can close the portals."

Kaci watched the subtle change that crept over Keres's features as she heard their tale. The slight furrow of her brows, the brief flicker in her eyes. "Our friend Micah—"

"*Your* friend," Lady Durya interjected.

"*Our* friend," Kaci reiterated, "believed that he had inadvertently caused the rift when he lost his amulet. He tried, unsuccessfully, to repair it. We came here on his suggestion, seeking help."

"Of course he did." Keres rolled her eyes.

"Wait, I thought you said you had never heard of Micah?" Kaci inquired, stepping closer to the woman.

"And I still haven't," Keres replied calmly. "I simply meant that it's not surprising that some witless fool might cause a rift. No one else would be so careless."

"He is not witless." Kaci defended her friend. "Micah is quite clever!"

Keres disregarded her comment. "Isdralan is the space between spaces. Any gateway created between worlds would have to pass through it. Your friend was likely correct in coming here to fix it." She tilted her head and the shadows and lights surrounding her swirled more rapidly. Kaci wanted to ask Lady Durya if she saw them, too, but decided against it in this woman's presence.

"I am deeply troubled by these occurrences and have brought them to my mother's attention. Regrettably, she dismissed my concerns." Keres paced back and forth. "Her mind is clouded with the aftermath of childbirth, and she cannot see the gravity of the situation. These portals could spread to other worlds and perhaps even tear apart the very fabric of the universe."

"That sounds awful," Kaci responded quietly. While she didn't trust this woman, her logic appeared sound, and the notion of the universe unraveling was indeed terrifying. They didn't have to like one another to be united in their cause, right?

"I can stop it from happening." Keres said confidently. "But I will need your help."

"Our help?" Kaci asked. "But we are nothing. Lesser beings, you said so yourself."

"Which makes you the perfect pair to help me. You can go unnoticed in these lands. Most will assume that you are lost in a dream and will return to your home upon waking."

"I have no wish to be deceptive." Kaci frowned. "Twisting the truth never ends well."

"You do not have to twist any truth," Keres answered, almost too quickly. "I just need something. An object of power that was supposed to be mine."

"Be clear." Lady Durya was losing her patience now. "What is it you want from us?"

"The newborn babes," Keres spoke urgently. "My mother is to name them her successors in their awakening ceremony. This cannot happen. Only I can stop these portals, and I should be her successor. This awakening ceremony needs to be stopped."

"Wait," Kaci frowned. "Are you just bitter? Because Mir did not choose you to be the next god?"

Keres's dark eyes flared with black fire. "Of course not," she snapped. "But how will a baby know the gravity of the situation? I need time." She paused. "And the amulet."

"So you want us to steal an amulet?" Kaci replied.

She thought of Micah's charm and wondered how common twins were in The Wilds. Did he know he had new siblings? Did he know Keres? *Oh, Micah, please be okay.* She sighed audibly.

"Oh, stop. I will not make you go against your morals," Keres said. "Perhaps your task will even be something you find righteous."

A great gust of wind blew in from the sea, causing the beached ship's loose sail to catch and dance in the air. Kaci didn't like how *righteous* sounded on Keres's lips, but she inclined her head, willing to listen.

"Mir has bespelled the father of Aion and Ananke. All he wants is to go home. He has an ailing father to tend to. Once the children are awakened, he will be of no use to Mir and will be cast out. He will wander the lands, lost in Isdralan until he perishes, or find a way home where he will not remember his children. He will have a hole in his heart forever. It does not end well for her consorts once she loses interest."

"How do you know?" Kaci asked.

"Because she is my mother."

The woman appeared almost sorrowful now. Kaci couldn't help but contemplate how strikingly human

Mir appeared to act, despite being a goddess. This side of her personality seemed to starkly contrast the image of the Great Mother, benevolent and wise. It was no wonder the humans worshiped Mir, who seemed to take what she wanted and discard what was no longer beneficial to her.

As Kaci observed the situation, a mixture of emotions washed over her. She felt a twinge of empathy for the woman standing before her, but Kaci's unease remained. She couldn't shake the feeling that there was more to the story than what they were being told.

"All I need is for you to distract her, so I can help the father escape with his children."

The shadows danced oddly around Keres as she spoke, their forms blurring and twisting and causing a subtle ripple in the air. Something about Keres was off—something shifted beneath the surface—yet Kaci couldn't decipher it. It was as if Keres were weaving a veil, thread by thread, right before her eyes.

"Request an audience with Mir. You do not even have to be deceitful. You can ask her to help you close the portals." Keres smiled bitterly. "Who knows? She may even say yes." The dark woman turned to Lady Durya. "I will need your strength to help with the escape."

"No!" Kaci interrupted, "Durya and I should stay together." She would go through with this plan but tell Mir everything. It was only fair to hear all sides of the story, and she did not trust Keres alone with Lady Durya."

"It is okay, Kaci," her friend replied. "I will help Keres."

"No," Kaci argued, "It's not a good idea to separate."

Lady Durya rose to her full height, eyes glistening. "These children have the right to their childhood and should not be pawns in some political game."

"What political—" Kaci started, but she could see the similarities to Durya's own childhood. If her friend needed to help these children, then so be it. If Mir's story proved different, there would be time to make things right. Kaci took a steadying breath. "Okay. I understand."

In an unexpected display of affection, Lady Durya closed the distance between herself and the small elf, wrapping her arms around Kaci in a tight embrace.

"Thank you, Kaci. For understanding."

As the wind shifted once more, Kaci realized that her decision, whether right or wrong, had irrevocably altered their path. Much like the ship below, caught in a magic they didn't yet understand, they too were now swept up in the currents of a destiny they couldn't control. She glanced toward the half-submerged silhouette of the Golden Gull. It was a potential escape, a backup plan should things spiral out of control. Especially if Lady Durya's connection held true and the ship somehow "liked" her.

Keres escorted them to a modest cottage where they could rest and refresh themselves. Inside, separate bedrooms awaited them, each with elegant clothing laid out for them. Kaci's dress was a rich green, the bodice adorned with intricate silver leaves that reminded her of Arba Vitae. Stepping out of her room in her new attire, Kaci inquired why such fine clothing was necessary.

"You're meeting the guardian of the West. Mir adores luxury and is drawn to beauty. She's even more fascinated by mystery. Your blend of allure and power will pique her interest enough that she will grant you an audience."

Kaci blushed, unaccustomed to being described as beautiful and powerful. Perhaps she had misjudged Keres after all.

Lady Durya emerged next, beaming with pride. She had donned a rich plum-colored garment that perfectly complemented her skin. Strangely, the outfit was not a dress but a divided skirt that swirled and changed hues as she moved.

Keres provided a large looking glass, and Durya twirled before it, mesmerized by her reflection.

"Isn't it divine?" Lady Durya asked Kaci, who nodded, feeling the excitement in the air. Why was she excited? She had never cared about clothing, beauty, or power. Something was wrong.

She took a second glance at Keres, and the balls of magic were vibrating ferociously, smashing into each other and exploding into tiny, shadowed fireworks.

A welcoming fire crackled in the room's corner, drawing Kaci's attention away from the mirror. She sought a moment of solace to find her center. She softened her gaze, allowing the flickering flames to captivate her. The vision that followed was brief but insistent.

A small man with a mischievous expression and twinkling eyes sat on a stone wall, playing the penny whistle. The man's attention was fixed on a young boy strolling down a dirt path. He watched the child intently, even as he took a swig from his flask.

Suddenly, the man tensed and turned his head, locking with Kaci's inner gaze.

Beware, daughter of flame. She has ensnared you in a spell.

Kaci snapped out of the vision, and a rush of fear overwhelmed her. The shadows and light still danced around Keres's head, but Kaci was no longer overcome with the odd sensation that had gripped her before. The spell was broken. She said a silent prayer of thanks to the little man in her vision and stood.

Kaci had been reluctant to leave Lady Durya in her current state. The tale of her husband's demise was still fresh in her mind. Lifting that weight of lies must have been a relief for her friend. But she would be raw and vulnerable without even knowing it. What kind of friend was Kaci to leave Durya with that woman, shrouded in shadows?

Keres was a conundrum. Kaci studied her, trying to understand her motivation. Keres didn't seem evil, just shadowed. Kaci knew the concepts of light and dark were not as simple as good and evil. Light was akin to the warmth of the sun, radiating hope, knowledge, and positivity. Darkness was like the depths of the forest at night, shrouded in mystery and potential danger, representing the unknown and the potential for negativity. Both were important. Both light and dark were necessary for life to exist. Without darkness, there could be no light, and without light, there could be no appreciation for the mysteries and complexities of darkness. Perhaps the balance between the two was key to finding harmony and understanding.

She would do it. This was the best for everyone. She would go to Mir and ask for help, and she would ask Mir's side of Keres's story.

Chapter 16

Guardian of the West

"The Guardian of the West, a bastion of strength and unyielding power, is like the ocean tides that ebb and flow, mysterious yet inexorable. Impartial and resolute, she draws upon the sea's might to protect the realm with steadfast devotion, an enigmatic force to be revered and respected." - Bataku Raama, *The Birth of Magic*

Keres guided Kaci and Durya along a steep path that meandered toward the rocky shore. Lady Durya was silent, her face etched with apprehension.

"Is this your ship?" Kaci inquired, taking in the vessel's elegant lines.

Keres regarded Kaci with a mysterious smile. "There are moments, Kaci, when Isdralan unveils its secrets through mystery. It's a land of contradictions, where the boundaries of reality and dreams intertwine and meld."

Puzzled, Kaci studied Keres. "What are you saying?"

Keres responded with a cryptic air, "The Golden Gull's arrival here is far from a random occurrence. Isdralan has a way of summoning the resources and situations to assist us."

Kaci contemplated Keres's explanation. "So, the ship is here because it's what we need for our journey?"

"Precisely," Keres affirmed with a nod.

The group boarded the Golden Gull, and with Keres at the helm, they set sail across the expansive sea. Lady Durya's expression of concern slowly softened as they continued. She appeared relieved that the waters were calm and the skies were clear. The mysterious power of Isdralan seemed to guide them, ensuring a safe passage.

Keres provided concise directions at the shoreline, gesturing toward a narrow trail that wove through the trees. "Follow that path, and you'll discover Mir. She is preparing for the twins' awakening ceremony."

She pivoted toward Lady Durya, whispering something that caused Durya to gasp in surprise. The woman gave a curt nod of understanding.

Keres raised an eyebrow at Kaci. "Why are you still here?"

Despite her concerns over the influence Keres appeared to wield over Durya, Kaci exhaled and shifted her focus toward the forest trail. It felt disrespectful to interrupt Mir during such an important ritual, but she was at a loss for any better ideas, especially as a stranger in this land.

The sound of cascading water reached her ears before she entered the clearing. A waterfall poured from the side of a sheer cliff, filling a crystal-clear pool below. The mingling scents of earth and sea hung in the air, rich with mystery. Beneath the waterfall, a woman stood, allowing the water to flow over her face and body. Her hair seemed to blend seamlessly with the stream, making it difficult to tell where one ended and the other began.

Emerging from beneath the falls, the woman dove into the pool and swam gracefully toward Kaci.

"I've been expecting you," she said, her voice reminiscent of the delicate chime of tiny bells. Her body was smooth and pale, emanating a silvery glow that enveloped her. The colorful orbs Kaci had noticed around many individuals since arriving in The Wilds appeared more pronounced around this woman, and her aura seemed to dance and shift around her like quicksilver, constantly changing in hue and shape.

"You expected me?" Kaci asked, confused. "Did Keres tell you I was coming?"

A shadow rippled on the woman's face, and she frowned, but it quickly shifted and merged with the nimbus surrounding her. "I have been awake for a long time. I can sense the ebbs and tides of my domain as clearly as those in my body. You, child, are quite the disturbance."

Kaci stiffened. It made her think of Belan every time someone called her child. She had to quell the anger when Keres had called her that. With Mir, it was mostly sorrow that bubbled up like the churning pool where the water fell.

Mir followed Kaci's gaze and inclined her head. "This water can be cathartic. Step in and rinse your troubles away."

The refreshing water enveloped her feet as Kaci waded into the pool, and she exhaled forcefully. Her purpose came rushing back like a flood. "I can't afford to waste time. I have something to tell you and a favor to ask."

"Time is an illusion. All instances can be accessed, and all moments explored. The path isn't straightforward; it twists and turns. You, child of flame, are not confined to this singular moment. It exists only at the crossroads of chance and circumstance."

There it was again. Why did everyone here insist on calling her the child of flame? She could recall the face of the man from her visions who had saved her twice.

"He is your father," Mir said with a smile.

"Father?" she whispered to herself, tasting the word, savoring it. It was foreign on her tongue, yet it held a familiar echo, like a long-forgotten melody. Her father. The Guardian of the South. Her chest felt tight, and her breath hitched. The man she'd seen in her visions—was her father.

Unanswered questions lingered in the air like specters, but a new one began to form. Elena. She could see the woman's features in her mind's eye, how protective she had been of Kaci when she stood outside the circle in her vision, calling Kaci home. Could she be…?

She looked up at Mir, eyes glistening with unshed tears, desperation and hope straining her features. Would the knowledge change anything? Her voice was just above a whisper when she spoke again.

"Is Elena my mother?"

But Mir did not answer that question.

"Father might be an overstatement for his role in your life," she continued about the Guardian of the South. "More like a guiding force. He has never been one to be directly involved unless he is looking for amusement." Mir raised an eyebrow. "But label it as you wish."

"Was it a mistake for him to not take a role in my life?" Kaci mused, her mind drifting to her vision of Elena and the man. She couldn't help but wonder if Elena *was* her mother. She imagined what her life might have been like, raised by the two of them in a typical family setting, surrounded by love and warmth. The thought brought an amused smile to her face. "Should he have loved me?"

"*Love* is a fleeting thing," Mir replied, "and *should* is a useless sentiment."

"What about your children? Do you love them?" Kaci asked, trying to get back on track. Talking to Mir was like trying to solve all of life's puzzles. "I need your help, but I also need to tell you that Keres plans to help their father take them from you. She told me that after they are *awakened*, you will have no use for him."

"She is not wrong." Mir cocked her head. "He will be happier living his life the way it was meant to be."

Kaci found herself puzzled by Mir's reaction. The Guardian of the West didn't appear sad or angry, nor did she seem in a rush to rescue her children.

Mir regarded Kaci thoughtfully, then asked, "Is sharing your concern about my family the only reason for your visit? Is there something else you wish to discuss?"

Kaci hesitated for a moment before answering, "Yes, there is something else, but I'm not sure what to ask for and how to ask it."

"Tell me what you need." Mir spoke softly. "Then we shall see what will be."

"I need help to close the portals in my world," Kaci said. "Shadows are pouring out and possessing the beings they come across. I can banish them, but I don't know how to stop the rips from opening."

Mir gazed into Kaci's eyes, seeming to pierce her soul. "What gives me the right to choose your lives over those of the shadows?"

"They are evil!" Kaci cried. "And—" She paused, realizing the complexity of the situation. Wasn't that the way of things? Predator and prey, strong and weak, the circle of life. This was far bigger than one little Elven girl. Then she remembered Belan. He had sacrificed everything so they could be here. "We just want to survive," she whispered.

Mir stepped out of the pool and draped a gossamer dress over her surprisingly dry body. "Come, child, let us observe the outcome of Keres's plans, then we shall speak more."

Kaci trailed behind Mir as they followed a path that led to a secluded inlet with a sandy beach. The entrance to a cave was nestled almost invisibly in the cove. Two woven baskets sat side by side near the entrance, their tiny occupants swaddled in seaweed. One infant wailed loudly while the other lay at rest.

A dark-haired man approached the baskets cautiously, whispered something inaudible over them, and picked up the crying infant. He sang a gentle lullaby until the child quieted, then reached for the other.

My progeny. Mir's voice echoed in Kaci's mind. The strange sensation caused Kaci's breath to catch as she turned to face the woman.

"Did—"

As Kaci continued to observe, she noticed the colors surrounding the infants. They seemed to be connected, their orbs dancing and intertwining as if they shared an invisible bond. Mir placed a finger over her lips and gestured for Kaci to keep watching. The woman appeared almost proud of the children. Keres had mentioned Mir's lack of empathy, but this didn't seem to align with her current demeanor. However, there was still a certain detachment about Mir. Kaci's mind was flooded with thoughts and colors, making it difficult to think clearly.

Aion and Ananke. Time and fate. Mir's lips didn't move, but she was undoubtedly projecting words directly into Kaci's head. The colors swirled around Mir and seemed to dance in response to her mental communication, enveloping the two of them in a gentle white mist as the words echoed in Kaci's mind. *They are the future and will become the all.*

The all. Such a curious way to phrase things, but Kaci was getting used to this woman's way of talking, and every time Mir spoke, Kaci could watch the thoughts as they flowed between them.

She observed the mother's aura of light dancing around her and attempted to speak directly to Mir's mind in the same fashion. This was probably a bad idea, but as Belan had once told her, you never learn without making mistakes. And curiosity is vital.

Are they being prepared for their awakening?

You learn fast. Mir looked unfazed. *Keres told you much. I am surprised. She holds her secrets close. Be wary. She often speaks in half-truths.*

Is she your daughter?

A look of contemplation passed over Mir's face before she inclined her head. *She is. Her heart is good for one filled with such a tempest.*

This did not seem like a mother that held disdain for her child. There was almost a reverence there, buried under a blanket of indifference.

You may believe that I am indifferent, child of flame, but that is not the whole truth. You see what lies before you—a path, a journey. But I see something far greater, the tapestry of infinite possibilities. The events unfolding have occurred countless times before. You may assume I wield extraordinary powers, but it is merely an awakening that has granted me this vision.

Just as what will happen to you and your children.

This ceremony is simply a formality. They will either

awaken on their own or they will not.

Mir turned back to the children.

"Richard!" she called aloud to the man as she remained at Kaci's side.

A small creature, resembling a cross between a bear and a wolf, burst from the brush and transformed into the familiar woman with pale, silver-flecked hair. Keres approached the man, speaking urgently and pointing to the cave—the same cave that Kaci and Durya had stood in front of with young Muirenn. As Keres urged him toward the entrance, one child remained in the man's arms. The man turned, gesturing to the second child, but Keres shook her head. He grew frantic, and they exchanged heated whispers.

"Are you okay?" Mir called out to the man but remained where she was.

"Shouldn't you go to them?" Kaci asked, leaning forward, but Mir simply observed, undisturbed.

Keres hastened the man along the path and shifted back into her animal form. As the man turned his back, Kaci watched in horror as Lady Durya scooped up the other child and vanished into the woods.

Reaching into the folds of her flowing robes, Mir

produced two small medallions. She closed her hand around them, squeezing gently, and when she opened her fist, there was only one. The stately woman attached the trinket to a slim silver chain and handed it to Kaci.

The necklace felt warm to the touch as Kaci turned it over, examining the symbol—three spirals meeting in the middle—a triskelion.

"This was meant for your children," Kaci whispered. "Why are you giving it to me?"

"It will find its way home." Mir smiled and turned back toward the pool. "You'd best find your friend."

"Wait—" Kaci called, more confused than when she first spoke with Mir. "What do I do with it? What about your child?"

But Mir didn't answer. The trees enveloped her, light and shadows dappling and dancing, creating patterns on her smooth skin until she vanished into the forest.

Kaci paused, feeling the warm earth under her feet and breathing in the salty sea air, when a rush of movement broke the serenity. A dark-haired man came crashing out of the cave like a phantom was close at his heels. For a moment, she thought it was the same man that had followed Keres, but the familiar flop of hair, and the fact he was calling her name, quickly squashed that misconception.

"Kaci! Lady Durya!" Micah called frantically. "Where did you go?"

His face was stricken with worry as his eyes darted this way and that. He let out a deep sigh as Kaci jogged to meet him. "Why did you two rush off?" Micah cried.

"We didn't!" Kaci shook her head. "We waited days for you, Micah. I thought for sure we had lost you!" All the emotions, fears, and sorrow she had bottled up flowed out at that moment. Big, ugly tears streamed down her face, and snot bubbled out of her nose. But Kaci didn't care. She wrapped her arms around her friend, squeezing him tight. "I am so glad you are alive! Where did you go?" she choked, the words muffled by his shoulder.

"I am glad to be alive, too." Micah's voice was soft, his reply coming out as a breathless chuckle. He pulled away after a moment, a crooked smile gracing his lips.

"In the caves, I saw a man…" Micah started after a moment, his gaze distant as he was pulled back into the memory. "For a moment, I thought it was Cirden. But it wasn't him. It was someone much more interesting.

"Who did you meet?"

A spark of excitement dancing in his gaze as he met Kaci's eyes. "It was the man from the book. Bataku Raama—" Micah glanced around as if he were expecting an eye roll. "Wait, where is Durya?"

"Oh." Kaci fidgeted and tugged at her braid. "She is helping some lady named Keres with a task, and then she will help us close the portals.

Micah's face went white. "Did you say Keres?"

"Yes," Kaci nodded, feeling a wave of nervousness. "Do you know her?"

Her friend was now muttering under his breath, so she repeated, "Micah, do you know Keres?"

Snapping out of his daze, Micah gave a curt nod. "She isn't supposed to be here. We sent her back." He began pacing, anxiety etched on his face.

"Muirenn and I sent her back, and…" His voice faded into the heavy silence. He seemed to focus on something distant, something Kaci couldn't see. His fingers flexed and unflexed at his sides, a testament to his turmoil.

At that moment, something changed in Micah. A

sudden jolt, like the snap of a tautly pulled string. "That has yet to happen in this timeline. We really need to find my mother."

"Where is your mother?"

"Here, probably. She stays on this island and—wait. How did you find your way here? We were searching for the entrance under the tree."

"We found the tree," Kaci replied. "Then we took a ship, and Keres guided us here."

"Where did you get a ship?"

"It was Durya's ship."

"Here?" Micah's face displayed confusion.

"Yes," Kaci beamed. "The Golden Gull!"

"Kaci," Micah paused and stared at her for a long moment, struggling to find words. "I don't even know where to begin. Keres is bad news. Fortunately, this is where we can usually locate Mir."

"Oh!" Kaci smiled, "I forgot to mention, I just spoke to Mir! She gave me this. It has the same symbol as the crowns."

Kaci pulled the pendant from her pocket and handed it to Micah. He turned it over, traced a finger along the spirals, and gently wrapped his fingers around it.

"I wonder if this Mir—" He seemed to be grappling with a thought, the pieces coming together in his mind. "Can she see the future paths?"

The thought hung in the air between them, an unanswerable question for the moment. Micah looked up from the amulet to meet Kaci's in a determined gaze. He gripped the amulet a little tighter.

"Thank you, Kaci," he said, the words raw and earnest. "With this, I might be able to help to make things right. I know for sure that I have a lot to learn."

"Belan said that when you realize this, it's the beginning of wisdom."

"Who?" Micah looked confused, and Kaci's heart ached. Belan deserved to be remembered. Why did he choose this path?

"Hey," Micah continued, "are you okay?"

Kaci nodded. "Micah, are you and Muirenn twins?"

"Yeah," Micah said. "But we were separated at birth. I didn't meet her until I was twelve."

"Oh no," was all Kaci could manage before Durya

came crashing through the trees, shouting.

"I messed up. We need to go!"

"What have you done?" Micah demanded.

"Micah!" Durya retorted.

"Why do we have to go?" Kaci interrupted.

"No time," Durya panted, "But Keres is as mad as a—"

A great roar emerged from the forest before Lady Durya could finish her sentence.

Keres's furious footsteps echoed across the rugged terrain as Micah, Kaci, and Durya ran for their lives. The ground beneath their feet shook as a powerful blast of energy narrowly missed the trio.

"You cannot escape me!" the dark woman roared.

Kaci ran as fast as she could toward the edge of the cliff, her heart pounding with a mixture of fear and excitement as the wind howled in her ears. The path ahead was steep and treacherous, but they had no time to waste.

As they approached the cliff's edge, Keres suddenly materialized in front of them, ablaze with fiery rage. She summoned a dark vortex that crackled with ominous energy, sending a barrage of black bolts hurtling toward the group.

Durya gasped as the energy surged toward them, but Micah was already in action. He pushed his friends out of the way with lightning-fast reflexes, allowing them to continue toward the ship as the blast sailed narrowly past them.

Below, the Golden Gull bobbed in the rough waters, her sails billowing in the wind. "Come on, we're almost there!" Kaci shouted, urging her companions forward.

Just as they were about to reach the ship, Keres appeared again in their path, this time surrounded by a pulsating aura of dark energy, eerily similar to the dark shadows they were trying to defeat.

"We can't take her head on," Micah said, his eyes darting as he sought a way out.

Suddenly, Durya noticed a nearby outcropping of rocks. "Follow me!" she yelled, diving in their direction.

The trio quickly scrambled up the rocks, using them as cover from Keres's onslaught. From their vantage point, they could see the Golden Gull clearly.

"Let's make a run for it!" Micah yelled, taking the

lead.

With Keres hot on their heels, they made a mad dash toward the ship. The world seemed to blur around Kaci, a cacophony muffled in her adrenaline-fueled focus. As their boots thudded onto the ship's wooden deck, it started to pull away as if by magic.

She could feel the surge of energy building behind them. Keres gathered her power for one final assault. The air crackled as she let loose the blast of dark energy, her power radiating outwards in a furious vortex. It sped toward them like a predator, hot and terrible, the energy humming with menace.

The blast missed them by a hair's breadth, a residual heat singing the ship's stern as it hurtled past them and slammed into the open water. A towering geyser erupted into the air, both terrifying and awe-inspiring. The sparkling droplets cascaded down like liquid diamonds. Then as quickly as it had arisen, the pillar of water fell back into the sea, the disturbance rippling outward, waves rocking the ship as they radiated toward the shoreline.

Breathless and battered, Kaci, Durya, and Micah stumbled onto the deck of the Golden Gull. They had narrowly escaped Keres's wrath, but what now? Sweat dripped down Kaci's face, and her chest heaved with the exertion of the treacherous climb down the cliff.

As the ship sailed toward the safety of the open sea, her mind raced with questions. Who was controlling the ship? She and her friends were the only people on board. The thought sent a shiver down her spine.

Had someone snuck on board while they were fighting Keres? Or was this some kind of trap? Kaci couldn't help but wonder if they were sailing into even more danger.

Chapter 17

Secrets of the Sky

"In the birth of magic, we find the essence of those who dwell in the heavens; transcending our comprehension, they guide without dominion, harmonizing with the cosmic tapestry." - Bataku Raama, *The Birth of Magic*

W e've searched the ship thrice over," Lady Durya said, her voice weary. "There's no one here but us." They had explored from deck to hull, making sure not to miss any of the bulkheads or cargo holds. Every shadow seemed to hide a lurking threat, but they found nothing besides worn wood and salt-streaked walls.

"Do you even know how to sail this thing?" Kaci breathed as she gripped the rail. They could still hear Keres's howls as the Golden Gull drifted further from shore. "What if we float out to sea and get lost forever?"

No sooner than the words were spoken, the Gull

lurched, its sails billowing with unseen forces as the sun dipped below the horizon. The ship's timbers creaked and groaned as it followed the curve of the land, as if sailing of its own volition.

Kaci's unease grew with each moment. She rubbed her temples. "How can this be? A ship can't sail itself." Part of her wanted to feel shocked, but few things could surprise her now.

Micah leaned against the ship's railing watching the endless horizon. "I think my mother is behind this," he said, his voice distant.

"This is her realm," he continued in a hushed tone. "She is in control and will do as she thinks is best." His voice was bitter, yet tinged with respect. Kaci reached for him, and he turned away, looking out over the water.

"Just once, I would like to think that Muirenn and I could have grown up together, in some version of my life, anyway. And that somehow would help me better understand this place. Perhaps even feel Mir's love." He shook his head and punched the rail.

Kaci frowned. "Why would she help us now? She seemed indifferent to what's happening in our world."

Micah hesitated, staring into the dark waves.

"Maybe she's finally taken a side. Or perhaps she's guiding us for her own reasons. I don't know why she's paying attention now. I don't even feel like I exist to her."

A gust of wind caught the sails, and the ship surged forward. Lady Durya tightened her grip on the railing, her knuckles white. "Regardless of who's behind it, the ship sails on. We can't stop it. We need to be prepared for whatever lies ahead."

"How could you have done that?" Micah turned to face Lady Durya, his eyes full of fire. "You helped someone kidnap children!"

Durya took a step back, sneering at Micah as she began to pace. "And just what were we to expect, Micah? You vanish without a trace, leaving us in the dark about your past. How were we to anticipate you were one of those infants? It's not like you are the only set of twins ever to exist."

A growl echoed in Micah's throat as his gaze anchored to the distant sea. "I assumed you were smarter than that, *Lady.*"

Inhaling deeply, he collected his emotions before swiveling to face Durya. "I left because I believed I saw Cirden, and you were too consumed by your anger to react." A sigh slipped from him, laced with disappointment. "I don't understand why your disdain for me is so intense. In all our encounters, you've never shown me an ounce of trust. I kept my past hidden, hoping it would give a future version of myself a chance to earn your respect."

Durya scoffed, her expression frustrated. "This is foolish. I was under the impression that aiding Keres was a noble cause, that it would benefit Isdralan and in turn, us." She paused and glanced at Kaci. "Now it feels like I've been walking blindly, and suddenly the blindfold's been ripped off. By the time my sight returned, the man and the boy had already left. I was stuck with the girl. For what it's worth, I ensured she was returned to her mother."

Kaci noted the tumult of emotions playing across Micah's face. He stuttered for a moment, struggling to keep his rising fury and pain at bay, then he shook his head and turned away from Lady Durya, back to Kaci. "I…I assumed you would have waited for me in the caves."

"Micah," Kaci said. "We waited for as long as we could. But the world does not wait—"

"It's fine," he said with a sigh. "I know time is strange in that place."

"You shouldn't have left us," Lady Durya interrupted. "This," she waved a hand toward the mainland, "is your fault. And as for helping Keres," she paused, her voice quivering with anger, "I—I am not sure what happened."

Underneath her fiery indignation, a current of embarrassment seemed to flow. "There's an unsettling aura to this place," she confessed, the bitterness in her voice subsiding. "I was deceived, and I regret it deeply."

Micah's shoulders loosened, and his breathing steadied as he took in the vast expanse of the sea before him. As Kaci observed, her thoughts strayed toward Lady Durya. She wondered if Durya had been ensnared by the same enchantment that her father had cautioned her about in the vision.

As if reading her thoughts, Lady Durya scoffed, her voice dripping with sarcasm. "Oh, please. It's not like I had a choice in the matter. I imagine Keres cast some sort of enchantment on me. If only someone had been there to protect those poor, helpless infants, like perhaps their mother? Or the person who knew they were in danger?"

Micah's anger flared once more, his fists clenching at his sides. "You have no right to speak like that," he snapped. The fragile peace between them shattered like glass.

Micah scowled and stomped toward the bow of the ship. "I'm sick of being everyone's scapegoat. Come get me when we arrive somewhere." He sulked toward the cabin and made a show of slamming the door behind him.

"Well, that tantrum was unnecessary." Lady Durya sniffed.

"Durya," Kaci sighed, not knowing what to say. Instead, she turned to watch the sea. No words would change Durya's feelings, and any advice would be in vain. The three of them needed to have a common goal. Find Cirden and close the portals. All she could do was trust that Mir was sending them where they needed to be.

Dusk fell, but the heavens never grew dark. Instead, they were bathed in a perpetual twilight between night and day,. The Golden Gull sailed onward, guided by unseen hands, its deck bathed in the soft, eerie glow. This was not the sky Kaci grew up under, yet it still felt like home. Although they had only been on the ship for a few hours, she missed the feeling of earth under her feet.

Lady Durya, on the other hand, looked at home on the ship. She stood at the bow, her hands gripping the figurehead as if commanding the vessel herself, a queen presiding over her realm.

After some time, the lady joined Kaci at the starboard railing. "We should probably try to get some rest. Who knows what is coming next?"

"I'm surprised you didn't kick Micah out of the captain's quarters." Kaci attempted to smile.

"Bah," Durya flicked a hand dismissively. "It still has too much of my late husband's energy. Once I burn all the furnishings, that room will be mine," she said with a wicked grin.

"Wouldn't it have your energy? You slept there too!"

Lady Durya laughed bitterly. "Don't forget, our marriage was not like that. I was his wife in name only. All my late husband needed was my holdings and an heir."

Her words trailed off, and Durya joined Kaci at the rail, staring out over the sea.

"I'm sorry," Kaci whispered. There were no other words to give. If only Micah knew, maybe he wouldn't be so quick to judge.

In the end, neither of them opted for sleep. They stood quietly together, watching the sea, their shared sorrow forging an unspoken bond between them.

It wasn't long before the Golden Gull gave a lurch and turned toward the shore as if drawn by some magnetic force.

Kaci knocked on the door to the cabin and paused. "Micah, it's Kaci. We're approaching land."

"Come in." His voice was low, and when she opened the door, he was sitting on a luxurious four-poster bed, staring at the wall.

"Have you been here all night?" she asked, sitting on the bed next to him. His eyes were dry, but tears stained his cheeks, and he held the triskelion pendant in his hand, fingers tracing over its intricate swirls.

"I would like to think the pendant is why she let us be separated," he said slowly as he studied it. "Because she knew I would need it here and now. But who knows with that woman? She is weaving this great tapestry, and all we can see are a few threads. I wish sometimes she would tell me her plans."

"You don't learn to be a master overnight." Kaci put an arm around him and squeezed his shoulders. "But she trusted you enough to give it to you."

"How is it you seem to accept these things so easily?" Micah asked, laughing bitterly.

"I was born to the mysteries," Kaci smiled. "I've been told since I was a wee thing that you will never be wise until you realize just that. Come, let's meet our destiny."

The morning light was warm and bright as the Golden Gull pulled in, water gently lapping at its hull. A giant mountain loomed on shore, so tall its peak was obscured by the clouds that gathered around the mighty summit.

On the dock, a single person stood awaiting their arrival, obscured by a large crate. The figure was short and stout, and it gave off a soft glow. Kaci couldn't tell if it was the same type of energy that surrounded everyone here in Isdralan or something new entirely. There was a purity and innocence about it that made her smile.

As the gangplank lowered of its own accord, Durya and Micah glanced at her, avoiding each other's eyes. The trio walked down together, and Kaci's gaze remained fixed on the glowing figure.

"Belan!" she exclaimed, running to the man and

wrapping her arms around him in a warm hug. "You're alive!"

He gave a smile and a slight nod. The others seemed to look right through him. Micah glimpsed the figure, his brow furrowing in confusion, but he twisted away, unable to hold the memory in his mind. Durya did not comment on the Earthborn's or Kaci's excitement. It was as though they could see him, but they forgot as soon as the moment passed. He was a memory—a ghost.

"Why can't they see you?" Kaci asked her friend before glancing back at her companions.

"I do not exist," he answered simply, clasping her hand. His skin felt warm to the touch, like any living being.

"Then how can I see you?" she asked. "And feel you?"

He gave a knowing smile and gestured toward the mountain peak. "I have touched the sky."

"What does that mean?" she whispered, knowing that was a question he wouldn't answer.

"They are expecting you," he said, pointing to the mountain again. "In the tower at the peak."

Then he turned away.

"Wait," Kaci called. "Aren't you coming?"

Belan turned back and took a step toward her. "No, my child, I cannot." He gently touched her arm. "I no longer exist on your plane."

If this were so, how could she see him? Kaci had so many questions floating in her head. One, in particular, floated to the top and won out.

"Are you lonely?"

Belan swept his arm toward the trees ahead, and for the briefest of moments, Kaci could swear she saw a grand city bustling with light and life. Then it was gone.

"I'm not alone," he replied as he faded from view.

"What now?" Lady Durya's voice jarred her from the spell she had been under. The moment had been bittersweet—Belan was here, but just out of reach in some ghostly city that Kaci couldn't touch. Oh, how nice it would be to give up and live there with him. Instead, she pointed to the mountain.

"We need to go there."

Durya rolled her eyes. "I am not dressed for climbing. How do you even know?"

Micah had been silent during this entire exchange. "I think she is right," was all he added.

The ascent had looked treacherous, with a narrow trail of switchbacks winding through the trees up to the precipice of the great peak. But once they arrived, none of them quite remembered the journey.

As the last of the trees parted, Kaci felt as though a fog had lifted from her mind. Before them stood a grand tower reaching into the sky, with nothing but vast expanses of azure beyond. The sight was both breath-taking and terrifying. It possessed a surreal quality that made her feel suspended between worlds.

A grand archway led into a pristine chamber made of gold-lined marble, stretching from the floors to the ceilings. There was no furnishing save for a massive marble table at the center. Three otherworldly beings sat around the table, their gaze fixed on the new arrivals. They appeared to be human but exuded a transcendent quality that made them seem more than mortal.

With dark hair cascading in waves down her back, Mir gave them a nod, and her lips turned up slightly. She looked over the group, but lingered on Micah the longest. She warmed, her eyes crinkling as her smile widened.

Kaci recognized the man instantly. He was tall, his golden hair intermingled with flames, and his eyes held an impish sparkle. He gave Kaci a wink and nodded at Micah, but said nothing as he leaned back casually.

The third being was a mystery. Black, piercing eyes seemed to drill directly into Kaci's soul. Their dark hair was cropped short. This entity was ageless and timeless. Grim and ancient, a jewel rested on their brow. It surprised Kaci when an echo interrupted her thoughts.

We are the maiden, the mother, and the crone. We are the warrior within and without. We are what we need to be, when we need to be.

Kaci shivered, feeling simultaneously chastised and educated. Lady Durya had dropped to her knees, unable to meet the powerful being's eyes. This was entirely unexpected.

"Rise, Durya." When they spoke, their voice was rich and musical.

The clicking of hooves echoed on the floor behind them as a fourth figure entered the room. A magnificent stag with intricately twisted and branched horns walked toward them and morphed into a man that seemed to be made from the mist surrounding him. Silvery hair crowned his head in wisps, and a crown of light rested on his brow. He took his place at the table and waved the three to join the group.

"You are the guardians?" Kaci asked and blushed. She was stating the obvious. So many questions arose, and she had to wait and listen.

"Elena has taught you well," the man with the fiery hair said.

"Listen, learn, and then ask," Mir continued.

Durya interrupted. "What should we call you?"

"Impulse magnified," the warrior-like being said with a laugh. "Being raised by the humans did you no favors there."

"We have as many names as worlds that exist. But you may call me Brennon," the misty man whispered.

"Connie." The fiery man spoke now, and Micah smirked, almost imperceptibly.

The being with dark eyes scanned the group before answering, "Fia."

"You all know me as Mir. That will do nicely."

"Why did you summon us?" It was Durya who finally spoke. She had risen, shoulders thrown back in determination, meeting Fia's intense gaze.

Connie threw back his head in laughter, his bright hair moving like the crackling flames of a fire. "We do not summon."

"It is not as though we sit on a podium ruling the masses," Mir added. "As much as people would like to think it, we are not gods."

"But what about the powers and abilities you have?" Durya asked.

"They do not differ from your own," Brennon said softly. "Our lives come into existence just like yours, and in the end we will be part of the whole once again."

"If you do not want to be seen as gods, why let people worship you?" Micah asked.

Brennon raised an eyebrow. "I do not *let* them do anything. Worship or not, good or evil—it makes no difference."

"That seems bleak." Kaci frowned. "If that's so, then what is the point?"

Brennon's lips turned up in a slight smile that reminded her of Belan. "That is a lovely thought that would probably take eons to discuss. However, we will end up circling right back to the same question. We are part of the whole, and when you realize that, it will free you."

"But what about the portals and the lives that are being stolen?" Kaci pressed.

"In the beginning," Fia began, "there existed many worlds filled with different entities, separate yet always intertwining, bound by the thread of existence. They were unaware of each other, but when *the First* harnessed this thread, the universe reeled and shifted. Like all youthful entities, the First found power intoxicating. Eventually, he recognized his missteps and sought to contain the energy he had unleashed, but it was too late. The world had taken on a life of its own, and many beings sought to control it. He tried to contain this power and those that sought to control it, the world around him exploded and collapsed inward simultaneously, giving birth to Kashara. Into this void, he imprisoned his world in darkness, and he placed himself at the epicenter."

Kaci's mind flashed to the dark place in her vision, the intense quarrel between the man and woman. Could she have witnessed the genesis of this tale?

"However," Fia continued, "he neglected to remember that darkness is merely one facet of existence. Wherever darkness arises, light must also follow."

"Like Newton's third law!" Micah interjected, feet bouncing with excitement.

"Indeed," Fia affirmed. "Simultaneously, Isdralan was born to counterbalance the darkness. Prior to his creation of Kashara, the First had dispatched his kin to another realm. When his own world met its catastrophic end, they were wrenched from their space and time, and transformed into beings of light, and propelled to Isdralan. These were the first guardians, the foundational stones upon which Isdralan stands today," Fia declared.

"In the grand cosmic design, who exists where holds no significant consequence," Fia further explained. "The souls entrapped within Kashara are part of the universal whole. If they were to escape, the void would have to be replenished."

"But they want to possess you!" Durya objected. "If they succeed, all will plunge into darkness and despair!"

With a mere raise of her eyebrow, Fia silenced Durya, who immediately bowed in reverence. "The dawn of consciousness within Kashara was mirrored in Isdralan, creating the existence of guardians like us to uphold balance. Should one of us fall, the universe will find a way to replace us, restoring equilibrium once more. That is the way."

"So be it," Brennon answered. "The whole will continue with or without us; we are small parts in a great tapestry."

"Then why be guardians? Why even talk to us?" Kaci asked, balling her fists. She felt the familiar heat in her belly, and small puffs of smoke seemed to come from her hair. "Why bring us here?"

"We are guardians because it was what we wanted," Connie answered simply. "Isdralan was put into place because those who came before us had the desire to shape existence. You brought *yourself* here, child of flame, because you wanted to shape your reality."

"How do we stop it?" Micah asked, pulling the triskelion pendant from his pocket. "Why do I need this to use my abilities?"

"It's just a tool." Mir smiled and fluffed his hair. "A crutch you may someday shed."

"You have many of those crutches and pendants." Connie laughed as Micah glowered. "Oh, don't be so glum. I admire your experiments."

"So," Micah faced Mir. "It wasn't you who guided the ship?"

Mir shook her head.

"So, if you didn't summon us and aren't willing to help," Durya interrupted, "Why did the Gull bring us here? Why waste our time?"

"Time is yours to do with what you will," Brennon answered. "The four of us are here because we chose to be."

"I have a question." Kaci interrupted. "Since we arrived, I see orbs and clouds of light and color surrounding people. It doesn't happen all the time, but no one else can see it." Kaci looked at her friends and blushed. "There are other things I see that no one else can."

"You can see the thread. The soul reflects the color of its contemplations," Brennon answered simply.

It had become clear to Kaci that the guardians were not going to help directly, so she might as well garner as much information as they would give. The worst thing they could do would be to refuse to answer.

"How do we close the portals for good?" Kaci asked the guardians.

"You know this already," Connie answered, his demeanor suddenly tired. "Back where it all started."

Their eyes locked for a fleeting moment, and she gave a nod. Connie and the other guardians had confirmed what she suspected. To counterbalance the darkness, she would need to harness light. Though unsure of the method, Kaci knew the task was hers and hers alone. *You have a duty to fulfill. A destiny,* Elena had told her. Perhaps their estrangement had roots in this foreknowledge—that Kaci's light would be offered to the abyss.

Kaci felt a deep sadness as her gaze swept over her friends. Was this how Belan felt when he discovered what opening the gateway required? Kaci resolved to keep them in the dark. She didn't wish for them to bear guilt for her actions.

"Cirden is there?" Kaci voiced her question aloud. In response, Connie simply nodded.

"Can you transport us there?" she asked.

Connie's curt *no* closed that line of inquiry.

Undeterred, the group maintained their discourse with the guardians until there was more silence than speaking. Their conversation with the guardians drawn to a close, Kaci, Micah, and Durya departed the majestic expanse of the great hall. The resonant echo of their footsteps lingered in the air until Durya's voice cut into the silence.

"Well, this was all a colossal waste of time." She scoffed and rolled her eyes as the group descended the steps of the towering structure. "Tell me, why did we bother?"

Chapter 18

Hope's Fading Light

*"Guarding those we cherish can be a dou-
ble-edged sword. In our fervent desire to protect, we
may unknowingly bring discord. Tread softly and
be wary, for love can inadvertently bury."* Bataku
Raama, *The Birth of Magic*

With the sunlight filtering through the trees, the trio stepped onto the lush forest floor. They all knew what needed to be done and that their only course of action was to return to Elyndris and put an end to the portals on their own. While their purpose was clear, the path forward was riddled with complexities and confusion. No one seemed to want to voice their thoughts about the journey ahead. Kaci quietly wondered if Connie's advice meant more than going back home.

"It *was* impressive that we received an audience with the gods," Lady Durya mused aloud, breaking the silence. Her voice was awed but tinted with frustration.

"They are not *gods*," Micah interrupted.

"Meeting Fia…" Lady Durya breathed, ignoring Micah.

Kaci, caught in her thoughts, barely heard the two bickering. Connie's words echoed in her mind. *Back where it all started*—a simple phrase, but everything he spoke was so cryptic. Had he meant Elyndris? Home? Aeloria? She puzzled over the advice, but then a realization hit her like a bolt of lightning. The fire. Arba Vitae. That's where they would find Cirden.

Her sudden sharp intake of breath drew the attention of her companions. "I think I know what Connie meant," she said, her face aglow. "He wasn't just talking about a place, but a time. The fire, Arba Vitae, that's where we started. And that's where we'll find Cirden!"

"You may be on to something. But how do we get there?" Micah asked, his voice filled with uncertainty.

Micah's question hung in the air, leaving a momentary silence while Lady Durya regarded them.

"Going back to the caves," she proposed, the words rolling off her tongue with practiced grace. "If they exist outside our known time, maybe they hold the key."

"I—I really don't want to go back to those caves. There's…" Kaci's eyes shimmered with a mix of fear and sorrow as her voice trailed off.

"Well," Durya responded, tilting her head in a forced effort to appear kind, "it's not as if we're inundated with options. We mustn't overlook any possibility."

The memory of the dark, twisted paths of the Caves of Chaos sent a shiver down Kaci's spine. It was because of the caves that Belan had been swallowed from existence. What else would that place demand as payment, and who might be the next to vanish? She glanced at Lady Durya and then at Micah. Neither knew the pain of loss that Kaci was feeling. And yet the fate of their world hung in the balance. The silence grew heavy, like a suffocating blanket. Finally, Micah broke the quiet, his voice cracking with determination.

"I have an idea," he said.

Micah's excitement was contagious as he shared his plan. "I might get the pendant to take us back to Kaci's world," he said with a mysterious smile.

"Really? How?" Kaci's voice rose in surprise.

"Using the same concepts that got me here." Micah hesitated for a moment, attempting to gather his thoughts as they boarded the Golden Gull. "You see, the pendant is attuned to different worlds and dimensions. I've been studying it for a long time, trying to figure out how to manipulate its power."

"I don't know," Kaci thought out loud. "That didn't go so well the first time."

"We can always revisit the cave plan." Micah gave a half smile.

Durya frowned. "So you think you can change it to take us back to Elyndris?" she asked.

Micah nodded. "Exactly! But I'll need to do some tinkering with the ship's figurehead to make it work."

As they approached the ship, Micah scrutinized the golden bird. Its wings were outstretched, creating an illusion of motion as they seemed to catch the wind. The feathers were delicately etched, each one distinct and shimmering in the sunlight. The bird's eyes were made of two small, gleaming gemstones that captured the light, making them appear as though they were surveying the vast expanse of the sea before them. Micah made his way over, working quickly and skillfully. His fingers danced over the intricate metal parts as he made adjustments.

Kaci and Durya watched in fascination as the figurehead emitted a pulsating blue light. Micah stepped back, wiping his forehead with the back of his hand.

"Okay, that should do it," he declared, looking satisfied with his work. "Touch it and think of where you want to go."

Kaci moved toward the figurehead, her fingertips grazing the cool metal surface. Her eyes fell shut as she focused her mind on her homeland. Images flooded her thoughts; the flickering bonfire, Cirden's fury, Arda's anguish, and the vitality of Arba Vitae.

Durya's intervention was sudden, her voice full of alarm. "Wait!" Her body was taut with what Kaci could only interpret as panic.

Micah turned to her, a look of puzzlement etched across his face. "What's the matter?" he asked, eyeing Durya.

"There's something wrong," Durya stated, her gaze fixed on the figurehead as if she could perceive something within it. "It's—it's resisting. It doesn't want us to meddle with time."

Suddenly, there was a blinding flash of light, and when the group could see again, they found themselves in a foreign environment. The Golden Gull had transformed, now a vessel of sleek and smooth contours, with sharp angles and curves. Kaci noticed strange symbols etched into the side of the ship but couldn't make sense of them.

"What just happened?" Kaci asked, her voice trembling.

"I may have messed up the coordinates," Micah admitted sheepishly, looking down at the pendant in his hand.

Somehow, they were now indoors. This baffling collision of the familiar and alien was made all the more surreal by the sudden emergence of a small mechanical portal. A strange figure entered the room from the portal. It was humanoid, with feathers protruding from its arms and a beak-like nose. It turned to face them, and Kaci could see that it had piercing blue eyes that seemed to glow in the darkness. Next to it was an old man. His face was etched with wrinkles, and his jacket was worn, the fabric frayed at the edges from years of wear. There was something familiar about him that Kaci couldn't put her finger on. Only when her eyes met his did the realization hit her. This old man *was* Micah. A very old Micah.

"Greetings, travelers," the man said in a melodic voice. "May I assist you?"

Durya and Kaci exchanged a confused glance while their Micah stepped forward with a hesitant smile. "We meet again."

"And we will, infinitely more times," the old man replied.

"We seem to have gotten lost," Micah explained. "Is there any way you can help us get back to where we came from?"

The man tilted his head, considering. "It is possible."

Lady Durya growled low in her throat, and the man burst into a resounding fit of laughter. Kaci worried he was having a seizure, but after a time, the man was able to contain himself.

"Very well," the man's eyes shined, and he gave them a wink. "I can assist you, but the journey may not be comfortable."

The group looked at each other, uncertain. But in the end, they had little choice. They nodded their agreement, and the man tapped a few of the strange symbols, seeming to set the ship's course.

They hurtled through the vast expanse of the multiverse, catching glimpses of strange and wondrous worlds, each more bizarre than the last. Finally, they emerged back into their own time and place, the familiar skies of Elyndris overhead and the Golden Gull once again a humble sailing ship. The man and bird person were gone. They could only hope they were in the right place.

Micah breathed a sigh of relief. "That was…intense," he said.

The group scanned their surroundings, searching for landmarks. The landscape seemed familiar, but Kaci couldn't shake the feeling of uncertainty. How would they know if it was the right time? She glanced at her companions, trying to gauge their thoughts. Micah seemed confident, his expression relaxed. Lady Durya, on the other hand, appeared unconvinced, her brow furrowed as she scrutinized every detail of their surroundings.

Durya's scanned the sea as the Gull sailed toward the horizon, and suddenly her expression brightened. There was a towering lighthouse, standing tall and proud against the cloudy sky. She let out a gasp of relief.

"Look!" she exclaimed, pointing at the lighthouse. "I recognize that structure. We made it back!"

The ship changed course and headed toward the

lighthouse. Kaci turned to Micah with a worried expression. "Are you sure this is the right time?" she asked, her voice tinged with concern.

Micah nodded confidently. "I'm positive," he said. "I trust the old man wouldn't steer us wrong."

Durya let out a small sigh of relief as the structure loomed closer, its beacon guiding them safely home.

To Kaci's surprise, Smeadon greeted the group as the Golden Gull approached the dock, followed closely by Jeth and Meshach. The goblin looked worried and anxious, his slight frame quivering.

"Incomin'!" he shouted, his thick accent making his words difficult to understand. "Yarrr, ye been gone for months! The world's gone topsy-turvy!"

The group exchanged a worried glance, wondering what could have happened during their absence. "What do you mean?" Durya asked, her voice tense with concern.

Smeadon looked around nervously, his beady eyes darting from side to side. "Arrr, the shadow portals," he said, his voice trembling. "They be openin' everywhere, and society be crumblin'! But us gobl'ns seem be immune to possession."

Kaci felt a chill run down her spine. If Smeadon recognized her and the portals existed, then they were in the wrong time. Why hadn't the old man dropped them earlier? She glanced at Micah, but his face was blank.

As they walked, Kaci glanced around the streets. It was unusual for humans to allow such a multitude of goblins into the city. They must be afraid indeed to let so many in!

"And what about my mother? And my brother?" Durya asked, her voice barely above a whisper. "Are they safe?"

Smeadon's expression turned grim. "I tried me best to protect Lady Evelyn," he said, his voice filled with regret. "But the shadows be too powerful for me to handle. Your brother is fine, and awaitin fer you." Smeadon brightened. "Lady Kaci, she be a fierce warrior. She be able to fight off the shadows and protect, right?"

Kaci felt her heart break. Durya had loved her mother in her own way. That she had fallen to the shadows was a sobering reminder of how they had failed.

As the group made their way through the bustling streets of the small port town, they could see the devastation wrought by the shadow portals. Buildings lay in ruins, and the streets were littered with debris and rubble. But even amid the chaos, there were signs of hope. Small groups of goblins were banding together to protect the human homes and families from the shadows.

Kaci turned to Smeadon and said, "It's amazing to see so many goblins working."

Smeadon blushed at the compliment and responded in a gruff voice, "Aye, they be a determined lot. They are. They wanted to help protect the homes and the wee ones. And, well, the extra shinies didn't hurt neither," he added with a sly grin.

She couldn't help but smile. Gold was a powerful motivator, and if it meant that the goblins would fight against the shadows, then she was all for it. They needed as many allies as they could get.

"Smeadon," Kaci said, turning to the goblin. "Have you heard anything about Belan? He was the Earthborn priest. Do you remember him?"

Smeadon looked at Kaci, his brow furrowed in confusion. "Belan the priest? Harrr, I'm sorry, I don't know what ye be talkin' about," he said, his accent making his words difficult to understand.

Smeadon looked at the group with a heavy heart, and his voice filled with sadness as he spoke. "Aye, but the Earthborn kingdom has all but fallen to the shadows," he said in a low voice. "Their defenses were strong, but the shadows were stronger. It be a tragedy, it be."

Kaci felt a pang of disappointment. She had hoped against hope that maybe since goblins could not be possessed, Smeadon might have remembered Belan.

Smeadon continued through the twisting, narrow streets, his body darting nimbly through the crowds. After several minutes, they arrived at a nondescript building on the outskirts of the town.

"This be the safe house," Smeadon said, then turned to Lady Durya, his voice low and cautious. "Your brother and his man are inside, tryin' to keep the peace."

Marcus and Sharn huddled around a table, poring over maps and documents. Marcus looked up as they entered, his face tense and drawn, but brightening at the sight of his sister. "I wish we were meeting under better circumstances. The king's forces are mounting defenses that are only going to be possessed. They won't follow me because—well—and mother is—"

"I know," Durya said with a heavy sigh.

Kaci had always known that Durya and Marcus's status as orcs would make it difficult for them to gain the trust and respect of the humans they governed, even with the family name to back them. Still, it was painful to see it play out.

"We need to unite the people," Durya said, her voice determined. "We can't let the shadows tear us apart."

Marcus sighed, his expression pained. "I wish it were that simple, sister," he said. "But you know as well as I do the people won't follow us. They see us as savages, not as leaders."

As they talked, Sharn sat quietly in the corner, often glancing nervously toward Durya. Kaci could tell that he was still smitten with her friend, even after all these years, and gave him a sad smile. If only they had time for love and life.

"I have a plan," Durya said, her voice firm, then turned to Marcus. "Edward is dead, but no one knows this yet. Mother and Father intended for Westerfield to go to him and my heirs. I will rule using his name. The goblins and townspeople will be my messengers. I will buy their loyalty—let the goblins keep a share of whatever plunder they find. And," she added, turning to

Smeadon, "I will make you the goblins' leader."

Smeadon looked stunned at the idea. "Me? The leader of the goblins?"

Durya nodded. "Yes, you," she said. "You have proven yourself to be an…ally. I know you will lead the goblins as long as the coin keeps coming."

He laughed, gave a vicious smile, and bowed deeply. "This be the beginnin' of a profitable relationship," Smeadon said, his voice filled with enthusiasm. "I be at your service, Lady Durya. I make sure the goblins on your side. Together, we make those shadows wish they never came here!"

Kaci's focus drifted, and as she stared at the fire crackling in the fireplace, a strange sensation washed over her. Suddenly, she was transported back to the moment at the bonfire, where everything changed—the beginning. This time it was different than what she remembered.

Connie's cryptic advice came rushing back: *Back where it all started.*

Cirden appeared before her, hunched with sorrow and regret.

This vision was different—not a glimpse of the

past, nor a view of the future. It was as though Cirden were there with her in the present.

"At Arba Vitae," he said, eyes weary. "Slipping. There is not much of me left. Please—"

Then he was gone, replaced by someone or something else that stared back at her from within Cirden's body.

Darkness consumed her. You are mine, a voice echoed. It seemed to come from all around and inside of her. Kaci was certain this was the dark entity, Javina—the one in charge of it all.

Cirden's dark, hollow eyes looked at her as he gave an awful grin. "Mistress, this is the one."

Suddenly, Kaci was back in the room with her friends. She shuddered, fear washing over her as she emerged from the vision. Kaci couldn't let it control her. She had to make things right. She had to do it now. A voice in her head warned her not to go. If Javina wanted her to come, wasn't it best to stay far away? But Kaci pushed that voice down, determined to face the darkness.

Turning to Micah, she said, "Time is of the essence. We must sail the Gull to Aeloria here and now. I saw Cirden in a vision. He tried to tell me something."

Micah looked at her, filled with concern. "Are you sure, Kaci? Before you said we had to go back to the time where it started. We don't know what we'll find there."

Kaci nodded firmly. "I'm sure. We have to find Cirden. He is the key, and his knowledge can help us stop things once and for all."

Lady Durya frowned. "Kaci, I understand how important Cirden is to all this, but we need you here," she argued, her voice firm. "Our world is falling apart, and thus far, you are the only one who can close these portals. If you leave now to chase after Cirden, who knows how long we will survive? With you here, we at least have a chance. Please reconsider your decision."

In Isdralan, there had been a united resolve, an unspoken agreement to trace their steps back to where it all began. But now, inexplicably, they were urging her to remain behind and close the portals in the same way that didn't work before. The more she tried to make sense of it, the more confusing it all became.

Kaci met her friend's gaze and spoke formally, noticing the surrounding company. "I understand your concerns, Lady Durya, but I believe that if I don't go now, there will come a time when I won't be able to help at all," she said, her voice steady. "By going to the source, confronting Cirden and whatever force is behind him, I hope to end the shadows once and for all. I know it's risky, but this is our best chance to save our world. If we can cut off the head of the snake, so to speak, then perhaps we can stop the shadows from spreading any further."

"I will go with her," Micah's voice was quiet but firm. "I won't let anything happen to Kaci."

Lady Durya clenched her fists, visibly struggling to contain her feelings as she looked at Kaci and Micah. She scowled and sighed before finally relenting. "Fine," she growled, the word dripping with frustration. "You two go on this fool's errand. But mark my words, Micah, if any harm befalls Kaci…" she paused, her voice lowering to a menacing growl, "I will rip your limbs from your body and use them to beat you senseless before I feed them to the wolves." With a final, begrudging nod, she gave her consent.

Lady Durya turned to Smeadon. "Marcus informed me you have some skill in sailing. I would like you to captain my ship, the Golden Gull, and take Kaci to Aeloria. You choose a crew and go with her. You all will be well compensated."

Smeadon nodded, a grin spreading across his face. "Aye, lady, consider it done. We'll find you a crew that'll make the shadows shake in their boots!"

Kaci smiled weakly at the goblin's enthusiasm, but it did little to dispel the heavy sense of foreboding that hung over her like a dark cloud. She knew they were facing a treacherous journey, and the shadow of impending doom seemed to loom ever larger on the horizon. How she wished she had Belan at her side. What would he tell her? *Find your light, child.* But Kaci knew where she was going. There was no light.

She collapsed on the deck of the Golden Gull, her mind and body utterly drained. Smeadon had assembled a motley crew of goblins and other unlikely allies, and they set sail for Aeloria with grim determination on their faces.

Leaving Durya, Marcus, and Sharn behind in Westerfield was difficult. They showed concern for Kaci, but they had their own important work ahead of them—forging an alliance with the humans to halt the insidious shadows' continued encroachment upon their shared world. All Kaci could do was hope that her friend's plan would work.

Durya's determination to prove herself a capable

and strong leader was a flickering candle in the all-consuming darkness, and Kaci knew that Marcus and Sharn would support her. Together, they would build tenuous bridges between the fractured factions of their world. She hoped they could escape ever-advancing shadows.

As Kaci closed her eyes, she felt herself slipping into a twisted and disquieting dream. She was peering into the heart of darkness itself. There she watched the malevolent puppet master controlling Cirden, and the terrifying visage of Javina. Javina's cold, unblinking gaze met hers in the depths of the abyss.

"Who are you?" Kaci asked, her voice trembling. Darkness surrounded her.

"I am your destiny," the voice replied.

"What have you done with Cirden?" Kaci demanded.

"General Raelon has prepared the way for me," the voice said. "He has found you. You will be my vessel."

"No," Kaci said firmly. "I won't. You can't possess me."

"What makes you think I haven't already?" the voice asked, and Kaci felt a chill run down her spine.

"I would know, wouldn't I?" Kaci replied, her voice growing stronger.

Javina laughed eerily, and Kaci felt fear tightening around her.

There was fire everywhere, and Kaci felt herself being pulled toward it.

"Why me?" Kaci asked, her voice barely above a whisper.

"You are born of the darkness and born of the light," the voice said. "You are the perfect vessel for my power."

"No," Kaci said again, her voice growing stronger. Flames began to lick the air around her, chasing away the darkness.

Awakening with a start, Kaci's heart hammered against her ribcage, each thud echoing the terror that gripped her. In the dark confines of her mind, the pieces of a terrifying puzzle were coming together into a dawning realization that brought with it a chilling understanding. The danger was far more sinister than she had ever imagined.

Kaci's lineage, her being the child of a Guardian, made her a desirable vessel. Her body and mind were keys to unlocking a power much more catastrophic than just the fall of Elyndris. She was leading Micah, another child of gods, into the belly of the beast, blinded by hope and determination.

If he were also to be possessed by these dark souls, the consequences would be disastrous. Elyndris would fall, Micah's world could be consumed, and even Isdralan might not escape unscathed. Micah's power, though fresh and untrained, was equal to hers, if not greater. Kaci couldn't bear the thought of him succumbing to Javina's grasp. She was stronger, and this was a burden she had to bear alone.

The night weighed heavily upon them, and the Gull lay anchored near the desolate shore of Aeloria, but Micah slept peacefully under the starry sky, unaware of what lay ahead. In the oppressive darkness, Kaci penned a letter to Micah, folded it neatly, and placed it by his head.

Dear Micah,

I pray this letter finds you well when you wake. I have reached the painful conclusion that I must forge ahead on my own.

I know you blame yourself for all that has happened,

but if it weren't for someone as caring as you, then perhaps we would have been doomed from the start. Your mother is a formidable guardian, but you are an even better guardian because you will sacrifice everything to protect our world. I cannot risk you falling prey to the darkness. I must confront this nightmare alone. I hope you can understand my reasons.

Please convey my love to Durya, Marcus, and Sharn if the worst happens. I trust they will continue defending our world until the last.

And to you, Micah, I have one request. Never surrender. Regardless of the obstacles you encounter, never abandon the fight. We are guardians in our own right, sworn to shield our worlds from the darkness. I believe you will continue to grow into a powerful force for good.

With love,

Kaci

With a heavy heart, she slipped over the side of the boat and disappeared into the inky abyss below. As she swam toward the shore, to where it all began, she felt the crushing weight of despair and the icy embrace of hopelessness.

Chapter 19

Torn Asunder

"Shadow of spirit shall bind you to this place.
It shall keep you from death but also life. People will
know this place as Kashara, Darkness Eternal."
Bataku Raama, *The Birth of Magic*

As Kaci emerged from the water onto the rocky shore, she looked back at the ship, anchored in the harbor, rocking gently in the tide. The warm glow of lanterns illuminated the deck, casting strange shadows across the water. Kaci felt a pang of guilt and sadness as she realized she was leaving Micah behind, but it was for the best. He would stay safe as long as she was alone.

She couldn't help but think about Belan and wonder if he would approve of her plan. His time in her life had been short, and now he was gone, ripped from the fabric of time. Why did he make the choice he did, and what had his sacrifice accomplished? She pushed the thoughts aside, focusing instead on the task at hand. She needed to find Cirden and, through him, make a bargain. If Javina wanted her, she could have her, but not the world. With a steadying breath, Kaci turned and started toward her old home, her senses on high alert for any sign of danger.

She scanned the beach until she found the trail that would take her to Arba Vitae. She made her way into the woods, using her intuition and the faint moonlight seeping through the canopy to lead her way. As a child, she had walked this route so often that she could traverse it with her eyes shut. A hoot from an owl in the distance caught her attention, and she smiled, comforted by the familiar sound. The crash of waves lapping the shore grew fainter as she walked, replaced by a serene silence. It was as if the forest itself was holding its breath, waiting for Kaci to reach her destination.

After miles, she entered Arba Vitae's clearing. The sight of the great tree gave Kaci a familiar sense of awe and reverence. There she was, her friend and confidant, now a solemn monument to the impermanence of life. She still held her majestic aura, but her weariness was evident. Her once sprawling branches hung heavy, burdened not by age but by sickness. The leaves rustled in the soft wind, whispering not only secrets but tales of impending finality. Her verdant green was marred with dark patches, much like cancer on the once flawless skin.

As Kaci neared the ailing giant, she could feel the air, once vibrant with life, now pulsated with looming dread. She closed her eyes, steeled herself, and pressed her palm onto the rough bark, and a shudder coursed through her.

At the touch, she felt the dark tendrils, like some insidious poison, spreading within Arba Vitae. It was agonizing, but the tree bore it with grace. It knew of its waning vitality, yet it sought to comfort. Its essence was still that of a mother cradling her child, soothing its fears of the darkness.

Opening herself to their bond, Kaci found herself enveloped by sensations. Its pain was her pain, its dread, her dread. Isdralan's connection to the tree echoed in her mind. That fateful day of the bonfire had done more than just bring darkness into the world; it had severed their tie with the divine. When Arba Vitae perished, Elyndris's path to Isdralan would be forever closed.

Despite the sorrow that twisted her heart, Kaci understood. Arba Vitae was dying, and there was nothing she could do to change it. This sliced through her heart.

Belan, swallowed by the flames. Fate's cruel hands seemed determined to tear away everyone she loved. How was she supposed to shoulder such a weight if it promised nothing but sorrow?

In the distance, a flickering candle caught her attention, signaling Cirden's presence. He walked toward her and the tree with measured steps. Kaci watched his slow steps until he stood just a short distance from Arba Vitae, occupying the same spot where the bonfire had once blazed.

His stance was casual yet commanding. He followed Kaci's every movement, but he did not speak. As she approached, she noticed the wrinkles etched into his weathered face, as if every moment of his long life had left a permanent mark. His eyes flickered back and forth between pools of black, empty voids and a piercing blue, and Kaci imagined he could see straight through her. She could almost see the elder she once knew, but he was forever changed.

A wave of emotion crashed over her. Fear mingled with curiosity and a desperate desire to find answers. As she continued toward Cirden, Kaci drew a comforting breath. Cirden regarded her with a knowing expression.

"You came," he said in a gruff voice that seemed to

carry the weight of ages. Solid black now consumed his eyes. "I have been waiting."

Kaci nodded, her throat too dry to speak. She had so much to say, yet she didn't know where to start.

She glanced up at the tree behind him. It was said that Arba Vitae held the knowledge and memories of all those who had come before. Drawing from its strength, she let her body relax and allowed her thoughts to drift back to the warmth of the bonfire that had once burned nearby.

She gazed at Cirden and her brow furrowed. The dark orbs surrounding him seemed to win the battle against the few remaining motes of magic that swirled over his head. It was strange that she could see them outside of Isdralan, but there they were, plain as the stars above. Each time a flash of color emerged, the shadows quickly swallowed it. Kaci could sense the struggle within Cirden—two opposing forces battling for control of his soul.

She gritted her teeth, steeling herself for what was to come. "Hello," she whispered. "I don't know who you are. Does Cirden still exist?"

"We are one." The voice that answered didn't sound like that of the man she remembered, and the eyes turned to her were dark and empty. "As you will be with my empress."

Kaci's heart raced as she stood before Cirden, or rather, the man who possessed him. "What should I call you?" she asked, her voice trembling.

The haunting echoes of her dreams and visions from the night before were clear. They told a tale of Javina's desperation, a yearning for freedom from her Kasharan confines. Kaci contemplated the dangerous bargain she planned. If she surrendered to the empress, she was confident she could harness her magic to limit the fallout. Her power had surpassed Cirden's—she was sure of it now.

It was a compromise Kaci did not take lightly, but it was the lesser of two evils. She would sacrifice her-self for the people of Elydris. She could not risk Micah stopping her. He would doubtless declare her insane if he discovered her plan. In a way, perhaps she was. The gamble was dangerous. If she couldn't retain control, all she loved would be lost.

"Names mean nothing. Only Javina matters," the man replied, his voice cold and detached. "You may call me whatever you wish."

Kaci shivered at his words, then asked a question

that weighed on her mind. "Will it hurt?"

The man gave a dry laugh. "Life is pain. To suffer means you are alive. I would worry more about the lack of it if I were you."

Kaci took a deep breath and straightened her shoulders, reaching into her pack and brushing her fingers over the book she had taken from the great library. *I hope you are right, Bataku Raama, whoever you are.*

"I agree. My body for the Empress Javina," she declared, meeting Cirden's eyes. "And Elyndris is free. Your people will no longer possess their bodies and souls."

"Done," Cirden replied, and Kaci braced herself for the ancient ritual.

The old traditions had long since fallen into disuse, and it was only through a passage in *The Birth of Magic* that she had stumbled upon this age-old binding ritual.

It was a relic of a harsher era, a blood pact symbolizing an unbreakable commitment, dating back to a time when clan rivalries were fierce and mistrust was as common as the air they breathed. The stakes were dire; breaking your word meant facing a severe consequence—an abrupt and forceful expulsion from this existence.

Cirden drew a long, curved knife from his robes, and Kaci eyed the blade. "Is there a need for this?" she asked. "From what I understand, it is the words that matter, and if I break them, my fate is death."

The man tilted his head as if considering her. "We learned this blood pact from Cirden's mind," he said, gesturing at himself with a mocking smile. "If you break your word, death would be a gift. My mistress's wrath knows no bounds. If you break your word, it unshackles Javina, giving her full control to do as she will. Elyndris will most certainly feel her wrath if you break your end of the bargain."

Cirden muttered the words of the binding as he grasped Kaci's wrist. She took a sharp breath in as the cool knife blade sliced through her skin. The brief sting was followed by a similar cut into Cirden's own flesh. A shared sacrifice, a bond forged in spirit. She watched as droplets beaded up, mirror images of each other, until they started to blend into one.

As their blood mingled, she felt a warmth surge through her that gradually spread from the site of the cut and reached out to the furthest parts of her being. It was an odd sensation—not unpleasant, but otherworldly.

It happened without warning. Kaci struggled in the darkness, a sudden force yanking her toward Javina. Her hands flew up as a protective barrier. Surrendering herself to another entity proved more challenging than she had anticipated, and her instincts would not just let her give in. She thrust forth a fierce wave of fire and light in Javina's direction, a desperate attempt to repel the woman or, at least, diminish her strength. But the empress's power was overwhelming. The blazing assault was futile. Her flames dissipated as if they were mere wisps of smoke.

In Kaci's attempt to retain a sense of self, she was caught in a ceaseless tug of war, and the odds were stacked heavily against her. Javina's presence was pervasive, a specter that haunted the dark corners of Kaci's mind. Her essence intertwined with Kaci's, taunting and tormenting.

Yet Kaci was far from defeated. She steadied her mind, mustering every shred of strength and invoking the light and flame that blazed within her core. She had sworn to yield her body, yet she was determined to preserve her essence. For a fleeting moment, hope flared and the darkness seemed to wane. A flash shone in the distance. This had to be her inner light.

Kaci moved toward the light, but as she neared, a chilling realization struck her. The light was not a haven, but a trap, contrived by Javina to ensnare her. It was no manifestation of her inner self but a corruption. She had walked right into Kashara!

In a panic, Kaci attempted to retreat, but it was already too late. Javina's power had enveloped her and taken control of her body. Trapped in the dim recesses of her own mind, Kaci could only watch, powerless, as Javina emerged from the darkness, stepping into the world with a triumphant stride. Her menacing laughter echoed in Kaci's ears, a dreadful symphony that marked the beginning of a new, uncertain era.

Javina hummed a tune, pleased with her victory. With a wave of her hand, she opened Kaci's vision, allowing Kaci to see through her own eyes, but forbidding her from speaking or acting. With her view of her own world returned, light and hope flowed in. Kaci knew she had to push harder if there was any chance of breaking free from Javina's grasp.

In control of Cirden's body, General Raelon strode cautiously toward Kaci. "Is it really you?" he asked.

A smirk played at the corner of Kaci's lips. It was disconcerting to feel her body move but have no control. "Indeed," she confirmed, her tone smooth as silk, laced with unmistakable confidence.

The general furrowed his brows. "And what of our promise? The blood pact?" he asked. "How do we ensure vessels for the others without breaking our word? We swore not to possess anyone else."

Javina, in Kaci's body, let out a low, triumphant chuckle. "Your concerns are rooted in their old ways, Raelon. Now that I am here," she gestured to herself, "our power will evolve. Our knowledge transcends the primitive boundaries of their magic. We'll find a way."

While the general and the empress engaged in their dialogue, Kaci retreated into the confines of her Kasharan cage. She could perceive other entities around her, vague and ephemeral, yet she could not communicate with them. It was a desolate place, echoing with loneliness. Javina's ability to communicate with General Raelon from within this prison was a puzzle that Kaci had yet to solve.

In this spectral form, Kaci's power seemed limited only to sight. She could see through her own eyes, but witnessed the world as a silent observer, unable to influence it.

As she ventured further into the confines of her

peculiar prison, Kaci made a startling discovery. She was not in Kashara in the truest sense. Instead, she was in Javina herself, caged within the empress's essence. The sensation of being trapped within another being sent a wave of fear rushing over her.

Settling in to explore her prison, Kaci noticed tiny shimmering bubbles, like the ones she had encountered in the cave where she'd relived Micah and Muirenn's memory. Each of these bubbles also seemed to represent a memory—a fragment of Javina's past. The darker ones were ominous and murky, indicating times spent in Kashara. The bright ones were much fewer in number. They were vibrant and saturated with color. They painted a more joyful picture, showing instances of happiness and contentment in the empress's life. Each bubble was a window into Javina's soul, providing Kaci with insight into her captor's life.

One bubble caught Kaci's attention in the vast sea of Javina's memories. She approached it cautiously, not daring to touch it, drawn by the vibrant hues swirling within.

Then the bubble's hues morphed into a coherent scene of tenderness. A man of considerable stature and commanding presence stood, addressing a young girl who peeked shyly from behind the safety of her mother's skirts. The mother, visibly pregnant, watched the interaction with a loving gaze.

"Are you coming with us, da'maien?" the child asked.

The man rested a hand on the girl's head, a soothing gesture of paternal love. "No, ma'chien," he responded to the child.

"Perhaps today, I can be just father. What do you say?" His question coaxed a shy smile from the girl.

The scene blurred, and Kaci found herself once again surrounded by the countless bubbles of Javina's other memories. As she approached another bubble, something familiar turned her attention back to the world outside.

A familiar voice called out from the forest, "Kaci, is that you? This is not your task to bear alone!"

Kaci cringed. *No, Micah, why didn't you listen? You should have stayed on the Gull.*

Javina's essence gleamed with a newfound hunger as Micah approached. A cold sweat broke out on Kaci's forehead. She wanted to tell Micah to be careful, but she struggled against this dark entity that possessed her body. Trying to speak was like trying to push back a tsunami.

As Micah drew closer, Javina reached out a hand, her eyes glowing with an icy fire. Kaci could feel the elation in Javina's heart, the desire for power, for control. The sensation was overwhelming, a tidal wave of darkness threatening to drown out Kaci's thoughts and feelings.

Her own essence was bombarded by every emotion, every thought that Javina experienced. They were truly merged. She felt Javina's deep, dark loathing and knew the terrifying truth. The Empress had never wanted Elyndris. It was only an end to a means. It was Isdralan she loathed and would burn to the ground. Kaci's feelings mixed with the darkness surrounding her. The danger was so much worse than she had imagined.

Isdralan, the heart of dreams, the birthplace of imagination. To destroy it would be to snuff out the beacon that linked all realms together. Its demise would mean the death of dreams, the end of possibilities. Each world would be left adrift in the cosmic sea, disconnected from any another, solitary and desolate.

This was exactly what Javina craved. She didn't just want to conquer, she wanted to isolate, to sever the ties that bound the worlds together, and she knew Micah was the path to achieve this. The realization sent a fresh wave of dread over Kaci. It had never been about her;

Micah had always been the end goal. She did not have the ability to travel between worlds in the way Micah did.

Her success was more important than ever. Once Arba Vitae passed, there would be no way for Javina to get to Isdralan. The fabric of time, the delicate thread tying together all of existence, would remain intact. This was a glimmer of hope in the storm. *Micah, please just go away!*

Kaci felt the emptiness and hatred that consumed Javina. The empress had spent an eternity in an endless night, chained alongside the souls that had supported her, shrouded in perpetual darkness. Time here was a cruel joke, stretching out into an unending bleak void that swallowed all hope, all sense of self. Her eons in the shadow trap had warped her beyond recognition. The entity she once was had long been lost, distorted, and twisted until she became a creature more shadow than substance, more hatred than heart.

During these long, empty stretches of nothingness, one gnawing truth had consumed Javina—while she languished in the darkness, her mother and siblings had escaped to a world bathed in light. They had found refuge in Isdralan, a haven in a realm that was the polar opposite of the desolate trap she was confined within.

Her mind would often conjure images of that place, vibrant and teeming with life, its air humming with magic and imagination. She imagined her family living there in blissful harmony, free and unburdened, under the bright sky of Isdralan. The thought twisted in her like a knife, each mental image a sharp sting that reminded her of the paradise she had been denied.

The injustice of it all was a poison that dripped steadily into her psyche, warping her mind, inflaming her hatred. Why should they bask in the light while she was left to wither in the shadows? If she couldn't have Isdralan, she would ensure that no one else could.

Even in the face of such darkness, Kaci refused to give up hope. She tapped on that brightest of memories, and she sensed Javina hesitate outside for the briefest moment before snapping her focus back to Micah.

As Micah's power radiated off him like a beacon, Javina's hunger intensified. Kaci could feel the pull, the desire to harness that energy for her own purposes. She couldn't let that happen. She summoned all her strength. Her mind focused on pushing back the darkness and breaking free. The fate of her world hung in the balance, and she refused to let it fall into the hands of Javina.

With a sly smile curling her lips, Javina greeted him. "Micah, how delightful of you to join us." Her voice dripped with insincere warmth as she gestured to the man beside her. "Meet Cirden, the venerable elder of the Terra Clan."

Cirden responded with an inclination of his head, a flawless imitation of the Elven greeting down to the subtlest nuance. Yet his eyes were devoid of the usual Elven warmth. They were dark, as cold and unfathomable as a moonless night.

Micah raised an eyebrow, sensing that something was not right. "Hello, Kaci. Happy to meet you, Cirden." He gave a polite nod to Cirden, then continued, "Can I see the crown?"

Then he watched as Kaci, or what he thought was Kaci, approached him with a smile.

"Micah, my dear friend," Kaci said, her voice sweet and soft. "The crown is safe for now. We need your help to get to Isdralan. You have the power to take us there, don't you?"

Micah eyed her warily. "What's going on, Kaci? You don't sound like yourself."

Kaci's smile faltered for a moment, but then it was

back in place, bright and cheerful. "I'm fine, Micah. Really, I am. Just tired." She gave him a rueful chuckle. "However, I need to get to Isdralan. I have to convince the guardians. They must understand the gravity of our predicament."

Micah shivered. "We already tried, and they won't help! Remember?"

Her smile morphed into a smirk, sharp and almost predatory. "Then we simply must try harder." She reached out, fingers closing around his wrist with an iron grip, each word punctuated with a tightening squeeze. "You were the one who got me into this mess."

Cirden grabbed his other wrist, quickly pulling him away from Kaci and growling low.

Kaci—Javina—could feel her host's disquiet bubbling up from where it was buried. Kaci's knowledge was an open book to the empress, filled with secrets and powerful leverage. The Golden Gull, the guardians, Micah's mistake—Javina drank it all in, growing intoxicated on the heady mix of information.

But in her thirst for knowledge, Javina had grown greedy, allowing a slip in her guise. The mere mention of revisiting the guardians was an overstep, a little too audacious. Javina was masterful in playing to their motivations—Micah's insecurity, Kaci's inherent desire to help, and even Cirden's pride in his unique calling. She was weaving a web of deception around them all; her lies spun from their deepest desires and fears. However, in her haste and arrogance, she'd given Kaci a sliver of hope—an indicator that, while formidable, she was not invincible.

Biding her time, the real Kaci watched from the shadows as Micah hesitated, unsure of what was happening. She felt a thrill of excitement that was not her own at the thought of using him to get what she wanted. "Please, Micah," Javina said, her voice honeyed and persuasive. "We need your help. I know you care about Elyndris as much as I do. Isdralan is the only hope we have left." Existence was becoming more confusing by the minute as her memories seemed to merge with Javina's.

Micah looked at her for a long moment, his eyes searching hers for some sign of truth. Finally, he nodded, and Javina felt a surge of triumph. "Okay," he said. "I'll take you to Isdralan. But you have to promise me you'll be honest with me. No more secrets."

Javina's smile was cold and calculating. "Of course, Micah," she said. "We're all on the same side here. Come, Cirden."

As they approached the Golden Gull, conflicting emotions coursed through Kaci's veins. The weight of despair threatened to drag her down, while newfound freedom elated her. The battle between the two feelings left her disoriented and unable to come up with a solid plan. Every time an idea surfaced, Javina was there to push it away, like a thief in the night. Javina had no intention of keeping her promise. She had what she wanted and would use Micah to get it.

The morning sun peeked over the horizon as they arrived at the beach. Smeadon was on deck, saluting them with a goblin's awkwardness, trying to mimic a human. His tricorn was adorned with a bright red feather, a small reminder of their journey to Marshfield. Kaci fixated on the feather, its blazing crimson shade igniting a signal within her, drawing her closer to the echo of herself, submerged in the oppressive tide of Javina's will. At that moment, the feather offered a handhold, a grounding point in the whirlpool of Javina's possession, a reminder of who she truly was. Micah had been silent throughout their walk back to the boat, and as they approached, he took a deep breath before turning to face Kaci.

Kaci felt a chill run down her spine at the way Micah was looking at her as if seeing her for the first time, his expression clouded with suspicion and anger.

"You're not Kaci," he growled, his hand instinctively reaching for his sword. "What have you done with her?"

The smirk on Kaci's face broadened, delighting in the turmoil that clouded Micah's gaze. "Awe, Micah," she cooed, each word tinged with cruel delight. "So quick on the draw. Yes, I still hold pieces of Kaci. But I've transcended her. I've become something greater."

Micah's eyes hardened and his jaw set in defiance. His fingers closed tighter around his sword's hilt. "That's not true," he retorted. "You're not Kaci. The Kaci I know is…she's more than this."

He squared his shoulders, edging closer with a newfound determination shadowing his face. "And whatever you've done to her, I won't let it stand. We— we care about her. And I won't let you harm her any further." His voice had a rawness, a line drawn in the sand.

Cirden stood taller, placing his body between Micah and Kaci, but Javina flicked Kaci's hand and the man stood down.

"You think you can stop me?" she hissed, her voice

rising in pitch. "Micah. I am more powerful than you can imagine. More powerful than anyone in this world."

Micah stood his ground, his jaw clenched. "I know enough," he said, his voice steady. "I know you're dangerous, and I won't let you hurt anyone else. Not if I can stop you."

Kaci felt a surge of anger at Micah's defiance, but she kept her composure. She knew he was a formidable opponent and that she couldn't afford to underestimate him. Instead, she tried a different tactic.

She leaned in, a softer note seeping into her voice. "Oh, Micah, you are correct," she conceded, "I am perilous. But that's a matter of perspective, isn't it? We could harness this danger and turn it into something extraordinary. Imagine you and I pooling our abilities. Your raw power, my boundless knowledge."

Micah stared back at her, and Kaci saw a twinge, an echo of his uncertainty. She seized upon it, her words threading carefully. "Just consider the potential. As it stands, the guardians merely observe, don't they? You've tasted the bitterness of that truth in your quest."

Silence hung between them for a moment, tension crackling like a live wire. Then, softening her gaze, she continued, "We could step beyond mere observation.

We could mold reality and provide aid where needed. Envision all the good we could spread, the lives we could uplift."

Her words hung in the air; a tempting offer dangled before him, the gravity of which even Micah could not wholly dismiss. For a moment, Micah seemed to waver. Kaci could see the conflict written in his face, the struggle between his fear and his desire to do good. But then he shook his head. "I can't do that," he said, his voice firm. "Not with you."

Kaci's smile faded, replaced by a scowl of anger and frustration. "Fine," she spat, her voice venomous. "If you don't help me, then you're useless to me. But there are others who could use you."

Javina's lips curled into a wicked grin as she reached out to the shadows, and Kaci felt the power coursing through her veins. She knew just the man to give Micah's powers to—someone who would become her second-in-command, a loyal follower who would help her rule with an iron fist. With his powers at her disposal, they would be unstoppable.

"Take him, General," she said to Cirden. "He is my gift to you. So much stronger than this doddering old man."

The scene erupted into chaos as a monstrous shadow sprung from Cirden, lunging at Micah. With an almost instinctive reaction, Micah repelled the shadow. Thrown off its course, it spiraled back into Cirden, who staggered under the recoil.

Locked in a standoff, Micah and Cirden studied one another. Youth and vitality charged Micah's moves, while Cirden's loyalty to Javina gave him a raw, forceful power.

Fists met and legs tangled in a frenzied dance, each hit echoing ominously. Micah, light on his feet, avoided Cirden's brutal blows while using his agility to strike back. But Cirden was relentless, his resolve fueled by Javina's whispers and the tantalizing prospect of Micah's powers.

Watching from the sidelines of her mind, Kaci felt helpless as Javina delighted in the violence unfolding. She longed to break free from Javina's clutches, yearning to throw herself into the fray to help Micah.

The heavens chose to intercede just as the struggle between Micah and Cirden reached fever pitch. The sun crested the horizon, splashing the landscape with a golden light, and the world seemed to take a breath.

The silhouette of a man approached. Short, stout,

and strong with a long, flowing beard, he began to solidify against the dawn. As the morning light bathed him in its warm glow, he seemed less a man and more a personification of the day's birth, radiating power and strength.

Belan's presence ignited a blazing beacon of hope within Kaci. His resilience was like a hand extended to a drowning person. He smiled as he approached, his presence filling the air with a sense of calm and reassurance.

He spoke to them both, addressing Javina by name. "The binding ensures you keep your promise, Javina," he said, his voice like a soothing balm to Kaci's troubled soul. "Kaci gave you her body, but you ensured Elyndris is safe." He scooped up a handful of sand, letting the tiny grains slip through his fingers as he continued. "Remember that breaking the bond will mean your own death."

Javina laughed a cruel and mocking sound. "Oh, Belan, if only it were that easy. Death would be a blessing. Unfortunately, death has no hold over me. I am immortal."

"But Kaci is not," Belan countered. "And you are bound to her for eternity. Do not forget that she holds the key to your destruction." Despite Javina's physical dominance, Kaci's spirit was untouched, still brimming with life and resistance. The Empress was in a precarious situation; she had seized Kaci's body but underestimated its potential to bring her reign to an end.

Javina's eyes flashed with fury, but she kept her laughter in check. "Yes, Kaci," she spat the name like a curse. "She and I may be bound, but she is now trapped in Kashara. Do not think for a moment that she has any power over me."

"Are you sure?" Belan's voice rang out, filled with a quiet intensity. And then, in a sudden burst of motion, he flared into pure light.

As the light grazed Kaci, their entwined consciousness was inundated with a flurry of memories that prodded the depths of their shared psyche. Javina screamed in fury as she felt her grip on Kaci slipping away. Javina's essence flickered in and out of existence. "No! This cannot be happening!" she shouted, her voice echoing through the void. The world seemed to fold in on itself, the past and present intertwining, unfurling in rapid succession.

A little girl, eyes bright with curiosity, watched as her

father's hands danced, casting orbs of light into the air. Each touch sent warmth coursing through her. A sense of pride kindled in her father's approving smile.

A world ablaze, molten steel hissing and popping as it cascaded down to fill the crevices below. A mantra whispered amid the roaring flames: From fire we are forged, and from fire we are destroyed. A man swallowed by the inferno, her own heart ablaze as the cries ripped from her throat—was it sorrow or triumph?

Her father stood in a vortex of shadow and light. He uttered words of binding, and the world they knew became Kashara, Darkness Eternal. A chaotic symphony of screams echoed around them as the world plunged into a cold abyss.

A child, dancing with abandon beneath the sheltering boughs of Arba Vitae. A melody swept through the air, its notes dancing like fireflies, leading her toward a brilliant circle of light. A leap of faith, and she plunged into it, unafraid. Amid the wildflowers sat a golden-haired man. The gentle strength in his eyes, the love in his laughter, the warmth of his touch. She was lifted high, twirling in his arms, and they crafted crowns of flowers.

The scenes were vivid, saturated with emotions of love, despair, hope, and loss. Each memory pulsed, intertwined, and faded into the next until their boundaries blurred. The distinction between Kaci's and Javina's pasts muddled until neither woman could discern where one memory ended and the other began. Their experiences, although different, echoed similar themes of love, loss, and sacrifice, evoking a poignant nostalgia.

This fleeting glimmer of hope left Javina reeling. Seizing this moment, Kaci called upon her inner reserves. She summoned forth all the power she could muster and pushed back against the darkness.

Javina's anguished howl punctured the air, her grip on Kaci faltering as the light swallowed her whole. One moment, Kaci and Javina were joined as one, their souls interwoven in a surreal dance. In the next instant, they were torn asunder. Their identities split, then fused again. Kaci reeled from the confusion of this bizarre merger. Her mind was a whirlpool of emotions.

As one, the shadows plummeted back into the familiar abyss that had engulfed them for far too long. Victory had been within reach, tantalizingly close, but now it all unraveled before them.

As one, the shadows battled against the encroaching loss, desperate to keep a semblance of their power, but it was futile. The light had devoured them, leaving them feeble and impotent.

Ripped from Kaci's body, Javina tumbled into the shadow realm from where she had come in a last attempt to endure. The darkness encircled her, consuming her until only a faint echo remained in the void.

Javina defied her fate for a heartbeat, cursing the forces that had conspired against her. Yet, as she surveyed her surroundings, she saw the others that had been doomed along with her in Kashara, and they recognized they were not alone. They all dwelled here together—those who had been imprisoned in this shadow realm for an eternity, and the pioneers they had dispatched to prepare the path. Now they were forced to confront the consequences of Javina's fateful deal. The path out of the shadow realm had been sealed shut, casting them back into the darkness from which they had sought to escape. But *they had escaped*, if only for the briefest of months.

But the residents of Kashara understood they had not been vanquished. Time was on their side. They would discover an escape from this darkness, a way to reclaim their power and return to the world they were forced to leave behind. They refused to accept defeat, not now, not ever.

As the light swallowed Javina, plunging her back into the shadow realm, Kaci experienced an unusual sensation. She felt a fragment of the empress inside of her still, a residual essence clinging to her being.

At the same time, Kaci recognized that a part of herself was missing. It had been left behind with Javina. It was an odd sensation, like a piece of her soul had been ripped away. Yet even through her pain, Kaci felt its necessity.

Javina was not entirely evil. She had been driven by a profound desire to escape the shadow realm and reclaim her power, her life.

Similarly, darkness had always lived in Kaci. Its shadow had often threatened to consume her if left unchecked. Kaci tried to look for her light, but the familiar flame had vanished, replaced now by a fragile balance between light and dark, good and evil.

Kaci felt a raw, gaping wound where a part of her had been torn away—a loss that could never completely heal. Disbelief and confusion engulfed her like a dream from which she could not awaken. The world around her had become disorienting, its shape and meaning distorted.

The pain arrived like a tempest, searing and merciless, that coursed through her body and mind and left her shuddering and gasping for breath. It was an agony that refused to be silenced, demanding to be felt in all its intensity. A vital fragment had been wrenched from her being, leaving her adrift.

The sensation of loss was most harrowing—the stark realization that a part of her was forever gone. She felt hollowed out, a shadow of her former self. The portals had vanished, and with them, a piece of her. Though she understood she would eventually adapt to the loss, the pain of being torn asunder and losing a piece of her soul would forever linger in her memory.

In its place, she sensed Javina's experience. The sensation of being ripped apart was new to Javina, who had always maintained control. Now, as a piece of her essence separated from her and melded with Kaci, she grappled with foreign sensations of disorientation and loss.

Kaci felt Javina's intense pain intermingle with rage and betrayal. She had never intended to be connected to Kaci, only to control and dominate her. This inner light was her weakness, a sensation that incited a desire to scream and wreak havoc upon everything in her path. Having this light as an inescapable part of her was a fate worse than the shadow trap. Even as Javina railed against the unfairness of it, she knew that a part of her would forever remain connected to Kaci. It was a bond unbreakable, regardless of her efforts.

And then, suddenly, it was over. Javina vanished and Kaci was left standing there, quivering from her ordeal.

Weak and weary, Kaci looked toward Micah, her face displaying both appreciation and sorrow. Micah stood drenched in sweat, with the lifeless body of Cirden crumpled at his feet. Kaci felt a pang of sympathy for the real Cirden, who had become an unfortunate pawn in this struggle. "Thank you," she whispered.

Micah's brow furrowed in confusion. "I don't understand," he said, shaking his head. "What just happened?"

Kaci's smile broadened. "You knew it wasn't me, Micah," she replied. "Without you, Javina would have assumed total control. How did you know?"

"Don't forget—I have known you for years." Micah shrugged. "But that's in your future."

"This whole time and space thing confuses me." Kaci flopped onto the beach. "I always believed time traveled in a straight line, like an arrow."

"And fruit flies like bananas," Micah quipped with a crooked grin.

Kaci scrunched her face, puzzled. What did he mean?

"Those little insects. We have them where I live. They're fond of bananas."

"Ah!" Kaci laughed. "A play on words! It was a joke."

Micah simply smiled and nodded.

"Who told you that one?" Kaci inquired.

"My friend," Micah replied tenderly. "One of the best friends I've ever had."

Farewells and Destinies

"In every mortal heart lies a balance of light and darkness. Embrace this duality, for in their harmony, true magic awakens. Seek not to vanquish the shadows within, but strive for equilibrium, unveiling the mystic power of your soul." - Bataku Raama, *The Birth of Magic*

As they paid their final respects to Cirden, a solemn silence enveloped Kaci and Micah. With a prayer whispered into the wind, Kaci reached for the crown adorning Cirden's head. The piece of the triskelion pattern embedded in the crown's design seemed almost to pulse beneath her touch. She removed it, her hands trembling as she held the piece of metal that had cost Cirden his life.

"This is not how he should be remembered," she murmured, her voice barely above a whisper as she held out the crown to Micah. Her gaze locked onto his. "He deserves to rest free of this deception."

Micah's face softened, acknowledging her senti-ment. He accepted the crown, its weight symbolic of the heavy consequences of their recent clash. "I'll study the piece from my amulet," he promised. "Perhaps I could reforge it. Maybe even give it to you…"

The words hung between them and Kaci froze. She didn't want that amulet, didn't want to be reminded of all that had transpired. The responsibility, the deception, the power. It was too much. She wanted to escape it, to leave it behind.

"No, thank you," was all she answered.

With a shared sense of reverence, Kaci and Micah shouldered Cirden's body and bore it toward Arba Vitae. With only a small spark of life left in it, the tree bore a murmur of energy that seemed to encompass them.

They laid Cirden beneath the dwindling canopy and the soil beneath him yielded to their soft touch. As if responding to their act of love, Arba Vitae rustled gently, the sound like a lullaby that cradled the fallen man. It was as if she recognized the return of her lost son.

Her heart echoing with the grief of a thousand mournful cries, Kaci watched Cirden's peaceful repose.

She mourned him, mourned the fraying bond with Arba Vitae, mourned the heritage slipping through her fingers. This loss wasn't just Cirden. It was a piece of her, of the clans, of the ancient roots that had tied them to this earth.

"What happens now for your people?" Micah's quiet question shattered the silence.

"I don't know," Kaci confessed, her voice no louder than the gentle rustle of Arba Vitae's leaves. "We are a resilient people. And with the portals no longer a threat, we will carry on. But Arba Vitae…" Her voice faded into the wind as her gaze returned to the once-vibrant tree. A soft sigh slipped past her lips. "I fear the cost of losing her might be more than we ever foresaw." The weight of that unspoken regret sank into the silence.

As they drew near the sea again, the sight of the Golden Gull offered a glimmer of solace, a haven amid the chaos she had endured. Smeadon stood vigilantly on the deck, awaiting their return.

Kaci glanced at Micah, her voice barely above a whisper. "Do you think it's truly over? That we've seen the last of Empress Javina?"

Micah exhaled slowly, his gaze distant. "I don't know. I thought I had seen the last of Keres, but we both know how that ended up. Kaci, I don't think the people that touch us are ever truly gone. We may perceive time moving, but really it *just is*."

Pausing, Kaci recalled a memory that didn't belong to her. "Who is Keres to you, anyway?"

She observed as Micah's expression transformed, recognition and anger filling his features. "Keres," he uttered, his voice laced with bitterness.

Kaci stepped back, uncertain what was happening. "Micah?" she inquired cautiously.

Micah faced her, smoldering with fury. "Keres is my half-sister," he said, teeth clenched. "She abducted Mir and attempted to obliterate her. We defeated her— Muirenn, myself, and…"

His voice trailed off as he regarded her thoughtfully, then simply shook his head. "We vanquished Keres and banished her to the shadows."

Kaci's eyes widened in shock as Micah continued. "Keres eventually broke free," he said, his voice growing colder. "But her fate remained a mystery to me."

"The empress—she was acquainted with her somehow. Everything is hazy. Wasn't Keres the one we fled from in Isdralan?" Kaci questioned. "Had she already escaped by then?"

Micah's brow furrowed. "Time…it's been playing tricks on me. There's a tangle of past, present, future moments that all blend into a single ball. It's not easy to differentiate. Sometimes I think others remember events as I do, but when they don't, it's disconcerting."

He paused, lost in thought. "Keres, if everything were linear, would be trapped in your future but in my past. Honestly, I am not sure I completely understand it myself."

His words resonated with Kaci, "I understand the feeling," she replied. "There's someone, someone I remember who no one else seems to, also. It feels like he's been erased. But Javina saw him. He was here, Micah. Belan was here!"

Kaci's smile bloomed as she remembered. Despite her exhaustion, she scanned the beach for any sign of Belan.

"Who was here?" Micah asked, his eyebrows knitting in confusion.

Kaci turned to Micah, her voice hesitant. "Micah, do you remember seeing an Earthborn man during our fight with Javina? I felt him there, helping us." Had he been a figment of her imagination, a desperate creation in a time of crisis? Or had he truly been there, a silent guardian watching over her?

Micah shook his head. "I'm sorry, Kaci, I don't recall him. But, who's to say? I *was* a little busy." His lips curled into a half smile, and he gave a wink.

Disappointment crept in. She wanted to believe that Belan was real, a guardian angel sent to protect her in her darkest hour. Yet part of her feared that he was nothing more than a fabrication, her mind clinging to hope when all seemed lost. A realization hit her. To offer her this gift, this final beacon of hope, maybe Belan had to vanish. She felt the weight of his sacrifice like a boulder on her chest.

Her memories, her experiences, were so different from the others, and they were filled with Belan's presence—their journey through the Mountain Kingdom, the path to Marshfield, and everything that came after was painted with moments that included Belan. Were those memories nothing more than a figment of her imagination? The disparity between her memory and Micah's account of events made her question her sanity, leaving her more adrift than ever.

It was this dichotomy, especially concerning Belan,

that stung her. This chasm between what she knew and what others remembered distanced her from those she cared about. She felt herself retreating into a shell, a shadow of herself, carrying a piece of Javina as an additional burden. The empty solitude of her new role made her sense of isolation even more lonely.

As Kaci continued to wrestle with her doubts and fears, a whisper of Javina's lingering presence darkened her thoughts. *Is this the destiny you've chosen? Are you content in your loneliness, shouldering burdens that aren't yours to bear? Are you not tired of this endless sacrifice? Do you still think you're strong? You are alone. What strength is there in that?*

It was subtle, like the shadow cast by a flickering candle, but it was enough to send a shiver down her spine. Though she had emerged from her conflict victorious, Javina's influence still lingered. Kaci's heart raced as her mind filled with the haunting echo of Javina's voice, her cruel laughter. *See how quickly your world crumbles?* She glanced around, almost expecting to see the empress materialize before her. But there was nothing.

Kaci nodded, her eyes seeking Micah's. "I'm glad we all have each other. We can face whatever comes our way together."

Micah offered a weary smile. "You're right. Together-er." But he didn't meet her eyes, and the darkness inside her whispered, *he will not stay.* She remembered that this was not Micah's time or place.

"Welcome back, lady!" Smeadon called out from the deck, a wide grin on his face. "I was worried you wouldna be returning to us. Rough night?"

Kaci gave a tired smile. "You could say that. I just want to sleep for days."

"We should go to Westerfield," Micah commented, "and find out if any portals still exist." He opened his mouth as if to say more but quickly closed it.

Kaci nodded in agreement. "And we need to make sure they never come back again. But first, let's get some rest. It's been a long day. Smeadon, will you set sail for Westerfield?"

Smeadon gave a nod, "Of course, lady."

Kaci couldn't help but notice Micah's gaze lingering on her face as they descended below deck. He studied her with a mixture of curiosity and concern. She knew she hadn't been her usual self since they returned to the ship. The weight of her troubles had left her distant and withdrawn. A veil of uncertainty replaced laughter and bright smiles. She longed to ease his mind, to reassure him she would find her way back to herself, but the words remained locked away within her, unable to break free from the confines of her heavy heart.

"I'm just tired," Kaci said, sucking in a breath before opening the door.

"Please don't disappear again," Micah whispered. "I can help if you need it."

"You are one to talk." She attempted a grin and failed, then slipped into the room, letting the door close with a click. Could he see the turmoil she was feeling? When she was sure she was alone, she exhaled long and slow.

She sat in front of the ornate vanity, staring at her reflection in the mirror. Auburn hair fell in loose waves around her face, the freckles still dotted across her nose and cheeks, and her green eyes stared back at her. But somehow, it didn't feel like she was looking at herself. She was an imposter wearing someone else's face, and Kaci couldn't help but wonder how much of the empress still lingered inside of her. Fearing her friends would sense the change and reject her, she wanted to hide it away. She had always been an outsider, and now more than ever, she felt like she didn't belong. Would she ever truly feel like herself again?

To distract herself, she pulled the tattered book from her rucksack.

"Shadow of spirit shall bind you to this place. It shall keep you from death, but also from life. People will know this place as Kashara, *Darkness Eternal."*

Bataku Raama's words offered a detached, analytical exposition of the magic in Kashara, devoid of emotion. His writing didn't reflect the agony or torment that resonated with the name Kashara. It didn't hold the accusation of betrayal that echoed in her heart whenever she thought of the place.

She could almost feel the cold fear and burning rage that consumed her as her father sentenced them to an eternity in the darkness. But then it struck her—these memories weren't hers. Or were they? It was becoming increasingly difficult for Kaci to disentangle Javina's memories from her own.

Kaci snapped the book shut in frustration, the sound of its closing resonating in the stillness. Despite the discomfort it brought, she could not ignore a nagging hunch. There was something more to this Bataku Raama, something that intertwined his fate with Kashara, the Empress, and potentially the future of Isdralan. She made a mental note to research further, uncovering what lay beneath this mysterious scribe's words.

Finally, she succumbed to sleep.

When she opened her eyes again, she felt the gentle sway of the boat. She sat up, stretched, and made her way to the deck. Kaci felt a sense of relief as they docked. They had made it to Westerfield.

Lady Durya and Sharn greeted them on the shore. As they approached, Durya's expression was both somber and hopeful. "Yesterday morning," she began, "all the portals vanished without a trace. Those who had been possessed either met their end or found themselves liberated from their torment."

As she spoke, Kaci caught a fleeting interaction. It was nearly imperceptible, but the way Sharn's hand brushed against Lady Durya's suggested a new connection. Kaci smiled to herself and filed it away to ask about it later.

"I assume you accomplished your goal?" Lady Durya asked.

Micah and Kaci glanced at each other, then back to Durya, and both gave a quick nod.

The lady paused, choosing her words carefully. "The king is currently at Westerfield Estates, a guest. He has requested your presence and I believe it would be wise for both of you to join him."

Lady Durya led Kaci and Micah into the grand dining hall at the estate. Kaci couldn't help but feel overwhelmed by the opulence of the room. The walls were lined with intricate tapestries, and the long table was set with fine china and glittering silverware. At the far end of the table sat a man dressed in regal robes with a crown of gold resting on his head. Fortunately, it did not have the triskelion symbol. Lady Durya led them to seats beside the king, who smiled warmly at them.

"Welcome, Lady Durya, Kaci, and Micah," the king said, his commanding voice filling the grand hall. He sat straight and tall, his golden robes cascading down like a waterfall and his crown glistening with the finest jewels in the kingdom. "I am honored to have you as my guests. I have heard much of your exploits, and you have done a great service to our kingdom by ridding us of these silly shadow portals and the cursed crowns."

Kaci blinked at the man's flippant nature, taken aback by his casual dismissal of the dangers. The king's joviality seemed at odds with the gravity of the situation, and his words flowed with practiced ease, each syllable carefully chosen and delivered.

She felt a growing sense of discomfort as he continued to heap praise upon her, Micah, and Durya. She knew her actions had helped to save their world, but she didn't feel like a hero. Everything that had happened weighed heavily on her, and the king's words felt shallow in comparison.

Despite her tension, Kaci forced a smile and thanked the king for his kind words. She tried to focus on the food in front of her and the pleasant conversation, but her mind kept drifting.

The king shifted his attention to Lady Durya, his eyes softening with empathy. "I'm terribly sorry to hear about the passing of your mother and father, Lady Durya. However, your husband will make an excellent Duke."

Kaci's heart clenched at the mention of Durya's husband, knowing that the truth of his demise was a secret shared only between the two friends. She caught Durya's eye, offering silent support.

Lady Durya smiled politely, though her eyes betrayed a hint of fear that only Kaci could recognize. "Thank you, Your Majesty," she replied, her voice steady despite the weight of her secret. "Unfortunately, my husband is unwell and cannot attend tonight's dinner."

The king's face fell slightly, but he quickly recovered, maintaining his kingly composure. "Oh, I see. Well, I do hope he feels better soon. We were looking forward to his company."

Kaci couldn't help but feel a twinge of guilt for her part in concealing the truth. *You are lying to the king.* Durya had earned the right to rule on her own. She didn't need to hide behind the face of a man. Humans were so strange in their customs, but she knew that, for now, they had little choice. The stability of the kingdom depended on their silence, and they would bear this burden together, no matter the personal cost.

At that moment, a tiny voice whispered to her—a voice that had become familiar in the preceding hours. *You are poised perfectly on the cusp of dominion. Can you not feel the world trembling at your fingertips? The power to mend all that's broken—it's within you.* Kaci fought to repel the voice, to bury it in the recesses of her mind. *Wouldn't it be fulfilling to shape this world as you see fit? To cast off the chains of others' expectations and wield your own authority? The world could be molded in your image. You could reign with the might of a tempest and the resolve of steel. Bend this world to your will, for who knows it better than you?* Despite her efforts, Kaci found it difficult to silence the siren song of Javina's voice.

She swallowed, realizing that this voice would always be a part of her, a darkness she would have to battle for the rest of her life. For now, she knew she had to focus on the present and take things one day at a time. She took a deep breath and pushed the voice to the back of her mind, determined not to let it control her.

Micah's charm and sense of humor put everyone at ease as the meal progressed, including Kaci. He told stories and jokes, making those at the table laugh until their sides ached. Even Durya gave a few chuckles. Kaci was grateful for the distraction and felt herself letting go of the tension that had built up in her.

Afterward, Lady Durya led them to a sitting room where they could relax and talk privately. Micah poured them each a glass of mead while Lady Durya settled into a plush armchair and Kaci curled up on a couch. She relished the warmth of the fire and the softness of the cushions.

Micah continued to be charming, making small talk with Lady Durya, who pointedly rolled her eyes at him while Kaci listened quietly.

Kaci finally broke her silence, curiosity lacing her

voice. "Durya, I couldn't help but notice… you and Sharn?"

Lady Durya smiled bashfully, a blush creeping onto her face. She cast a glance at Micah, whose eyebrows were raised in question. Clearing her throat, Durya shook her head dismissively. "I do not know what you are talking about."

Kaci understood that the topic was off limits and changed the subject. "We should go to Isdralan. Even if they seemed not to care, we should at least tell the guardians the outcome."

Lady Durya smiled and shook her head. "I am needed here, Kaci. I must lead my people."

Kaci's shoulders slumped, but Lady Durya grinned and quickly added, "But you know, we could always use a lady-in-waiting at court. You would be most welcome."

Kaci shook her head vigorously. "No way. You know I couldn't stand being cooped up indoors all day."

The voice in the back of her mind whispered again, telling her to grab power while she had the chance. Lady Durya seemed to sense Kaci's inner turmoil and spoke up again.

"I understand, Kaci, believe me. The Gull, Smeadon, and crew are yours to do what you want with, so long as you leave time for their own…side projects." Durya gave a wink. "Just understand my deal with the goblins allows for avoiding certain laws. If ever you change your mind, you have a place in court. And who knows, perhaps I will join you once matters have stabilized here."

"I will go to Isdralan with you," Micah said warily. The brightness in his eyes had dulled a bit, and a look of sadness had come over his face. "It would be best if I returned to my place in time from there."

The silence that followed was filled with unspoken emotions. Despite the laughter and easy conversation, Kaci could feel the tension between Durya and Micah. Micah's desire for an apology from Durya for helping Keres was palpable, and Durya's stubbornness only made things worse. Kaci knew these unresolved issues cast a shadow over their last moments together, and in the end, each returned to their own quarters with unspoken words.

The next day, Kaci and Micah boarded the ship and set sail for Isdralan. The sea was calm and the breeze was gentle, but a heaviness hung in the air as the trio parted ways.

As they approached the coast, Kaci felt a wave of anticipation wash over her. Even though she had been here before, the idea of returning to Isdralan made her anxious. What if Javina was just biding her time, waiting to show her face the moment they reached Isdralan's shores? Kaci took a breath, trying to calm her nerves.

The ship dropped them off near Mir's cave, and they made their way up the rocky path. Mir was waiting for them at the entrance as if she had expected them.

"Are the babies okay?" Kaci blurted out without thinking.

Mir raised an eyebrow at Kaci's question, the corner of her lips curling in amusement. "The babies?" Kaci's face flushed with embarrassment, realizing her mistake. Did they not exist at this time? It was so confusing. "I'm sorry. I don't know why I said that."

Mir nodded, her eyes glinting with understanding. "Feelings can be powerful things. But don't worry, Kaci. The future is not set in stone. It is up to us to make our own destiny." She turned and walked toward the cave.

Kaci turned to Micah and whispered, "I will never get used to time being so fluid."

Micah replied tenderly, "It gets easier with practice.

But when you meet me in the future, be gentle. I may need a friend."

Kaci smiled and nodded at Micah. They followed Mir far into the cave, where their breaths echoed quietly amid the soft sound of dripping water. Mir gestured to a large triskelion on the floor as they entered a vast chamber. "You may rest here," she said simply before turning and nodding at a shadow in the corner.

Kaci and Micah settled onto the ground, leaning against the wall. The coldness of the air and the silence were almost oppressive. Micah must have sensed her unease because he placed a comforting hand on her shoulder. "It's alright," he murmured. "We're safe here."

She glanced around the room, but there was no one else there. Something about her fear was odd. Was it she or Javina that felt fear in this place? She shivered and pulled her cloak tighter around her.

"Are the guardians here?" Kaci asked, her voice echoing in the chamber.

Mir remained silent for a moment before she spoke. "It is just the two of us."

Cornelius stepped out of the shadows with an amused grin.

Kaci and Micah explained to Mir and Cornelius about their encounter with Javina. The two guardians listened intently, their expressions neutral as the story unfolded. After Kaci and Micah finished, there was a moment of silence before Cornelius spoke up.

"Be careful, little one," he said, his voice low and gravelly. "There are still powers within you that you do not understand. Powers that could be used for great good or great evil."

Kaci looked at Cornelius, sensing something familiar in his words, but she could not fully understand their meaning. A chill ran down her spine, and she wondered if Cornelius knew more about her than he was letting on. "Roots dig deeper than you realize. In fact, they are entwined with the very fabric of the cosmos.

His eyes twinkled as he continued, "We're all part of a grand game, aren't we? Of balance, of power. You hold a potent hand, child. The choice to play it—now, that's all yours."

"Thank you," she hesitated, not sure what he was getting at. "I will try to be careful."

Cornelius nodded, then turned and disappeared into the shadows of the cave. Kaci and Micah exchanged a look.

"Mir, what if the empress keeps trying to get to Isdralan?" Micah asked, his voice filled with concern. "What should we do?"

"Nothing," Mir stated simply.

Micah blinked, taken aback by Mir's response.

"I know what Mir means," Kaci said softly. "We can't control everything, Micah. Sometimes we have to let things unfold and trust that it will all work out in the end."

Micah frowned, still looking uncertain. "But what about Javina? What if she comes back?"

"Javina is not your concern," Mir reprimanded. "Don't dwell on it. You have much to learn. Focus on that."

Kaci and Micah exchanged a glance, realizing the dismissal.

"We'll do our best, Mir," Kaci said, determination in her voice.

Mir nodded, a hint of a smile on her face. "I know you will."

As the two of them walked out together, Kaci turned to Micah and spoke, her voice tinged with regret.

"As much as it pains me to admit, perhaps Mir has a point. You know the empress could only be here because of your attempt to fix my sad childhood."

Micah cast his gaze downward. His expression was pained. "I know," he replied quietly. "I was hoping to make things right."

Kaci placed a comforting hand on his shoulder. "I know you had good intentions, but maybe next time, you should let things unfold as they will."

Micah nodded slowly. "You're right. It's hard to accept that I can't always fix things, especially when I can return and revisit them again and again."

Kaci offered him a sad smile. "I know." An image of Belan flashed in her mind, and that tiny voice whispered again. *Yes, you can. You can fix things.* Kaci squeezed her eyes and shoved the voice down deep.

Micah looked up at her, gratitude in his eyes. "Thank you, Kaci. You always have a way of putting things in perspective."

Kaci regarded Micah with a curious expression. "So, what's next?" she asked. "How do you feel about showing me Isdralan?"

Micah sighed wearily and reached up to touch the

amulet around his neck, his fingers tracing its smooth surface. "I have to go back to my time," he said, his voice heavy with regret.

Kaci's heart sank at his words. "Back to the future?" she asked, hoping there might be a way to convince him to stay.

He giggled, then nodded solemnly. "I'm afraid so. Muirenn is waiting, and I promised I'd bring her amulet back."

Kaci nodded. "I understand," she said with a small smile. "Thank you for everything, Micah."

"Likewise, Kaci. We will meet again," Micah gave a wink, then returned her smile, though with a hint of sadness. "Stay safe and keep the light shining."

Kaci blinked. That was exactly something Belan would say.

With that, Micah walked a few steps away from Kaci and removed the amulet from his neck. He closed his eyes and focused his energy, channeling it into the pendant. A small light formed at the center, growing bigger and bigger until it became a glowing circle. He turned back to Kaci. "It's time for me to go back."

Kaci nodded, feeling a pang of sadness as she

watched Micah step through the portal and vanish. With a sigh, she walked down to the beach, searching for the Gull and gazing out over the sea. Above, a dragon soared through the crystal-clear sky.

As she watched the beautiful creature, she heard the empress's voice. It murmured like a seductive melody: *From light we are born, and to darkness we return.* Or was that Belan's voice? Kaci couldn't tell anymore. Would she never be free of Javina? As the words echoed in her mind, she could almost feel Belan beside her. She didn't dare look, worried that his presence would vanish the moment she turned her head.

She could imagine what he might have said. *You can let go of the darkness and embrace the light within you, or let the darkness consume you. The choice is yours.* With that, the illusion of Belan was gone, leaving Kaci alone with her thoughts.

The sunset painted the sky with a brilliant orange and red glow like a fiery beacon signaling the end of another day. On the horizon, the dragon soared, its silhouette a stark contrast against the bright colors. Kaci felt a tinge of excitement mixed with a darker, more powerful urge she could not name. She climbed aboard the Gull and asked Smeadon to follow the dragon, wondering what it could signify.

Her village, her past life, was not her destination. Not yet. She had more of herself to discover, to understand, especially in the light of recent revelations. For the first time in what felt like an eternity, she was unchained, free to dance on the whims of the wind, to explore the vast unknown.

As the crew prepared the boat for departure, they expertly hoisted the sails, allowing them to fill with the wind's steady push. The boat eased away from the dock, with the rudder skillfully guiding its path through the calm waters. Once a safe distance from the shore, the helmsman set the course, aligning the vessel with its destination. The boat carved through the waves with grace and purpose, embarking on its journey across the vast sea. While the Golden Gull chased the dragon across the vibrant horizon, Kaci's heart swelled with anticipation, embracing a destiny forged by the intertwining of light and darkness, ready to face the unknown.

Beth Connor

Beth Connor lives in the Pacific Northwest and loves to share stories through voice, dance, and the written word. She is the author of *Hollow City* and the Isdralan Chronicles series. She has narrated several audiobooks, and hosts the podcast *Crossroads Cantina*.

You can follow her at:

http://twitter.com/jbethconnor

http://facebook.com/jbethconnor

https://www.instagram.com/jbethconnor/

https://www.bethconnor.com

Additional Titles:

Hollow City

Whispers in the Mycelium

The Isdralan Chronicles:

Micah and the Candles of Time
The Golden Gull (Coming Soon)